Holding Out for PARIS

GABRIELLE ASHTON

PLAYLIST

These are the songs I listened to on repeat while I wrote *Holding Out For Paris*. Enjoy!

24/7/365 - Surfaces

Arkansas - Garrett Kato

bad guy - Billie Eilish

Best Friend - Rex Orange Country

Better In Yellow - Ferris & Sylvester

Blue Jeans - Lana Del Rey

Body Electric - Lana Del Rey

Call Out My Name - The Weekend

Girl Crush - Harry Styles

Green Light - Lorde

i love you - Billie Eilish

I Wanna Be Yours - Arctic Monkeys

Kiwi - Harry Styles

La Di Da - Lennon Stella

Liability - Lorde

New Light - John Mayer

PILLOWTALK - ZAYN

PLAYLIST

Since I Left You - Joy Crookes
So It Goes... Taylor Swift
Someone New - Hozier
Sucker - Jonas Brothers
Sweet Jane - Garrett Kato
Take Me To Church - Hozier
Teenager in Love - Madison Beer
Vibes - Six60
Wildest Dreams - Taylor Swift

Chapter One
LIZZIE

Elizabeth Hastings was wearing a trench coat, black pumps, and nothing else.

She'd never done this before. She wasn't usually the sort of girl to go out of her way to impress a guy—she'd never had anyone worth the effort before. But boy, was Amaury worth the effort. At least that's what she told herself every single, terrifying moment there was a bump or quick turn on the metro that threatened to send her toppling forward, giving her fellow passengers a more intimate glimpse than any stranger on public transport should ever see.

When you don't have a car, Versailles is actually quite difficult to get to from Paris. For Lizzie, at least. She'd never had to worry too much about public transport where she grew up, and to be honest, thanks to her generous trust fund, shouldn't really have to bother with it here. But when she'd moved to Paris, she had wanted the starving-artist experience. There was no way she could write a masterpiece of the likes of Hemingway or Fitzgerald if she was living it up like some sort of luxury travel blogger. She needed to live a Paris city life in all its glory, inconveniences included.

That is how she found herself on a one-hour, two-train journey from central Paris to a quiet street on the outskirts of Versailles, praying that an errant wind didn't put her ass on display to Metro Line 4.

She took a deep, nervous breath as she exited the train, holding a little box with his favorite pastries from that shop he loved in Montparnasse. She turned her mind to Amaury to ease her nerves during the walk from the station. It was six months since their first date, six months since he'd swept her off her feet and made her move to Paris unforgettable.

With olive skin that made him look permanently sun-kissed and those striking gray eyes, he was one of the most gorgeous men she had ever seen, with a French accent thrown in for good measure.

She sighed and couldn't help but smile to herself when she eventually reached his street. Whenever she thought of him, she felt a rush of pure warmth flood her system. He was exactly what she'd fantasized about when she dreamed of finding love in Paris… Older, commanding, mysterious. And so sexy. So unapologetically French.

She glanced up and fidgeted with the belt on her jacket when she reached the picket fence outside his house. They didn't usually meet up here. Amaury was a successful lawyer and based in Paris, so he'd bought a little apartment there for when he didn't feel like commuting, which was most of the time. He preferred the city; he thought it was so romantic. Lizzie agreed. That's why they always spent the night there when they saw each other. The only time she'd been to his house in Versailles was once, after a spontaneous message, instructing her to pack a bag and set aside a weekend… But even then he'd only popped into the house to grab a few things for himself and then they drove off toward the wineries in the south.

He didn't know she was coming here today, of course. That was the point of a surprise. But she knew he was here this morning; he always was on Sundays. Anyway, she didn't think he'd mind; she was doing something special for him and it was their anniversary, for crying out loud.

Well, their six-month anniversary. And the anniversary of their first date, not the moment they'd decided to commit to one another.

Not that there had actually *been* a moment like that; they'd never had "the talk"—they didn't need to. It was obvious from the moment he told her he loved her, and that he'd never met a woman as captivating, as *magnifique*, as her. Lizzie wasn't exactly lacking in self-confidence; she didn't need the poor man to spell out the words *be my girlfriend* for her to validate their relationship. She could be mature about it all.

"Enough stalling," she berated herself in a half-whisper, strutting forward through the gate. "Just do it."

She shook her head, fluffed out her thick, dark hair a bit, then walked up to the door and pressed the bell. Lizzie fidgeted and rocked on her heels; she must have switched positions five times in an attempt to somehow land on one that was casual yet sexy. She would be content to find a position that halfway achieved that.

"Delivery for Ama—" she began but abruptly stopped as the door swung fully open.

"*Voulez-vous parler avec Papa?*" a small, pajama-clad boy piped up, standing at the threshold. He looked about six years old, with a tuft of dark brown hair and piercing gray eyes that looked just like Amaury's.

"Hello? Can I help you?" a blonde with features so flawless, her face looked like it had been sculpted by freaking angels, asked in heavily accented English as she joined the boy.

"I...Um..." Lizzie could barely speak, could barely see. "I think I have the wrong—"

"*Qui-est-ce?*" She knew the voice that asked, "Who is it?" in French. It was Amaury's. But that couldn't be right. He lived alone. This couldn't be his house. She must have confused it with a neighbor. Lizzie took a step back and glanced toward the house next door. It didn't look like Amaury's. Maybe his neighbors were just visiting his place?

"She looks like a lost tourist looking for the palace. I'll help her out. Why don't you go put Nicolas to bed?" Amaury's voice rapidly

3

fired off in French, cutting through Lizzie's haze. He deftly stepped in front of the woman and child then closed the door behind him.

His hand was still on the handle. On his ring finger was a gold band she'd never seen before.

She blinked a few times, but it didn't move.

"What are you doing here?" Amaury demanded. She'd never heard his voice so hard.

"It's our anniversary," she said, still not quite believing this was really happening. She hoped he didn't hear the tremble in her voice.

"Anniversary? What?" Amaury stepped forward and his long, elegant hands grabbed onto her shoulders. "What were you thinking, showing up here? If my wife found out—"

That snapped her out of it. She gasped as she pushed him away. "Your *wife*? Your wife! You didn't think that was an important thing to mention to your *girlfriend*?"

Amaury laughed. It wasn't a nice sound. "Girlfriend? You think you're my girlfriend, *cherie*?" He laughed harder. "Oh, Americans."

Her eyes stung, and Amaury's beautiful face blurred. She felt sick. Ruined. He had a family? What the fuck? She was a *mistress?* The other woman? Lizzie gulped down the acid that rose in her throat. This couldn't be happening.

"You said you loved me. You said I captivated you."

Amaury cut her off. "A man will say a lot of things to get a woman in bed." He laughed some more. "Did you think you were the only one I fucked in that apartment?"

She didn't respond. She couldn't get the words out. They stuck in her throat, choking her.

Amaury turned back to the door. Apparently, he was finished with her. With his hand still on the brass handle, he glanced back over his shoulder at her.

"Come here again and I will have a restraining order filed against you."

Well, then. That relationship was well and truly over.

Chapter Two
LIZZIE

She called a cab for the ride home. For her sanity, dreams of living as a struggling artist could be put on hold. The drive seemed to last forever, but that could have been because she was trying her best to blink back the tears. She would *not* cry until she was back in the comfort of her room. She just couldn't, because if she opened that dam, she knew it wouldn't let up for hours, at least. If ever.

Lizzie was numb. It was as if this was all some horrible nightmare that she had yet to wake from. Every few minutes she pinched her hand, but no luck. It was still real—she was still sitting in an overpriced cab, watching the city pass by in a blur. Still holding that stupid box of pastries. The store always sold out by mid-morning, so Lizzie had made sure to wake up early to grab Amaury's favorite picks, then she had gone all the way home and painstakingly wrapped it for him. In her bag was orange juice she had hand-squeezed because that's the only way he liked it. Some cross between a laugh and a whimper escaped her throat.

The pink ribbon of the box stared up at her, mocking. It looked so silly, so girlish, so hopeful. It was just like her.

And let's not even get started on the whole trench-coat thing. Why on earth had she ever thought that was a good idea? Amaury was so mature, so worldly, she had wanted to do something that would shock him, excite him, that would show she wasn't just some ditzy twenty-something—she was a *woman*. Well, clearly he already had one of those. And a kid, to boot. *Fucking hell.*

AS THE CAR APPROACHED THE LITTLE CORNER STORE NEAR HER apartment, she called it to a stop and paid the ridiculous hundred-euro fare. The May morning was brisk on her bare legs, but she welcomed the pain. At least it meant she was feeling something.

The little store had a green façade and stands of fruit and vegetables spilling out from it. Lizzie bypassed all that and walked directly to the back, to the wine. *Hello, old friend.* Crouching down, she picked up the cheapest, filthiest red wine she could see. It was only two euros a bottle, and the label looked like it had been made on Microsoft Word. Perfect. She grabbed two.

Ten minutes later she was sitting on her couch, sipping red wine from the bottle in her favorite old T-shirt. It was actually one of her brother Sebastian's old college tees that she'd stolen. She loved feeling dwarfed by it, and there was something comforting about having a piece of Seb with her when she was feeling so undeniably crappy, thousands of miles away from her family.

Lizzie had three older brothers: Joshua, Sebastian, and Dylan. She loved them to bits, but they were part of the reason she had decided to pack up and move here all those months ago. They were all just so *successful*. It made her feel an extra, almost suffocating, pressure to achieve something.

But the areas her brothers thrived in, that's where Lizzie drowned.

She hated business, hated economics, and found anything remotely related to law or investment or management utterly boring. She loved literature, theater, language, and losing herself in a story. While other kids had played computer games or run around outside, she'd always been curled up in her favorite window seat with a book. Sometimes she would become so caught up that her family wouldn't hear from her for hours on end. Once her mother had been so worried, she had called the police to report her missing, and they had eventually found her sitting under a desk, so absorbed in the final Harry Potter installment that she hadn't even heard everyone calling for her. With three brothers, she'd learned pretty quickly how to zone out.

The memory brought a smile to her lips at the same time it brought a pang to her chest.

Boy, did she miss them.

~

HOURS PASSED. RAIN WAS POURING DOWN OUTSIDE, TURNING THE sky a bleak shade of gray that she felt down to her core. Lizzie left the windows open so she could hear the water pounding down on the pavement and feel the few stray drops splash her skin. She was about halfway through the first bottle of wine and the tears were pouring almost as freely as the booze. Gone were the shoulder-curling sobs from when she had first arrived home. Now she was just sitting still, staring out blankly past her little Juliet balcony onto the dreary street.

When her computer sounded with a Skype request from Sebastian, she didn't think twice about answering it. Lizzie had barely spoken since leaving Amaury's and his last words to her were playing on an incessant loop in her head. She needed her family.

"Hey, Lizzie girl!" Seb cheerfully began when the call went through. He was sitting at his desk and she could see the skyline of New York in the background. It looked early; he must have just arrived at work.

"Hi," she croaked back and forced out as much of a smile as she could muster.

The initial pixilation of the screen cleared enough for him to see her face properly and he let out a growl. "Lizzie? What happened? Are you alright?"

"I'm fine—just a rough day."

She didn't want to tell him about Amaury. He most certainly wouldn't approve. She was twenty-four, Amaury was almost thirty-six. And fucking married. Of course, at first Seb would just be furious with Amaury, but eventually, that would progress into berating Lizzie for being such a gullible idiot. Why hadn't she questioned never meeting his friends or family? Why did she think it was normal for him to only see her in a little apartment when he had an entire house only an hour's drive away?

"You're clearly not fine," Seb bit out, glaring at her as if he could telepathically communicate how unimpressed he was with her bullshit. "Look at your face, for fuck's sake."

He turned away from the camera and yelled out, "Josh, you better get in here."

Josh and Seb worked together at the company that had made her family almost obscenely wealthy.

Her grandparents had started out in real estate on a small scale, mostly dealing with low-cost housing on the outskirts of New York. When her father took over, he upped the ante and transformed their little business, Hastings Properties, into one of the largest real estate developers in the country. Now they owned hundreds of millions of square feet of real estate, and her dad had even gone and bought a few sports teams. As you do.

She sighed moments later when Josh's face joined Seb. "What the hell happened, Lizzie?"

"I'm just feeling homesick; really, there's nothing to worry about." Without even thinking about it, she picked up the bottle and had another sip.

That was the wrong move.

"Lizzie, are you *drinking*?"

"Isn't it like one in the afternoon in Paris?"

8

"Far out, she's almost finished that bottle."

"Talk to us, Lizzie, come on."

Her brothers' voices drifted around her and she smiled; it was nice hearing something familiar. Distracting too—it helped her keep her mind off—oh no, she was thinking about him again. She couldn't help but let out a small whimper, somewhere at the back of her throat, and felt fresh tears fill her eyes. Crap. Not again.

The boys immediately quieted down, and Seb said softly, "Lizzie, sweetie, I'm worried about you. Please tell me what's going on."

"Was it a guy?" Josh added, notably less softly, "Do you have his address? Just wondering—definitely not thinking about flying over there and bashing his face in or anything."

That almost earned him a laugh from Lizzie. "I love you guys, but I really don't want to talk about it. Plus, Sophia will be back from her nanny vacation by the end of the week so I'll be fine."

Lizzie had met Sophia at college and their friendship had been instantaneous. She was larger than life and always seemed to know what to do to cheer her up. That included supporting Lizzie's dreams of being the next J. K. Rowling.

She wanted to create and be renowned for it. To inspire little girls like the one she had been. She had her whole pen name lined up and was ready to stick to a minuscule budget, if only to prove a point. Talent wasn't something you could buy—then no one could throw it back in her face that Daddy had paid for it.

When Lizzie's writing rut entered what felt like its tenth year, Sophia had been the one to suggest they follow in the footsteps of her favorite authors and move to Paris. They'd rented the cheapest apartment they could find in *Saint-Germain-des-Prés*, and before the events of that morning, it had been the best decision she had ever made.

The frantic voices of her brothers shook her from her walk down memory lane.

"What do you mean she's still away?"

"You're *alone* over there?"

Well. Apparently, that hadn't been the best tidbit of information to share. *Whoops.*

"Guys, seriously, chill out."

Josh pushed Seb out of the screen and filled it instead with his indignant face. "How am I meant to *chill out* when my little sister is bawling her eyes out on the other side of the world?"

"I'm not that bad." She sniffed. Her eyes prickled again. *Fucking hell.*

"You can come home today. We'll even book your ticket for you." Seb's hopeful voice infuriated her.

"You don't even have a real job over there, so there's nothing holding you back," Josh piped up.

Of course they wouldn't consider it a real job. To help kill the time, Lizzie tutored a few students in English. It made sense with all she had read and studied. Editing came almost naturally. And when it was someone else's work, anything from an essay to a simple postcard, by kids who were just learning the language, she could take their ideas and transform them to something incredible.

But that wasn't good enough for her family.

Lizzie threw back her shoulders. "I'm not coming home! I'm fine. I'm an adult. I can get past this."

"No, you're our *baby* sister!" Josh's voice turned sing-song and every note drove into her like a nail. Their insane over-protective-ness was just another reason she'd upped and left.

Lizzie hastily said her goodbyes and slammed her laptop screen shut. Another minute of that conversation would drive her even further to drink. And that was no mean feat at this point.

She had almost a whole day open in front of her.

Between her students, Sophia, and spending time with Amaury, her timetable had been pretty full.

'Had' being the operative word.

And it's not like she really had other friends here.

Now she had plenty of time—just when she wanted to be so busy that she wouldn't have a chance to sink down into a spiral of sadness and succumb to those feelings of worthlessness that hovered at the back of her mind.

She downed the rest of the bottle.

Chapter Three
SPENCER

I t was raining in England. Shock, horror.

Spencer Tate stepped out of his brand-new gym and groaned as he took in the gray skies above him. What could be less motivating to getting your ass off the couch and doing something with your life than *rain*?

When he'd decided to open up London's first 'Tate's Training', he'd planned for a late May start, assuming that with the summer months looming, people would be more inclined to kickstart their training.

The weather wasn't playing along.

Spencer ran a hand through his hair, debating whether he should just wait it out. He didn't have an umbrella. Yeah, it was a rookie move when traveling to England but he hadn't planned to be here that long. Spencer had just made the trip over for the gym's grand opening.

He stepped out onto the drenched footpath with a sigh but soon found himself grinning. Getting a little wet was a small price to pay to see his new baby in all its glory. Spencer turned on his heel, tipping his chin back to take in the bold letters of his name on the front of the building. They were dark blue with a line of red and white on the outline, a little taste of the USA smack-bang in the middle of London. The sign was back-lit and with the droplets of rain on the front, the glow looked fucking magical.

It had officially opened yesterday and he was still riding the high. Granted, the sign-up numbers weren't exactly where he wanted them to be but overall Spencer was pretty damn pleased with himself. Besides, with the crazy amount of Londoners using his fitness app, he knew success would come easily here.

Who'd have thought ten years ago his little football hobby would somehow lead him to heading up his own business? Aside from Hastings. Spencer shook his head. He owed his old college roommate big time.

The buzz of his phone vibrating in his pocket cut his musings short. When he saw the name lighting up the screen he grinned.

"Seb, man, I was literally just thinking about you!" Spencer hoisted his duffel over his shoulder so he could put the phone to his ear. He was flying back home today and had figured he'd kill the time between hotel checkout and heading over to Heathrow with one last workout.

"Still got that crush on me then?" Seb's voice rang out over the line. Spencer could practically *see* him winking thousands of miles away.

"You know it."

Seb Hastings had one of the biggest egos of anyone Spencer had ever met. To his credit, he'd earned it. He was crazy successful, had a brilliant mind, and the lucky bastard had somehow also won the genetic lottery in the looks department. Well, that's how he'd heard one of Seb's flavor-of-the-weeks describe it anyway.

"How's the empire treating you, your majesty?"

Spencer rolled his eyes. The magazines and talk shows loved to dub the rise to success of his little personal training business as a 'fitness empire'. One magazine had put him on their cover with the words 'the king' splashed across his chest. It was something Seb never ceased to find amusing.

"World domination is coming along nicely. Now, to what do I owe the pleasure of your call?"

"Listen…" Seb cleared his throat, "I need a favor."

"Anything. What's up?"

"It's Lizzie."

Oh boy. This was serious then.

Anyone who knew Seb even half-decently was aware of how much he adored his little sister. It was the same for all the Hastings boys. When he was living off ramen noodles and craving home-cooked meals in those first few years of college, Spencer crashed plenty of Seb's family dinners. Mary Hastings would love to tell the story that when she fell pregnant with Seb, little Dylan had begged for a sister. It had been the same every time she'd told them they were going to have a new sibling—all her boys wanted was a baby girl. When she finally gave birth to Elizabeth, her sons couldn't be happier.

That little girl had been loved before she'd been born. Before she'd been conceived, even.

Spencer would do anything for Seb. He owed him, for one, but also, he was his best friend. He'd give him his lung if he needed it. But when it came to Lizzie, he would go especially out of his way. That girl was Seb's *life.*

"Is she okay? What can I do?"

He heard Seb take a deep breath before he blurted out, "I need you to go to Paris. The train from London is only two hours—I checked. There's one leaving in fifty minutes; I booked a ticket with your name on it. I hope you don't mind—I just thought I should grab it soon before boarding closed, you know, and then I could tell you and even if you can't–"

Spencer cut him off. "Breathe, Seb. I'm on my way now. Email me the details."

Lucky he was only a few minutes away from St. Pancras station because this was bad.

Way bad.

Seb Hastings was looking at becoming the CEO of one of

America's biggest companies. He was ruthless in business. He dominated at pretty much every aspect of life. He did *not* stutter, and he definitely did not blabber.

"Talk to me, man. What happened?"

"That's the thing"—Seb let out a frustrated sigh—"we don't actually know. We skyped with her twenty minutes ago and I've never seen her like this. She was wrecked. We think a guy was involved. And her roommate is away." Seb's voice cracked. "She's all alone."

Spencer swore. "What's the name of the French jackass I need to punch in the face?"

He must have said that last line pretty loud because Joshua's steely voice rang out in the background. "Oh, we're finding out."

"Send me her address. I'll make sure she's alright."

"Can you stay a couple days just in case? Please? You're the only one she knows close by." It was killing him to hear Seb sound so desperate. "We've got a massive deal in the works over here and we can't leave, otherwise we'd be on the first flight over. Also, I think if we did, she'd try to kill us. She was so insistent on being all independent over there. This needs to be subtle."

"And why do you think she won't try to kill me?" Why hadn't he thought about this before? "I've barely seen her in years; she probably doesn't even like me."

Seb let out a laugh. "Don't worry on that front. She was obsessed with you back in the day. Wouldn't shut up. God, we had some fun messing with her about that." He paused and added, lower. "Don't get any ideas though."

Huh? Little Lizzie had been into him?

The girl he remembered was tiny, all scrawny arms and big glasses hidden by a mass of brown hair. She'd seemed to look perpetually thirteen years old; it was as if puberty never really hit. Was she even capable of having a crush at that age?

HOLDING OUT FOR PARIS

Lizzie never filled him in on it anyway.

"A good cover story." Apparently, Seb was still speaking. "All you need to do is say you're in Paris for a week or so, scoping out the market for a new gym. Easy."

Easy. Yeah, right.

Chapter Four
LIZZIE

How good is wine?

Seriously.

Who needs a boyfriend when you have *vin rouge*?

That's what Lizzie told herself anyway.

Although it's not like he'd been her actual boyfriend. What should she even call him? Ex-lover? Douchebag French *tête de nœud*? Fuck buddy who says he loves you but also has a wife and family hidden away? Is there a word for that? Maybe she should create one.

She was eight hours into her breakup and much more than an eighth through her second bottle of shitty red. Amaury didn't deserve her tears, much less her best bottle. No. He was worth the cheapest, most disgusting drink. Bottom shelf stuff. Yes.

She was drunk.

Okay, she was *very* drunk.

But what else could she do?

Sophia was away so she was no help. Besides, Lizzie was hesitant to tell her about the whole disaster anyway. Her best friend had never been a fan of Amaury, even after meeting him.

Lizzie couldn't bear to hear a single *I-told-you-so*. Nope.

Two more swigs later and her head was back against the couch cushions. She'd been horizontal for a few hours now and found she much preferred life that way.

Books weren't the answer today. No, Lizzie didn't want any of her favorite stories corrupted by her foul mood. Movies, she cared about less. Her first for the day had been *How To Be Single*. (Netflix had suggested it. She didn't care what anyone said—technology one hundred percent eavesdropped on you.) Next up was *Wolf Creek* because love didn't exist and why would she waste her time watching a stupid rom-com when it was all lies anyway? Now she was onto *Titanic*, because what problem couldn't be fixed by three hours of young Leonardo DiCaprio. That's right. *None.*

Leo was in the middle of dining with Rose's parents when her doorbell rung. *Huh?*

It couldn't be Sophia. They'd messaged just hours ago, and she was in Greece. Was it he-who-shall-not-be-named? *Tête de nœud?* Surely not. But if it *was* him… Lizzie had hours of liquid courage under her belt and quite a few choice words to say.

Bursting off the couch, she ran to do the door and flung it open, "How *dare* you—"

She stopped short. Blinked. Blinked again.

Spencer Tate was on her doorstep.

Spencer. Fucking. Tate.

The man she had spent her high school years crushing on. *Hard.*

Her brother's best friend.

She looked up. Way up. He was as gorgeous as ever. Pushing six foot four with golden hair and golden skin. The whole package. Eyes so blue they somehow brought you back to the happiest summer day you'd ever had. They were the *exact* color of the sky. How was that even possible?

Don't even get her started on his body. He had one of the most successful fitness apps in the world but there was another reason his Instagram account had millions of female followers—yes, Lizzie was one of them. Six reasons actually. They were on his stomach and ripped enough to cut glass.

Hang on. Spencer was *here*? In Paris?

No.

She was hallucinating; this was a red-wine-induced fantasy. Of course, she would imagine Spencer coming to her rescue. She'd been in love with him since she was barely fourteen.

Oh well. Her mind was doing her a favor; she wasn't going to complain.

In an ungraceful running leap, Lizzie threw herself into his arms, wrapping her legs around his waist.

Suddenly, her eyes were stinging again and tears threatened.

"Spencer," she bit out, "How could he do that to me? *How?*" Her voice broke on that last word.

"Uhhhh…Lizzie?" Spencer replied, a crease appearing between his brows. "Lizzie *Hastings?*"

"You think I'd make my fantasies more observant," Lizzie replied, lazily dragging a hand down his jaw. *Mmm.* He felt *good.* "Less talking. More ravishing. I need to forget about him."

Oh no. She was thinking about him again. The tears came back with a vengeance.

Spencer swore softly and suddenly they were moving. "Sweetie, how much have you had to drink?"

He set her down on the couch and soon she was horizontal again. *Bless.*

Moments later her head was being lifted and water poured down her throat. The cool liquid felt about as welcome as a fridge filled with mixed vegetables when you're severely hungover, but just for Spencer she decided to cooperate.

More time passed. She wasn't sure how much. Then she felt the presence of a warm body next to her on the sofa. Her body seemed to gravitate toward it of its own accord.

"Elizabeth, beautiful, can you tell me what happened?" Spencer said softly as he stroked her hair. She focused her blurry gaze on his lips as he spoke. The bottom was fuller than the other and she had this weird urge to suck on it.

"Can't you just hold me?" She half sobbed when she realized those glorious moving lips had been addressing her.

Spencer didn't say anything but sure enough, she soon found herself sitting on his lap, cradled in his arms. A scent, rich and clean, yet just so distinctly male, enveloped her. God, it felt good. So did his enormous biceps wrapped around her. His frame was just huge compared to hers. She was completely surrounded. Protected from her mess of a day.

It could have been a few minutes later or an hour. Time had ceased to be important to Lizzie that day from around her second bottle. But gradually she found herself talking, spitting out the whole, sordid tale.

"And to top it all off, I was naked under that trench coat, Spence. *Naked.* Ugh, I'm an idiot."

Spencer made a choked sound.

"What? You…you were na—" He let out a growl. "I'm going to fucking *kill* him."

Lizzie wasn't really listening, too caught up in finally letting it all out.

"He said he loved me. How can you do that to someone you love?" Her face was buried in that sweet spot between Spencer's neck and shoulder, and it was doing a decent job of keeping her calm. So was that scent. The man could make a killing if he found a way to bottle it. But it wasn't strong enough to completely take her mind off her mess of a day. "How could he let me be that person? I'm not that person; I'm not a homewrecker."

And just like that, she was overcome again, her body succumbing to those huge, wrenching sobs she thought she had all cried out already.

Spencer didn't say much. He just cupped the back of her head with his hand and held her, occasionally murmuring words of comfort or kissing her forehead. Somehow, it was exactly what she needed.

Her sobs eventually morphed into yawns and Spencer let out a chuckle. "Okay, princess, time for you to go to bed."

The next thing she knew she was tucked away under her covers and Spencer was touching her cheek. "You're worth so much more than that asshole, Elizabeth," he said so softly she could barely make it out. Or maybe she was imagining it?

"You deserve better."

Chapter Five
SPENCER

Elizabeth was still asleep when Spencer returned to her apartment. Good. She needed the rest.

As he quietly shut her door, Spencer made his way over to the kitchen with the groceries he'd just picked up. Navigating a French supermarket had not been on his top ten things to do on Day One of his Paris trip, but if it had been his sister in that state last night, he would have whipped her up breakfast in a heartbeat. But Elizabeth was not his sister. And thank God for that, because the thoughts he'd been having—

Nope. No. He would *not* think about Elizabeth like that.

But seriously. What the fuck.

How the hell did Seb's baby sister, scrawny little bookworm Lizzie, turn into the goddess from last night?

Calling her Lizzie didn't do her justice. That was a kid's name. Elizabeth was all woman.

Even with her eyes all puffy and her hair a mess you could tell she was stunning. The sight of her running toward him in a shirt, he could've sworn was his, had nearly short-circuited his fucking brain. It had been enough to make his cock stand at attention, that was for sure.

She still wasn't tall, but somehow the awkward skin and bones he remembered had turned into soft curves. He had never noticed the incredible chocolate brown of her hair until last night. It was rich and deep but when the light of the lamp hit her just right he swore he could see flecks of gold. Huge brown eyes almost the exact same shade topped it off. And those pink lips.

He let out a groan and attempted to distract himself whisking the eggs.

Everything seemed to be in slow motion as he processed it all. Then came the realization that the shirt, that looked just like his old college one, was not, in fact, his. It was Seb's. Her brother. His best friend.

That had been enough to pull his thoughts (and the blood flow to his cock) up short.

Well, until the moment she literally jumped in his arms.

What was he supposed to do? Push her away when she wrapped those incredible legs around his waist?

Come on, he was only human.

He'd put her down straight away.

Well, sort of.

Admittedly, holding that lithe little body in his arms on the couch was probably overkill when it came to comforting her. Would Seb have preferred him to sit on the opposite side of the couch? Not even a question. Would he have even attempted holding her if Seb were in the room? Fuck, no.

But even Seb couldn't deny that Elizabeth had been in need of a hug. That French fuckwit had really done a number on her.

The pan Spencer was holding made an unnecessarily harsh clang against the stove at the thought of him. The urge to punch something had grown stronger with every tear Elizabeth had shed. That fucker.

Cheating was bad enough, but doing it when you had a wife and a kid? And putting Elizabeth in the middle of it? Ama-whatsit—however the hell you pronounced that wanker's name—needed to die.

What kind of idiot was stupid enough to mess up a chance with

Elizabeth? She wasn't just beautiful, she was brilliant. Sure, Spencer hadn't seen what she looked like for years, but that didn't mean he hadn't been following along with how she was doing. Her brothers never shut up about how smart she was, how creative. The majority of Spencer's memories of her involved her face partially obscured by whatever book had taken her fancy. She must have an insane amount of knowledge in that head of hers. Miles more than Spencer, at any rate.

That was another reason why he needed to put a lid on those X-rated thoughts. Even without the whole Seb factor, she was way too good for him.

SPENCER WAS PUTTING THE FINISHING TOUCHES ON A HEARTY serving of eggs and bacon when he heard a surprised squeal.

"*Spencer?* Is that you?"

Turning around he spotted Elizabeth standing at the kitchen door, mouth wide open, still wearing that damn shirt.

"I'm guessing you don't remember much from last night and have a pretty nasty headache?" He put on his best, non-creepy smile. *Don't look at her tits, don't look at her tits, don't look at her...* Too late. He could see the outline of her... Fuck. Stop.

"Um. No. And yes." The most delightful shade of red took over her cheeks. Inwardly, he grinned. "How embarrassing was I?"

"Not embarrassing at all." Spencer cleared his throat. "You, uh, you had a rough day. I get it."

Suddenly his eyes were looking anywhere but her. He took in the ornate, albeit peeling ceiling, the tiles turning his feet to ice, the microwave that was frustratingly set on the wrong time. Sober, there was no way Elizabeth would have shared all of that with him. Hell, even drunk, if he wasn't her first human interaction post confrontation with that jackass, she wouldn't have said a peep.

When she didn't say anything he went on, "If you want to talk about it…"

"I don't."

Great, because if he heard another word about that douche, he would punch a hole in her wall.

He kept that thought to himself and instead replied with, "In that case can I interest you in breakfast and painkillers?" He turned so she could see the spread behind him.

Her face instantly softened.

"Thank God, that sounds like heaven."

"You can just call me Spence, it's okay." He flashed a shit-eating grin.

Elizabeth laughed and didn't it just sound amazing?

TEN MINUTES LATER THEY WERE SITTING ON HER BALCONY, GETTING into the food. Taking in the scene before him, he could understand the appeal of Paris.

It had this old-time feel like everything was in sepia, but somehow still vibrant. Nostalgic. All the buildings matched and had those fancy little wrought-iron balconies. Elizabeth's place was on this tiny street just off the main Boulevard Saint-Germain, and it was teeming with cafés and people, tourists and Parisians alike. She lived right on top of a boulangerie. The scents of fresh pastry, smoke, and flower boxes flirted with that crisp May air, and the result was so exotic he found himself inhaling a big gulp of air just to take it all in.

And that early morning light hitting Elizabeth's hair? Priceless.

He shook his head and realized the woman in question was currently speaking to him.

"What brings you to Paris anyway? I had no idea you were coming."

Of course she hadn't. Neither had he.

"Well, not sure how much Seb's kept you up-to-date, but I work in the fitness industry. I've got this app…"

Elizabeth's laughter cut him off. "Oh I know. I had your app."

She used his app? For some reason that filled him with this huge burst of pride. *Hang on…* "Had?"

"I lasted two weeks. So sue me." She threw her hands in the air at his questioning look. "It nearly killed me, you sadist. Who ends a workout with five sets of burpees?"

Now Spencer was laughing too.

"Well you're clearly doing something—your body is amazing."

Fuck. Had he said that out loud?

Elizabeth blinked.

Spencer blinked.

Time to back up.

"You know, from an objective, personal-trainer point of view."

She arched a single brow. "Right."

Okay, divert, divert.

"Anyway, last year I opened up a few gyms back home. This week I opened up my first one in London and now I'm scoping out a good spot in Paris." He couldn't look her in the eyes. "When I told your brothers about the trip, they sent me your address in case I had a spare moment to catch up."

Above all, Spencer hated lying. For little white lies, most people didn't sweat it. Not Spencer. Life was pretty black and white in his book. Dishonesty was dishonesty. There are no shades to it. But he also kept his word, and he had promised her brothers that he would be subtle about this. If it would help Elizabeth… He could put up with a little lie.

"Wow." Elizabeth sent the full force of a warm smile his way and he almost forgot how to breathe. "You've done so well, Spencer."

Spencer ducked his head and rubbed the back of his neck. "Yeah, not bad for a dumb jock, right?"

The success of Tate's Training had come as a surprise to Spencer. And to his immediate and extended family. And pretty much anyone who knew him at all before age twenty-one.

He'd never been exactly academic growing up. Spencer loved his football boots more than any book. Teenage Spencer didn't give two shits that he couldn't write a killer essay. He could outrun ninety-nine percent of the kids in school. He never understood why test results were always held up as the pinnacle of achievement anyway. It was football that landed him a college scholarship and set him up for life.

But sitting next to brainiac Elizabeth, whose trust fund made his considerable earnings look like pocket change, he felt inadequate beyond belief.

A frown creased Elizabeth's brow. "Stop talking yourself down. You're obviously not dumb." Her lips curved into a wry smile. "You have always been the epitome of jock, though."

Spencer laughed but it soon turned to a half-groan when she brought a cherry tomato to her mouth and he noticed the way her full bottom lip framed the red. A barrage of X-rated mental pictures swarmed his mind, and he began to imagine how those lips would look wrapped around something else.

Fuck.

He forced himself to examine the street below in great detail. The people walking by. The paint chipped on the sign outside the bakery. Anything he could latch onto, really.

"How long are you here for? Where are you staying?" Elizabeth's voice was like honey and it wasn't easing any of the tension in his jeans.

He guessed 'your couch' wasn't an acceptable answer to that one. Lie number two coming up.

"It's just up the road actually, on that big main street."

"Hotel Saint-Germain?"

Why not?

"Yep, that's the one."

"Such a great spot. It's my favorite part of the city." She had this adorable, dreamy look in her eyes. It was nice to see her mood lifted a bit. Just as the thought crossed his mind, her cheerful expression melted away and that light in her eyes dimmed. He would bet good money something had reminded her of the asshole.

Elizabeth met his eyes and he realized she had been putting on a brave front this morning. Yesterday's hurt was nowhere near healed.

"Thank you." She didn't need to say what for. Rearranging the cutlery in front of her nervously, she continued, "I really needed a friend."

Spencer reached out and stilled her hand. He couldn't help it.

"Anytime, Elizabeth. I mean that."

Breakfast passed by pretty pleasantly after that. They never seemed to be lacking in conversation. Soon enough Lizzie was ushering him out of the house because he must be really busy, you know, because of his 'gym', and Spencer was looking forward to getting some rest in a real bed.

He just needed to find out where the hell Hotel Saint-Germain was and cross his fingers it wasn't booked out.

Chapter Six
LIZZIE

Wine sucks.

Wine is the *worst*.

Immediately following Spencer's departure, Lizzie retreated back to the comfort of her bed, a bottle of water and packet of painkillers in tow.

The slightest sound—a floorboard creaking, the honk of a car outside, heck, even the faint hum of the dishwasher emanating from the kitchen on the entire other side of the apartment—was enough to intensify her splitting headache. It seemed to zoom in on whatever noise it could find, amplify it, then added in a matching throb.

It was as if an enthusiastic six-piece brass band had decided to use her head as their stage. And it was their first practice.

A painfully off-pitch violin suddenly joined the fray.

Lizzie groaned into her pillow.

Where to even start?

She was trying her best not to think about he-who-shall-not-be-named, but when that option was out of the picture, all she had left to turn her mind to was Spencer.

Freaking. Spencer.

Mortification did not even begin to describe how she was feeling about that little encounter.

Her memories of last night were patchy at best, especially once

Titanic had come on. In fact, her decision-making that night seemed to go down about the same way as the ship's captain.

Unfortunately, her brain decided to take that moment to delve deep into its hungover depths and bring up the memory of her opening the door to Spencer.

The poor man had probably just dropped in to say hey, and tick a best-friend brownie-points box so he could let Seb know that he'd caught up with her. Spencer would not have expected her to be in the state he found her.

He most definitely would not have expected her drunken, inhibition-less first reaction to his presence to be literally throwing herself at him.

Subtle, Lizzie. Real subtle.

In fairness, she couldn't believe that had been her first reaction to him either.

Mature, twenty-four-year-old Lizzie thought her crush on Spencer had long since passed. Sure, it had been love at first sight for her gooey-eyed teenage self, but she had eventually put a lid on it after five years of being subjected to story after story of Spencer's conquests whenever she eavesdropped on him and her brother. Seb had never discovered that the little air vent at the top of his ceiling was quite closely connected to the one next to her favorite reading nook in the neighboring room. *Whoops.*

Turns out, that crush was alive and well. Or maybe the ghost of her fourteen-year-old self had just come out to play. Who knows? It could just be the natural reaction of a full-blooded female in the presence of Spencer Tate. It possibly wasn't even the first time it had happened to him. She ignored the twinge of annoyance she felt at the idea of that.

The point was, she could remember leaping into his arms, cuddling and crying on him on the couch, and then everything afterward was pretty hazy.

Then the angel had made her breakfast. *Breakfast.*

Some girls weren't into food. They lost weight when they stressed because they didn't have an appetite. They stopped eating when they were full. What a concept.

Lizzie was not one of those girls.

Safe to say, fastest way to her heart was with a big, fat block of chocolate.

The eggs and bacon had been a great runner-up though.

How the hell was she supposed to quash her childhood crush when the object of said crush went ahead and did things like that? For God's sake, he'd slept on her couch to make sure she was okay! No mean feat for someone that tall. And the fact he had been able to make her smile, despite her heartbreak and hangover? Almost unbelievable.

But she couldn't dwell on that. The poor man had probably hightailed his way out of Paris the moment he'd left her apartment. Even if he hadn't, she couldn't face him again. What would she say? It would be humiliating.

Sighing, she decided it was high time to leave bed and do something with her day.

Lizzie was meant to be tutoring two students this afternoon, but one look in the mirror at the state of her blood-rimmed, puffy eyes put a stop on that. She called in sick. There was no way she could go out in public in this state.

Lizzie tried to ignore the fact that Spencer had seen her in a worse state.

The shower she took felt amazing, and painful and cathartic, all at the same time.

That feeling of being stripped bare, with the hot water cascading over her, was exactly what she needed. Here there was no judgment, no mask to put on for the rest of the world. The scent of her honey soap washed over her, the steam enveloping her like a warm embrace.

As difficult as it had been, to prevent even more of a breakdown, she had tried her best to avoid thoughts of Amaury this morning. But holding onto her feelings was taxing, and sometimes you just needed to let it out.

Lizzie put her back against the cool tiles, the contrast in sensation not unpleasant, and slid down until she was sitting on the floor.

It was only then that she let herself process the whole situation.

Naked, sober and small, she curled her knees to her chest and let the hot tears fall down her cheeks.

They mixed in with the water until they too were washed down the drain.

Chapter Seven
LIZZIE

The following morning Lizzie's eyes were still puffy. Her fault. That's what crying yourself to sleep got you. She had never imagined being the sort of girl to bawl her eyes out over a man, but then again, she had never expected to be betrayed like this. To put her heart in someone's hands and have them store it in a blender.

Still, she couldn't help but feel that she was letting herself down with her reaction.

To top it all off, she couldn't write a thing.

The unexpected sunlight had woken her early, and she had decided to take advantage of it by setting up at her gorgeous little antique writing desk. It had been one of her first purchases in Paris. Wandering along the tiny streets toward the Seine, she had come across the quaintest second-hand store, seen it in the window, and fallen immediately and irrevocably in love. This was how she pictured her Parisian life. It looked like the sort of piece one of the greats would have written at. It was so old; maybe one of them had.

Three hours had passed with her notepad in front of her and still, nothing.

Lizzie liked the idea of writing on paper. It felt traditional, right. There was something about the connection between mind, hand, and pen that seemed to resonate with her. She imagined Hemingway when he first moved to Paris with his wife, how he would furiously scribble away on the Left Bank, in a café, in his apartment. Being able to just pick up her book and jot away, whenever a brilliant idea came to her, just seemed like the essence of being a great writer.

But she had no great ideas.

In the back of her mind, during that whole Amaury mess, she had thought *at least this will give me something to write about.* Yet, at the peak of her pain, when she hadn't yet confided in her best friend, or had true closure from the man who had shredded her heart to pieces, she had nothing. *Nothing.* She could barely get a word out. Just pages and pages of crossed-out first lines.

The first line was the most important—any great writer would tell you that.

It was a bright, cold day in April, and the clocks were striking thirteen.

It is a truth universally acknowledged that a single man in possession of a good fortune must be in want of a wife.

Happy families are all alike; every unhappy family is unhappy in its own way.

Lolita, light of my life, fire of my loins.

Lizzie wanted a genius first line of her own. She wanted people fifty years from now to add it to their lists, their stupid Pinterest boards. And until she had a great one, she couldn't get anything else out. It was depressing as hell.

When her brothers wanted to get on the best sports team in school, they practiced, and repeated and tried again until they built muscles and learned strategy and became good enough. When she earned French, she first memorized verbs and conjugations and nouns, and then finally put it all together into sentence structures, until it resembled something she understood. But with writing... How do you teach talent? How do you learn brilliance?

And now she had come too far. In college she had majored in creative writing, much to the confusion of her family—*but why do you need to learn that? If you want to write, just write.* She had taken a year off between high school and college to travel and be inspired, to find herself. Well, she had found Europe and a lot of tequila. Now she had moved countries, uprooted her entire life to chase this dream. How could she then go and produce something sub-par?

She needed perfection, her *magnum opus*. And she couldn't even write one damn line.

~

SPENCER

THREE MILES TO GO. SWEAT WAS DRIPPING DOWN HIS BACK, EVEN with the cool weather, but it felt good. Paris was pretty flat so it made for an easy run.

But no matter how fast his feet hit the pavement or how loud the music blasted in his ears, he couldn't escape thoughts of Elizabeth.

That image he had of her face all blotchy and covered in tears would stay with him for a long while. Each time it popped back into his mind it felt like a knife to the gut.

He was meant to have left Paris already. All he had promised Seb was that he would go and check on her and make sure she was okay. She hadn't been, but he had helped her out, made sure she stopped drinking. He'd even given her breakfast for the hangover the next day. His back still hurt from sleeping on that damn couch. Spencer's duty was well and truly done.

But he couldn't leave.

He had never actually booked a return flight, only canceled the one from London. He was paying for the hotel on a night-to-night basis. It would be so simple to pack up and go.

Spencer slowed as he reached a traffic light and glanced up. *Fuck*. This was Elizabeth's street. It was as if there was a line between them, drawing him to her. First it had just been his thoughts but now his subconscious had somehow landed him outside of her fucking apartment building in the middle of his run. He was a moth and she was the flame. Christ.

Without really meaning to, he glanced up to where her apartment was and nearly jumped out of his shoes when he saw her sitting at a desk by the window. She was crumpling up a piece of paper in one hand, pinching the bridge of her nose with the other. She threw it next to a pile of more balled-up wads of paper. It felt like she had reached inside his chest and crumpled his heart instead.

He paused, breathing hard. Spencer pulled his phone out of his pocket and checked it for the millionth time. She still hadn't messaged him. He thought that was a bit strange. Spencer had half been expecting a thank-you text for helping her out the other day.

As he stared at her pinching the bridge of her nose, it suddenly occurred to him that she may not have his number. Why would she? They hadn't seen each other for years. And since he'd somehow found social media fame, he kept pretty tight security on his contact details. Of course, Elizabeth's brothers had passed on all of her info when they had sent through her address, so he quickly fired off a message.

It was like his whole body had become consumed with this need to see her. To do anything he could to make her laugh. Had he ever felt this much concern for a girl that wasn't his sister? He didn't think so. Spencer had never really had serious girlfriends. For him and Seb, it was never hard to find company on a Saturday night. Or any night, really. Between seeing his family, friends, and his work, he had never been interested in adding a relationship to the mix.

So he had no idea where the hell these thoughts were coming from. He was *obsessed* with her. Sure, if any girl he knew had gone through what she had, he would've felt bad for her. But not on this level. He just desperately wanted to see her smile.

Shaking his head, Spencer quickly changed directions and got the hell out of there before she noticed him. He was in way over his head.

~

LIZZIE

THE LOUD BUZZ OF HER PHONE ON THE DESK CAUGHT LIZZIE OFF guard. It was still early back home and Sophia was on a boat tour with shoddy reception. *Who the hell would be messaging?*

Unknown: *Hey Elizabeth! How's your day?*

Huh? No one she knew called her Elizabeth. A frown creased her brow as she shot off a reply.

Lizzie: *Who is this?*

She turned her phone back facedown onto the desk and tried to focus back on her writing, but not ten seconds later it was buzzing again.

Unknown: *Spencer*

Her stomach did an excited little backflip when she read his name, and her cheeks flushed. God, she was terrible. It was like she was back in eighth grade and a boy was texting her for the first time. Lizzie rolled her eyes and saved his number.

Lizzie: *Hey Spencer, you back home yet?*

Spencer: *Nope, I'm just up the road. Was wondering if you wanted to do something today?*

Teenage Lizzie did a happy dance. Spencer wanted to hang out with her?

Adult Lizzie quickly shut her down. It was a pity invite. Spencer was obviously sitting in his hotel feeling guilty about what a mess she had been. He had a sister; it was probably some residual fraternal protectiveness. Lizzie didn't need that; she had it in spades. Besides, there was no way she could trust herself seeing him again. The moment she caught sight of him, her cheeks would no doubt fall back on their go-to Spencer reaction... A tomato impersonation.

Lizzie: *Sorry, really busy today. Writing.*

Being rude wasn't her intention, but Lizzie really didn't want to encourage him. This was an easy out. He would take it.

Spencer: *I can meet up with you in a break, if you like?*

Ugh. Understanding too? He really needed to stop.

Lizzie: *No rest for the wicked!*

Lizzie put her phone back on the desk facedown, but she didn't immediately try to concentrate again on her work. A small part of her was just waiting for him to respond. Okay, a large part. Fine, she was actually sitting there just staring at her phone, volume turned on high, desperately wanting his attention. She was in a vulnerable state. She deserved some freaking leeway.

Almost an hour later Lizzie was leaning out against the balcony, searching for inspiration, when she heard the next buzz. With super-human-like speed she leapt inside to check it, while simultaneously trying to convince herself that she wasn't holding out to see the name Spencer light up her screen.

It did.

Making her way over to the kitchen to put the kettle on, Lizzie forced herself to wait a full five minutes until she opened it. She would *not* act like some desperate fangirl turning into a heart-eye emoji just because a hot guy sent her a message. She could be totally cool about this. After the water had boiled, with a mug of herbal tea in hand, Lizzie succumbed to the urge to read it.

A GIF of the most adorable puppy greeted her. It had its little face squished in the cushions of a couch, looking up, wagging its tail. The angle of it made it seem as if Lizzie herself was sitting on the couch, and the little fluffball was gazing at her specifically. It was chocolate and had a white star on its nose. Freaking. Adorable.

Also, highly confusing.

She typed out a response. Deleted it. Typed a new one, then repeated that process around four times before she finally replied.

Lizzie: *Was that meant for me?*

Her phone sounded seconds later.

Spencer: *It's an encouragement puppy. For your writing.*

She was staring at the screen, trying to process that when a second message shot through.

Spencer: *If you could only bring one French pastry to a deserted island, what would it be?*

A smile lit up her face before she was even aware it was happening, and this happy buzz of warmth swelled out from deep inside. It was that pure bliss of an endorphin rush, like when you sang, or had runners high, or ate chocolate. And she was getting it because Spencer sent her a picture of a puppy. Oh boy, this was not good.

Lizzie: *Kouign-amann*

Spencer: *That doesn't sound French.*

Lizzie: *It's a Breton speciality. Literally means "cake" and "butter." For some reason it's not in the Tate's Training meal plan?*

Spencer: *What's it like? Maybe I'll add it.*

Lizzie: *A croissant on steroids. Peak butter. The outside is gold and caramelized, and the inside is just soft, flaky buttery layers. Did I mention the butter? There's sugar too.*

Spencer: *That is definitely not going on my app.*

Spencer: *But you sound very passionate about it.*

Lizzie: *I'm passionate about all pastries.*

Smiling to herself while she sipped her tea, Lizzie strolled back to her desk. Writing was out of the question at the moment. If she hadn't accomplished anything yet today, another afternoon wasn't going to help. Instead, she brought up the latest work one of her students had sent her to proofread.

If there was one thing she hadn't expected during her move over here, it was how much she would enjoy her job. There was something about taking a student, who felt hopeless about their work, who wanted to improve but was at a loss of how to do it, to the next level. Seeing their faces, when they realized all hope wasn't lost, she felt that same endorphin rush.

Twenty minutes later, another GIF came through.

This one was of a big golden retriever. The camera zoomed in and a hand reached out to lift up the flap of the dog's ear and hiding under it, was an adorable napping kitten.

That picture was quickly followed up by one of a children's dancing concert. There were six-year-olds in tutus doing ballet, but one child, in the middle, was just ignoring everyone else and owning it, doing completely different moves super enthusiastically. It looked like she was singing, as well. It was freaking hilarious.

Where did this man come from? She sighed and got back to editing.

The rest of the afternoon passed in a blur as she caught up on the work she had missed when she canceled on everyone yesterday. Every half hour or so, Spencer sent through another GIF.

Every single time, she beamed. She couldn't help it.

When the sun began to set and that soft, golden-hour light took over her living room, she realized she hadn't thought about Amaury at all that afternoon.

Not even once.

Chapter Eight
SPENCER

Spencer had finally made it back to his hotel, his running gear completely drenched in sweat. He had practically sprinted the last few miles, needing to put as much distance between him and Elizabeth as he could.

Of course, sucker that he was, at every light where he stopped, he whipped out his phone to send her another message. Each time he saw her name on his screen, he felt butterflies in his stomach and it made him want to mentally slap himself.

Freshly showered, Spencer shook off the memory and lay back on the soft hotel mattress. He needed to do some actual work over here.

With a sigh, he pulled out his phone and spent some time checking in with clients and going through his Instagram. He let out a groan when he saw he had one thousand message requests since he had last checked yesterday. Tate's Training had even picked up a few celebrities and famous athletes as clients. It was insane. Part of him wanted to hire someone to handle all of the social stuff but it felt so fake. Like a slap in the face to everyone who had supported him.

When he had first started personal training, he hadn't even considered putting his business online. After Spencer made a bit of a name for himself, playing college ball and doing some small-time modeling gigs for extra cash, it was Seb who had insisted he capitalize on his newfound "fame" and sports science degree. He helped Spencer develop an online training program and website, so he could help clients all over the world. That man just knew how to make money. Obviously ran in the family. Seb didn't even try to claim a share in the program's success once it took off—no matter how many times Spencer tried to convince him otherwise.

Spencer exited out of Instagram and read over his messages with Elizabeth. He still couldn't shake that image of her crumpling the paper at her desk. Grade-A stalker, as it was, he wished he had been there to see her face when she saw his messages. Would she have smiled? Laughed? Spencer sighed and fired up his computer to check in with his sister. He was getting way too invested in Elizabeth Hastings.

Gracie answered his Skype call within seconds.

"Spence!" Her big, blue eyes appeared on the screen in front of him and he grinned. Her blond hair, the exact same shade as his, was adorably messy. They looked almost identical, except Grace was tall and lean where he was packing muscle.

"How's my favorite girl been?"

Spencer had always been close to his sister. Their mom had passed away when they were pretty young. One minute Mom was running out the door, insisting she needed to pop by the store to grab a few extra things for dinner, the next she was mowed down by a drunk driver. The bastard didn't even stay around to check on her and call an ambulance. He'd just bolted.

Spencer had been in his junior year but Grace had been at that age when puberty had just struck; she had been an awkward mess. When the news came about Mom, it had hit her hard. Grace went into a shell and she still hadn't fully grown out of it, even at twenty-five. Spencer could count the number of dates she had been on, on one hand.

Grace responded to his question with a yawn. "Pretty good.

Finished a new piece yesterday." She blinked a few times, bringing a hand up to rub the sleep out of her eyes.

"Yeah? What's it like?" Grace did a bit of work in film production but she was an artist at heart. She could spend days or weeks locked away in her apartment, caught up in a frenzy of painting.

"Come home and see it. Where are you anyway?"

"Paris."

Her eyes bulged. "Paris?" she asked incredulously. "Weren't you supposed to be in London?"

Spencer quickly explained about the situation with Lizzie. The two had met over the years and got along pretty well. They were only a year apart in age.

"That's actually why I was calling you. She seems like she needs a friend, and I want to go see her, but I don't want to be overstepping, you know?" Spencer got the words out quickly, before he lost his nerve. He needed a woman's advice.

Grace's mouth fell open and she made an excited squeal. "You *like* her!"

"Shut up. I don't."

"You *do*!" Grace was now laughing, hard. "Seb is going to murder you, Spence."

"Of course I like her, but I don't *like* like her," Spencer growled. Christ, he sounded like a twelve-year-old. "I just feel bad."

"Sure you do." Grace rolled her eyes. "I've seen what she looks like; I'm confident it's one hundred per cent honor that is driving you there."

Spencer threw his head back and groaned. This was not going to plan. Was he really that obvious?

"'Dammit, Grace. Even if I was looking at her like that I would never go there. She's Seb's *sister.*" He said the words slowly, enunciating each one clearly so she would get the fucking message. "I just want to know if you think I should go check on her tonight?"

"That depends—what are you planning on doing?"

Spencer blushed. He *blushed*. But finally, he gave in and told her what he had in mind. After putting up with a few more minutes of Grace being an idiot about the whole thing, she finally stopped teasing him and gave her approval of his idea, and a few suggestions.

If your sister couldn't give you inside knowledge on the female species, what was the point of having one?

Chapter Nine
LIZZIE

Lizzie was sitting on her couch in a face mask—self-care at its finest, right?—when her doorbell sounded.

Frowning, she debated whether or not to remove the frangipani-scented mud covering her face but then shrugged and started to make her way over. It was probably a delivery guy with the wrong address.

For the second time in just as many days, Spencer Tate was at her doorstep.

Lizzie shrieked.

His scent hit her first. It was intoxicating. He smelled like cinnamon and crisp autumn air with this hint of lemon that just drove her insane. She had discovered a whiff of it on her couch pillow earlier that day and had succumbed to a few guilty sniffs. Pure. Heaven.

"Want some company?" He smiled shyly. His golden hair was perfectly mussed, his eyes shone, and those cheekbones? *Wow.*

Damn, did he look good. He was sporting a casual, navy pullover, but it was tight enough to highlight his broad shoulders and hint at the muscles he made his living off of. His body looked like he had been a professional swimmer his whole life, then retired and decided to hit the gym six days a week. It was freaking spectacular. Her eyes continued their path downward to blue jeans slung low on his narrow hips, and dammit, now she was thinking about his crotch. Perfect.

"W-what are you doing here?" Lizzie finally got out once she was done ogling him. Her face grew hot as she realized how blatantly she had been checking him out.

At that point Spencer just decided to let himself in, strutting forward into her apartment while he threw back over his shoulder, "Well, when you told me your buddy Sophia wasn't home for a few days, I figured you needed a friend."

Lizzie pushed the door shut, still at a loss for words.

This didn't seem to faze Spencer, though. He was heading toward her kitchen bench and his hands were full of bags she hadn't noticed when she was, *ahem*, busy looking at other things.

She approached the counter cautiously, half-thinking this was all a figment of her imagination. Why on earth was he here?

Spencer turned the full force of those baby blues on her. "I've got your whole post-breakup recovery package right here."

Her eyes inadvertently traveled back down to below his hips and he chuckled. She decided it was better to look anywhere but him before she made even more of a fool of herself. That was when she noticed what he had actually set out on the counter.

There were multiple blocks of chocolate, some packets of chips, a giant tub of salted-caramel ice cream, a few bags of microwave popcorn, and *Dear God,* was that what she thought it was? Sitting next to the whole spread were three different *kouign-amanns*. It was obvious they were all from different stores.

Spencer must have noticed the direction of her thoughts. "I figured you would probably have a favorite baker, so I thought I better hedge my bets."

Lizzie opened her mouth. Closed it. Opened it again.

"Spencer, this is so thoughtful."

A smile pulled at the corner of his mouth and his cheeks turned a little pink. "I um, also picked up a few other things."

HOLDING OUT FOR PARIS

Spencer hoisted another bag onto the counter and it hit with a thud. Suddenly he was pulling out brand-new paperbacks. "Since you're such a bookworm, I thought these would work better than flowers, you know, for cheering up and all." At her gobsmacked stare he continued, "Don't worry—I know you have read literally every book on the planet so I only got new releases."

Her eyes were stinging. This was hands-down the sweetest thing any guy—no, any *person*—had done for her. Ever. He got her books? *Books?* He was a four-leaf clover. A diamond. A freaking unicorn.

"Am I being punked?" Lizzie found herself glancing around the room for cameras.

"Yep. The audience is gonna love that shit on your face."

Oh no. Dear God, no. In all the excitement of seeing Spencer, on her doorstep of all places, Lizzie had completed forgotten about her face mask. And while she was at it, she had also conveniently forgotten about the old T-shirt and sweats she was wearing, sans bra. Right. Awesome.

This was possibly the only time a sinkhole in the middle of her building would be a positive turn of events.

She pivoted around so he couldn't see her face but soon her shoulders were circled by big, warm palms as Spencer turned her back to him. His touch sent a shiver of awareness tingling down her spine.

"Don't worry, honey," Spencer drawled with a lazy grin that made his full bottom lip impossible to look away from, "I've got a sister, I've seen it all."

Lizzie's brain short-circuited. Did he just call her honey?

"Speaking of my sister—she's the one who made all the movie recommendations for tonight. So it really depends on what mood you're in."

"What are my options?" Her mind had at last decided to let her function as a human again. It was only ten minutes late. *Oh, well.* Beggars can't be choosers, right?

"Okay, if you want standard sappy romance crap, I've got *The Notebook*. But, you would owe me one for putting me through that." As he spoke, Spencer grabbed a bunch of DVDs and started handing them to her. "Now if you want funny, *Forgetting Sarah Marshall* is a good one—nice breakup theme to give you some hope."

At Lizzie's raised eyebrow, Spencer threw up his hands in defense. "Don't shoot the messenger! That's what Grace told me."

Lizzie rolled her eyes. "Go on then, what's next?"

Spencer scowled and mumbled something under his breath.

"What was that?"

"Magic Mike. For if you're, um"—he cleared his throat—"you know."

He looked so adorably awkward standing there, rubbing his hand against the back of his neck and keeping his eyes low that she couldn't help it. Lizzie surged forward and wrapped her arms around his neck—a wordless thank you.

At first he seemed surprised, all stiff in her arms but moments later he was hugging her back just as fiercely. Spencer wrapped his arms around her waist and pulled her closer, leaning down a little because of the height difference. His cheek brushed the sensitive shell of her ear and she felt his hot breath against her neck. Her own breathing quickened, and her hair stood on end. An oh-so-pleasant tingle made its way down her body, heightening her awareness of every single place her body touched his. Heat flooded her core. He felt divine. They fit together so perfectly.

Lizzie was on the verge of what could have been a sigh—or, let's be honest, a full-on pant—when Spencer suddenly jerked back and took a few steps away from her.

"It's not a big deal." Spencer's voice was distant, his face blank.

"I know Seb would do the same thing if it was my kid sister going through this."

It was like a bucket of ice had been poured on top of her head. *Of course*. Kid. Sister. Spencer wasn't doing this out of some sort of unrequited love for her. He didn't actually *care*. Lizzie reminded him of his little sister. Meanwhile, she was here, weak at the knees, over one hug.

"Of course. Let's watch *Forgetting Sarah Marshall* then." Lizzie smiled, but it didn't reach her eyes.

An hour or so later, they were settled on opposite ends of the couch, an array of greasy food in front of them, and the awkwardness had somewhat faded. Spencer wasn't as playful as he had been before, but maybe she had just worked that all up in her head. Lizzie had finally washed the mask off her face, and her misguided fantasies about the man in her living room went along with it.

Spencer passed the tub of ice cream back to her, his eyes locked on the screen.

Meanwhile, Lizzie's eyes never quite left his face, despite her best efforts. If you asked her the plot of that particular film, she wouldn't be able to tell you a thing. However, if you were to ask instead if Spencer had the cutest little freckle just below his left ear or whether his five-o'-clock shadow was working for him, she would have a bit more to say.

What? She was only human.

Chapter Ten
SPENCER

S pencer plucked at the cuff of his shirt for what felt like the millionth time, glancing up at the giant cathedral in front of him, its presence still awe-inspiring despite the fire's best efforts. He had a feeling it would stay that way for many years to come. His eyes scanned the crowds on the cobbled street outside the Notre Dame, searching for that head of hair he was way too good at recognizing.

The sun shone down past the clouds dotting the sky, striking the flowers that almost blanketed the ground. Pink petals were everywhere as the aftereffects of spring began floating down from the foliage. It was like that all over the city, the soft, rosy hues blending in seamlessly with the sandstone facades. Bloggers were just eating it up, posing with their fancy bags and shoes in front of professional-camera-toting friends. It kind of ruined the effect.

As his eyes made another round of checks, they caught on a little green shop, the windows filled with books. His mouth quirked up. Bingo.

Spencer ambled over to the store when he noticed the café attached to it. Sure enough, squashed onto a long table in between tourists was a big head of chocolate brown hair, nose buried in a small paperback. There was the Elizabeth he knew. The one he was comfortable with.

"You planning on standing me up, nerd?" Spencer purposefully used the nickname he and Seb had teased her with when they were younger.

A pair of guilty chestnut eyes and flushed cheeks appeared over the book as Elizabeth registered his presence.

"I'm so sorry! I was early so I thought I'd just read for a bit and…I must have lost track of time." In the process of scrambling out of the bench seat she almost knocked over her coffee cup, she was that flustered. It was adorable as hell.

In a completely platonic way, of course.

After nearly losing control from a goddamn hug last night, Spencer had reminded himself to rein it in. Way in. But when she had later suggested she give him a tour of the city to help him get a feel for possible spots for his gym, he couldn't say no. For one, he was pretty sure this was the first time she had actually left the house since her breakup. Two, he needed to be consistent with his cover story. Three—yeah, let's not go there.

Besides, on his own runs he couldn't help but notice how many other people were out and about exercising, much more so than when he had visited a few years ago. Maybe he actually would look into opening a Tate's Training here.

Elizabeth finally escaped the bench seat and began to approach him. He had seen her in an old T-shirt with tear-stained, blotchy cheeks. He had seen her hungover with red-rimmed eyes, smudged with mascara. He had even seen her with some weird mud crap on her face paired with a messy bun and sweats. Each time, her beauty was still undeniable.

But this. *This*. It was a whole new level.

His breath caught as he drunk her in. Those full hips were clad in a black leather skirt that fit tight at the waist and flared out until it touched somewhere high up on her thighs, putting her set of incredible legs on display. Tucked into it was a simple white tee, and she had pulled back the top part of her hair into one of those fancy braids girls loved, leaving most of it out and a few tendrils teasing her cheeks.

She hadn't even put much makeup on. She didn't need to. On most girls the outfit wouldn't earn them a second glance, but on Elizabeth... It was like she had stepped out in lacy lingerie for what it was doing for Spencer. He felt his jeans grow tight.

Spencer darted his eyes back to her face as she inched closer. Before she could go in for another disastrous hug, he lifted a hand and gave a little wave.

"Where to, tour guide?" Spencer fell in step beside her as she expertly navigated the throngs of tourists.

"The whole city centers around the Seine, so it's always a good place to start," she began, flicking her hair over her shoulder. A wave of whatever perfume she was wearing hit him and it smelled way too good. Like pretty flowers and cotton candy. Subtle, fresh, and just plain heady. He was itching to see if she tasted just as sweet.

"You listening, beefcake?"

Spencer blinked a few times to clear his head and sent a stern mental warning to his *other* head to tone it the fuck down. "Nope, this thick skull of mine can't process words."

The corner of her mouth twitched. "Was it the steroids?"

Spencer flexed his biceps. "You think you can achieve *this* level of perfection with an injection?" At Elizabeth's dramatic eye roll he added, "Besides. I got ripped before I could afford them."

A bark of laughter escaped her lips and it was the best sound he'd heard all day.

They began strolling over toward the bank of the river, and Spencer was careful to keep some distance between them. Elizabeth was wiping at the sides of her eyes, a huge grin still on her face. Spencer was smiling along with her when suddenly her expression slipped away and her eyes narrowed.

He looked in the direction of her gaze and saw a tall blond

woman, who looked to be in her early twenties, approaching them. She had bright blue eyes and a model's frame. Before his cock had decided Elizabeth Hastings was its true north, she would have been just his type.

The woman smiled shyly at Spencer, not even looking in Elizabeth's direction. "I couldn't resist meeting you Mr. Tate... I'm a big fan of your program." She glanced up at him from under her lashes and held out a hand. "Giselle."

Spencer plastered on a smile and let her know it was nice to meet her. He wasn't into the whole social media thing; all he really posted were workout videos and client testimonials. Somehow he'd amassed a huge following, and occasionally his app users or Instagram followers treated him like some kind of celebrity. He would never be entirely comfortable with it, but he wasn't going to throw their support back in their faces.

Giselle had her hand on his arm, animatedly talking about how it was so hard to find a good sculpting program when she already had such a tiny waist. His eyes darted to Elizabeth just in time to see her snort.

Suddenly Giselle was pressing herself up against him, pulling out her phone for a selfie. Her face was so close their cheeks were almost touching. He suppressed a sigh, threw on a tight smile for the picture, then carefully extracted himself from the arm she had hooked around his waist. Could the woman be any more obvious?

Apparently so, because her parting words were, "I'm in Paris for a few more days... I'll send you a message on Instagram." She bit her lip. "A picture message."

With that, Giselle was off. Thank. Fuck.

Spencer turned his attention back to Elizabeth who was shooting him a filthy look.

"Really?" her dry voice rang out.

Spencer shrugged. "I didn't want to be rude."

"And I bet if she was a three-hundred-pound woman with a face like Mrs. Doubtfire you'd let her be all over you, as well?"

"Why does it bother you so much anyway?"

Spencer hadn't meant it to come out sounding that sharp. Elizabeth instantly quieted down, mumbling something before continuing on with the tour as if nothing had happened. Spencer's brow furrowed as he noticed the tips of her ears and cheeks turning red. What did she have to be embarrassed about? Was she *jealous*?

Just as quickly as the thought occurred, he dismissed it. The woman had just had her heart broken, there was no way she would be thinking about anyone that way right now, let alone him... Someone as cultured as Elizabeth? Yeah, fat chance gym junkie was her type.

Soon enough, they were strolling side-by-side along the river in silence. Surprisingly it wasn't awkward; it felt natural. Elizabeth had stopped at every single book stand they passed. Spencer didn't mind. It was worth it to see those big eyes flash.

"Why do you always give the books a little shake?"

Spencer had noticed her doing it with every book she picked up.

Elizabeth ducked her head. "I like to see if there are any notes inside. Any stories from its past owner. I like that they have a history."

Well. Wasn't that damn cute. He wondered how many books she had bought just because they had some mysterious backstory.

"How long have you lived here again?"

"Around seven months now," Elizabeth replied absently, her eyes catching on a battered-looking paperback by someone called Camus.

"Does it get old?"

She thumbed the pages and her brow furrowed. "It's hard... At the start everything was so new, so exciting. I would see these carts for the first time and feel like I was one of my favorite writers,

59

scraping together a few coins to buy my reading material for the week."

Spencer lifted a brow at that and resisted a laugh. "When have you ever had to count coins?"

"That's the point." She scowled, and that little line between her brows only made her look cuter. "That's why I needed to come here, to live a real life and be inspired. How else am I meant to write?"

"Why did you have to move across the world to do that?"

Spencer didn't get it. His family had never been at the point where his parents couldn't put food on the table, but most of his childhood wardrobe was hand-me-downs, vacations were a rarity, and birthdays and Christmases were restricted to one present each. He'd still had it pretty good.

But Elizabeth? It wasn't just a new level... She was in a different universe. Spencer had been to her family 'house'. It had guest houses four times bigger than the three-bedroom apartment he and Grace had grown up in. Their garage was designed to fit twenty cars. No amount of playing poor could erase that sort of life from your system. He didn't know much about writing but if you couldn't be inspired by that, you were screwed.

"I want to be like them," Elizabeth was saying, flinging a hand out toward the old paperbacks stacked together in the cart, "they came to Paris and it changed them."

"Has it changed you?"

"Some things." Her expression clouded over, her face echoing that first night he had seen her.

Crap. He hadn't meant to upset her. He quickly grabbed her hand and pulled her toward the bridge ahead. "So, who does a guy have to kiss to get one of those little French pancakes around here anyway?"

Her mouth quirked up and she rolled her eyes.

"If you manage to lay one on the Mona Lisa, the crêpes are on me."

His eyes flashed. "You're on."

HOURS WENT BY IN A BLUR. SPENCER DIDN'T THINK HE HAD laughed so hard in years, and he felt it in his abs. He hadn't realized Elizabeth could be so witty. When they were younger and he was at her family's house all the time, she had been too young and shy to really talk to him, and the past few days she had still been so down about that French wanker.

But today? Today she was beaming. Her eyes shone. And she was cracking up just as much as he was.

They had made their way toward the Louvre in search of a crêpe stand. *Follow the tourists,* Elizabeth had instructed when his growling stomach became too much to ignore. Spencer had found a big sign advertising Di Vinci's masterpiece and planted a smooch on it, just to see Elizabeth smile. She also took a video. The sneak.

Afterward she put him into a boat that gave a city tour from the water. It was impossible not to get swept up in her enthusiasm for the city; her passion was contagious as she pointed out pretty old building after pretty old building. They all looked the same to Spencer, but he kept those thoughts quiet, looking more at Elizabeth than the architectural wonders she was fussing over.

They sat on the upper deck, and in between landmarks, they made up stories about the people sitting near them, competing to see who could come up with the craziest one. Friendship with her was like his favorite pair of jeans. Comfortable, an effortless fit, and when you slipped them on, they felt pretty damn perfect.

Now they were standing at the *Trocadéro,* a big plaza that boasted one of the best views of the Eiffel Tower in the city. Spencer was hyperaware of Elizabeth's small body next to his much larger one. The sun had just set, the temperature dropping with it, and he could see the hair on her arms standing on end.

Before he could overthink it, Spencer shrugged out of his jacket and placed it over her shoulders. His hands probably lingered longer than they should have on the slope of her upper back. He was going crazy. Over the course of the day, without even meaning to, he had found excuses to touch her. He knew it was wrong. He knew it would never go anywhere, but he couldn't help it. She was an addiction.

"My knight in shining armor." Her voice was sarcastic but when his eyes met hers, they shone. There was nothing but sincerity in those brown orbs. As he held her gaze, her pupils dilated. If he hadn't been focusing directly on her, he might have missed the way they quickly darted from his eyes to his lips and back. But he didn't.

"Anything for you, princess."

It could have been the kaleidoscope of colors painting the sky, making the sunset more than magical. Maybe it was the Eiffel Tower twinkling in the background, the shining lights just screaming romance. Perhaps it was all the couples around them, their love so obvious. He wasn't sure what made him do it but suddenly he was inching toward her, drawn by some invisible force.

Elizabeth's eyes sparked with something he couldn't quite name, but he felt it deep and low, and his body responded as if it were the most natural thing in the world. He let out a sharp breath as she tilted her face toward him. Could she be feeling this too? Those lips, that he hadn't been able to resist fantasizing about licking him all over, parted. Spencer's lids began to shut and he leaned in—

"Excuse me? Can you take a quick photo of us? While the sparkles are on."

With that nasally voice, Spencer's haze was broken. He flinched away, as if slapped, and focused all of his attention on the demanding tourist in front of him.

"Of course," he bit out, voice husky, as he took their camera and grabbed a few shots. He put his mind on shutdown; he could figure out what the fuck had almost happened there later.

Right now he needed to slam down the brakes… And pray to whatever higher power was up there that Seb never found out Spencer had almost made out with his baby sister.

Christ.

Chapter Eleven

LIZZIE

A couple of days later Lizzie was sitting with Spencer at *Café de Flore*, trying her best not to read into anything. And failing. Miserably.

She plucked at the flakes of the croissant on the intricate embossed plate in front of her. They had an outside table. It was the only real way to grab a coffee in Paris. Sitting on the bustling *Boulevard Saint-Germain* and people-watching added to the beauty of the whole experience. From locals, to tourists, students to celebrities, anyone and everyone could walk past. Lizzie loved to sit there, book in hand, and let the cacophony of different languages wash over her. Some of the greatest minds in history had sat at this very café and done the exact same thing.

Her eyes followed the path of her fork as she fiddled with it, stomach suddenly overcome with butterflies. It was hard to ignore them. Especially when it seemed like Spencer had been about to kiss her the other night. Now he had asked her to go for coffee. Was this a *date*? It couldn't be.

It just didn't make sense.

And yet, that image of his eyes all hooded, the feeling of his hot breath merging with hers... You can't make that stuff up. Sure, he could have been caught up in the moment. Lizzie knew all too well how the romance of Paris can send your better judgment to the back seat. Hell, hers had packed up, taken a dip in the Seine, and drowned the moment she set foot in the city. Hadn't even left a goodbye note.

That was the other thing. Amaury.

There was still a void in her heart where the handsome Frenchman had been. It wasn't nearly as aching as it had been a few days ago but it was still there. So was the knife in her gut. She had been thinking about him less and less, but when she did, it twisted. But if she had loved Amaury so much, how could she suddenly be so drawn to Spencer? Could she even trust what she was feeling, or was she just hurt and attention-starved?

Lizzie must have groaned out loud because Spencer's lips quirked. "Fancy croissant not to your liking, princess?"

"The food is fine, thank you, beefcake." Elizabeth sniffed, making a face.

"I'd sure hope so considering the price tag... Are they hand-churning the butter back there?"

"Don't be ridiculous." Her tone was haughty. "First they have to milk the cow."

Spencer chuckled, bringing his coffee to his lips. His hand dwarfed the cup, and Lizzie made a concerted effort not to imagine whether he also had a big... Foot. She meant foot. For stability and whatnot. It was a perfectly natural thing to think. There was absolutely no reason why her face should feel hot. Right.

"So how much longer are you here?"

For some reason, a shadow crossed Spencer's face. Maybe the gym plans weren't going so well after all.

"A few more days." Spencer cleared his throat. "I'm just playing it by ear."

"Where have you got to so far?" Lizzie had no idea what the process was, but it seemed odd that Spencer was here alone. Well, she assumed he was alone. He hadn't mentioned an agent or assistant or anything like that.

Spencer's answer was cryptic, and it matched the next few

replies he gave her when she pressed the issue. Wasn't this his passion? Shouldn't he be itching at the chance to share it with her? Eventually he raked his fingers through his hair and announced he was going to the bathroom, abruptly pushing out his chair and striding away.

Lizzie crinkled her nose. It was odd, to say the least. But, in fairness, when she was having difficulties with writing she didn't like to talk about it. Everyone went through the odd rough patch. She decided to let it lie.

The table made that annoying, amplified buzz that signaled a text message. Her eyes darted to the source and she saw Spencer's phone lighting up, the name Seb written above a text.

From the corner of her eye she took in the back of the restaurant, in the direction of the bathrooms. No movement there. She glanced back to the phone. She shouldn't. But curiosity was eating up a path along her spine. It *itched*.

Lizzie thought back to the other night. The chemistry that had been like pure electricity. Had Spencer told her brother? Was he asking Seb's blessing to pursue her? She scoffed but at the same time a happy shiver raked through her body.

Drumming her fingers against the table, she darted her eyes heavenward before she finally cracked. In the blink of an eye, Lizzie snatched the phone and squinted to read the message. Her stomach dropped, past her knees, past her feet. It sank into the ground, probably now buried somewhere in the catacombs of Paris.

Seb: *Good idea getting her out of the house. She still crying much or is she getting better? Thanks again for doing this, and for staying so long. I really owe you, man.*

Well. Lizzie hadn't been crying before but now she could feel the telltale hot sting as her eyes welled up.

She was an idiot. A stupid, gullible fool. She had seriously started to believe Spencer cared for her. Gorgeous, talented Spencer interested in little nerd Lizzie. Writer who couldn't write. Spoiled brat who had achieved nothing of note in her entire life.

A ragged breath escaped her and the loud street noises faded into the background. White noise took over as she thought back over every. Single. Moment.

Lizzie had opened up to him. She had let him see her vulnerable, let him hold her in his arms when she was dying inside. He was the only person she had confided in about the worst moment of her life.

The blaze of humiliation started in her cheeks but soon it expanded, seeping through her bones, taking over her whole body. She thought about how long she had stressed over the outfit she picked for their day out, the YouTube tutorial she had slaved in front of to get her hair just right in some naïve attempt to impress him. Meanwhile, Spencer was reporting back her every word, thought, and feeling to her damn brothers. All those moments, the sweet gestures that had meant the world to her, were nothing but a chore to him.

And what the fuck was that almost-kiss last night? *Pity?* She swallowed, tasting acid.

She hoped he would finish up with his stupid gym soon and leave… *Wait.*

Had he lied about that too?

Lizzie brought her palms up to cradle her forehead.

Was any of it real?

"Elizabeth? What's the matter?" Spencer's big, warm hand touched her shoulder and she flinched away.

"Don't," she spat out the word. It tasted vile.

Big blue eyes shining with concern tried to lock on to hers but she avoided his gaze.

Spencer crouched down next to her. His knee brushed her calf, and the spark it caused felt like pure betrayal. He reached out a hand to touch her, frowned, then lowered it.

"Elizabeth, baby, talk to me."

She gave a mirthless laugh and shook her head. "You don't get to call me that."

"You're right, I'm sorry." He held up his hands. "But you were upset before that. What is it? What can I do?"

Lizzie gathered up the emotions swirling around inside her, collected them into a net, then bottled them up deep in her chest. She worked hard to relax her face, and with a carefully blank expression turned her eyes back to Spencer. "You can go back to wherever you came from when you got the call to come and rescue me."

"Elizabeth, I—"

"No. You weren't honest. You pretended to *care*." Lizzie's voice cracked. She needed to leave ASAP or risk having another breakdown in front of this man. She pushed out her chair, coming to her feet. Spencer had been leaning against it and she felt a bitter sort of satisfaction when he stumbled forward. "You lied. You're no better than him."

There was no need to elaborate on who *he* was. She could tell the moment Spencer realized because his entire face just fell. His jaw clenched and those eyes clouded over with a mix between hurt and guilt.

Lizzie was almost at the door when she heard his last words.

"You really think that?"

She glanced over her shoulder, eyes narrowed. "I know it."

Chapter Twelve
SPENCER

H e'd fucked up.

Spencer knew it. Elizabeth knew it. The whole damn café probably knew it. You would have to be deaf not to hear the sharp scrape of Elizabeth's chair, blind if you missed her grimacing face as she tried to hold back tears, and just plain dumb if you were the man to put an expression like that on a woman like her.

He raked his hands through his hair, sitting on the edge of the bed at his hotel. It was an old, typically French building. The rooms were tiny but intricately decorated with heavy, embroidered bed covers and billowy white curtains. Spencer's room was pretty empty save for the duffel in front of him.

Each time he tried to call Elizabeth she didn't answer. It seemed like she was ignoring all of his messages too. Every little read receipt that appeared on his screen was like a punch to the gut.

Spencer had been close to Grace his whole life. When their mom had died, she had come to him with her problems. He felt he had a pretty fair understanding of the female mind. And he could see how bad this looked to Elizabeth.

He seemed like a total jerk. A liar. Every single kind word or gesture he had made would be immediately discounted. And she wasn't even giving him a chance to explain.

Spencer halfheartedly continued folding up his clothes. What explanation could he give her? That he couldn't stop thinking about her smile or her scent or the little furrow that appeared on her brow when she was especially captivated by a book? That he had been a split second away from kissing her the other night despite his best efforts to do the exact opposite?

That he came for Seb but stayed for her?

His eyes drew closed and he felt a headache coming on.

There was no way he was telling her any of that sappy crap. It was Seb's sister. His *sister*. You just don't go there. He would murder Seb or Dylan, and fucking destroy that little fuckboy Josh, if they so much as looked at Grace in the wrong way. It was rule one of the Bro Code. Anything less than asking for her hand in marriage was unacceptable. And yeah, that wasn't happening.

He needed to leave. If Elizabeth wasn't talking to him there was no reason for him to book in for another night tomorrow morning, the way he'd done every day since his arrival.

But deep in his gut he just *couldn't*. Suddenly that image of her crumpling up her writing at her desk, her face looking just as crushed as the paper, appeared again. He couldn't shake it. Elizabeth was strong, she could put on a brave face, but she had been through so much. And Spencer had just taken her already fragile trust and destroyed it. He'd taken that crumpled-up piece of paper and flung it straight into the fire.

That's how he found himself, ten minutes later, pounding hard at her front door. The cool wood wasn't the most comfortable to hit but the pain biting through his knuckles seemed so fitting. They couldn't leave things this way. Spencer had no idea what the hell he was going to say to her, but he figured he could wing it.

With the click of a few deadbolts sliding across, the door soon slid open.

"Elizabeth, I— Who the hell are *you*?" Nerves had eaten him alive on the walk over so it came out a little harsher than he had intended.

A tall woman with a heart-shaped face, amber eyes, and dark blond hair was standing at the threshold, raising a brow. She looked supremely unimpressed, if her pursed lips were any indication.

"Sophia. Her best friend," she drawled, as if it were the most obvious thing in the world, "and you are *not* her boyfriend."

"Some best friend you are. She doesn't have a boyfriend anymore." Spencer scowled at the thought of him. "I know her brother; I really need to talk to her."

Sophia ignored him. "Uh, yeah she does. He's tall, French, and hung like a—"

"The fuck also has a wife," he spat out. That shut her up.

"He *what*?"

Soon enough they were facing each other on opposite ends of the couch, Sophia's mouth gaping open as Spencer finished up explaining his time in Paris. Sophia had only arrived home from Greece a few hours ago, and Elizabeth was out tutoring so they hadn't yet had time to catch up. He felt a little bad for sharing Elizabeth's secret, but it had kind of slipped out. The briefest mention of that French wanker pissed him off enough to switch off the part of his brain responsible for reasoning. Besides, Sophia would have found out eventually.

The skin on her face was dark from her time away, her nose covered with a generous splattering of freckles. But that didn't stop the deep, angry scarlet from taking over. Spencer watched, fascinated, as the color slowly expanded down her neck. If steam suddenly began to billow from her ears he honestly would not be surprised.

"That FUCK. That DOUCHECANOE. I will *kill* him." With each word Sophia thumped a fist into the pillow she was clutching in her lap. *Jesus.* He didn't want to get on this woman's bad side. "I could tell he was sleazy, you know; I *told* her he was too good to be true."

Spencer remained silent. He knew from experience with Grace

that his input was not necessary here. The occasional nod or 'mmmh' would suffice until Sophia wrapped up her rant. Hell, he remembered the wave of fury that had hit him when Elizabeth cried out the story to him. That shit needed time to process.

After ten or so more minutes of indignation went by, with Sophia progressing from hitting the pillow to stalking around the room, muttering various threats to herself, she finally calmed down, and Spencer had a chance to get a word in.

"Look, she's pretty angry with me at the moment. I get it." He took a breath. "But I'm worried about her—it's a shitty thing to go through and I still want to be there for her, you know?"

"Do I want to know what you did to piss her off that much?" Her voice was low and dangerous. Calm Sophia was almost more frightening than enraged Sophia.

He grimaced. "Yeah, probably not." In the silence that followed Spencer pushed on. *Not much to lose anyway.* "I'm glad you're back; I really think she needs a friend."

More silence.

"Do you have anything planned to help her cheer up?"

Sophia sparked up at that. "Oh don't you worry, I'm doing a girls night."

At that it felt like a weight had been lifted off his chest. Girls night. Perfect. Elizabeth would be able to kick back, have a few drinks at home with her best friend, and get it all out. Maybe they'd watch a few chick flicks, have a laugh. It was exactly what she needed, especially when Spencer had helped aggravate her heartbreak.

"Can you keep me updated with how she's doing?"

"No."

Okay, not ideal but he could work with it. Best friends were protective—it was understandable. Spencer plastered on a smile and tried to mold his face into what he hoped was an expression that screamed 'this is a good guy'.

"Could you let her know I'd love to talk to her to clear the air? Even just a phone call." He let his face fall a little. "Honestly, at this point I'll take what I can get."

That brought a laugh to Sophia's lips, which he considered a pretty good sign. Finally, after a dramatic sigh she promised to put in a good word for him, then shooed him out the door.

Spencer's mood lifted a little as he made the walk back to his hotel. Sure, nothing had changed between him and Elizabeth, but at least he knew her friend was back. Sophia seemed loyal as hell, so there was no way she would let Elizabeth get too down in the dumps.

As Spencer walked into the lobby, he reasoned to himself that Sophia taking the reins was the best solution. Deep down he knew he shouldn't be trying to make up with Elizabeth at all. Should just walk away now. With the crazy attraction he felt toward her, no good would come out of a friendship between them. There was no way he would be able to resist her for long, and if he gave in, there was a good chance the Hastings boys would castrate him.

Spencer shuddered. Nope, he liked his balls right where they were, *thank you very much.*

Chapter Thirteen
LIZZIE

Lizzie closed the lid of her laptop and sighed. It seemed like every kid who walked into the library today was one of hers. Saturdays were always her busiest day. Exam season was coming up and with students in class during the week, Saturday was the day they all wanted to book in. When she had first come to Paris, she had posted in a few Facebook groups, offering her services. Now through word-of-mouth, she had close to twenty students she saw regularly. When they weren't meeting up face-to-face at the library, they were sending her essays and assignments to critique.

It wasn't just high school kids though; Lizzie actually had a few university students, whose second language was English, who needed a bit of help with grammar.

She threw her head side to side, cracking her neck then stretched out her back. Lizzie had been sitting at the same desk for close to five hours and it had taken its toll. But she didn't really mind. There was something about helping students that always seemed to brighten her day. They were old enough that tutoring was their choice, not some chore their parents had forced them into, and it made teaching them a breeze.

Despite the mess with Spencer the night before, somehow the kids had been able to cheer her up. She felt such a rush when she was able do something good for them, to provide a service that helped take their work to the next level. And the smiles on their faces when she praised something they had done, or helped them see critique from their teachers in a new light? Priceless.

But as she hoisted her messenger bag across her chest and ambled down the library steps in the direction of Metro Line Four it all came rushing back.

It almost wasn't surprising that she had ended up in this situation. What the hell had she been thinking, fantasizing about Spencer caring for her? It was like she was driving on a freeway of her hopes and dreams and decided to let her fourteen-year-old self take the wheel. Well, it seemed the little idiot had hit a guardrail and flung them both off a cliff. Typical.

The plus side was that Lizzie had already spent up her quota of tears for the week—the year even—so finding out that everything with Spencer was just in her head wasn't as upsetting as it would have been a few weeks ago. In comparison to fucking Amaury, the man was a saint.

And yet.

She had just begun to feel *happy* again. During that day, walking around Paris, she had smiled so much it had hurt. Seeing the twinkle in Spencer's eyes, his little smirk… He was infectious. And to find out it was all an act?

Lizzie shook her head. No. She would *not* think about that.

Taking a deep breath, she hopped off the metro, dodging through crowds as she made her way to her little street. She picked up a baguette and some camembert on the way, because, when in Rome, right?

When she finally made it through her apartment door, she let out a little squeal and dropped her bags in excitement as she caught sight of her best friend's beaming face.

"You're back!" Lizzie was still squealing as Sophia pulled her in for a tight hug. The tension left her body. All it took was a familiar face for Lizzie to feel like she could handle everything. She wasn't alone anymore.

"Don't be too mad at him but I met Spencer and he told me everything." The words came out all rushed and breathy as Sophia blurted them out, still embracing Lizzie.

That stopped her short. Lizzie jerked away. "He *told* you!"

As if lying to her wasn't bad enough, now he was going around sharing the worst moment of her entire life? He hadn't just broken her trust, he'd hurled it off the fucking Eiffel Tower so it smashed into tiny little pieces on the ground. Probably hit a tourist along the way too. Dangerous stuff.

Spencer was *so* dead.

"I told you not to be mad! It was an accident!"

"How does one blurt out my darkest day by *accident*?"

A guilty expression took over Sophia's face.

"Sophia." Lizzie's tone was a warning, her narrowed eyes driving the point home.

"I may have started talking about Amaury's giant monster cock." Sophia sighed. "And I think he just saw red."

Right. Lizzie would process that little tidbit of information later. But for now...

"So. What are we doing about my poor broken heart then?"

Sophia grinned and the glint in her eyes was slightly evil.

Uh-oh.

A FEW HOURS LATER LIZZIE LOOKED LIKE A DIFFERENT PERSON.

Sophia had made good use of her afternoon, hitting up the shops in the trendy *Marais* district. She had come home with what could only be described as pure magic.

The dress was skintight and a deep scarlet, strapless and short.

Somehow, it still managed to come across as classy. Every single lump and bump on Lizzie's body was transformed. Her waist looked smaller, her tits better, and when she turned around to glance in the mirror, even she would admit her small ass looked pretty damn incredible.

Sophia had also seen to her makeup. Lizzie didn't normally wear much, but seeing the effect it had on her face, she could completely understand why some girls did. A shimmery, brown, smoky eye with a few strategic strokes of lip liner, and some contouring, went a long way. A *really* long way.

Lizzie finished off the look with her favorite black over-the-knee boots, leaving only a small section of her thigh on display. She was going sans jacket. Tonight was serious.

After a long discussion (and half a bottle of red) she and Sophia decided Lizzie needed a rebound. A nice, mindless one-night stand to replace her memory of Amaury. Was it the most mature decision she'd ever made? No, probably not.

Was it a tried and tested method of getting past a breakup? Hell. Yeah.

Somewhere deep in the back of her mind, Lizzie realized that a part of her was doing this to get over Spencer, as well, but she never really listened to that part anyway.

She was ready for girls night.

The sounds of a remix of Lana Del Rey wafted through the apartment, definitely a few decibels higher than her neighbors would appreciate. There was one cheese platter on their small dining room table, and two bottles of wine. They still had a few hours until they were heading out because the clubs opened so late over here, but they were making good use of the time with drinking and talking shit.

"Okay. What are we feeling? Blonde or brunette?" Sophia was very into the rebound idea. She even volunteered to stay out super late so Lizzie would have the apartment to herself to 'go heels to Jesus', as Sophia had so eloquently put it.

"Redhead." Lizzie's reply was instantaneous. Amaury had hair so dark it was almost black. Spencer's was this gorgeous honey blond color that she longed to run her hands—

Nope. The man's hair was completely uninspiring. Not at all noteworthy. At all.

Sophia quirked a brow. "Interesting choice…" She hummed and made a big show of considering the issue, going so far as to pinch her chin thoughtfully. "Especially considering you practically go into heat at the sight of a tall blond."

Lizzie rolled her eyes but her friend wasn't done yet. "Hang on." Sophia fake-gasped, "Isn't *Spencer* blond!"

"Shut up." Lizzie grunted and swallowed another mouthful of wine, focusing on the bitter wild-fruit taste to try and drown out her best friend. It didn't work.

"Are we going to talk about how hot he is?"

"No, Sophia."

"I stalked his Instagram, by the way. Don't even pretend you haven't thought about running your tongue down those abs."

"Sophia."

"And the arms? His biceps are basically the size of your face; can you imagine what he could do wi—"

"SOPHIA."

That shut her up.

Lizzie stood up, grabbed the bottle of red, and poured her friend a generous glass. "We are *not* talking about that." She nudged it toward her. "If your mouth opens for anything other than drinking, you're no longer my best friend."

Chapter Fourteen
SPENCER

Spencer folded up his favorite blue shirt and placed it at the top of his duffel. After much twiddling of his thumbs and pointless procrastination, he had finally made up his mind.

His flight home was booked for mid-morning the next day and he knew it was the right thing to do. Elizabeth didn't need him. She didn't want to speak to him. And now she had her best friend so there really was no reason for him to stay. No, scratch that. There was no *acceptable* reason for him to stay.

Spencer looked around the hotel room. He was actually going to miss this city and all its intricacies. Over the past week Paris had drawn him in almost as much as Elizabeth had. It was just as charming and beautiful, and there was so much of it he had yet to explore. Just like there were so many parts of Elizabeth... Yeah. Leaving was definitely a good idea.

It was around eight and he had almost gone forty minutes without thinking about Elizabeth. It was kind of a record. Of course, the episode of *How I Met Your Mother,* he had put on to entertain him while he packed, had helped a little.

Now with his most pressing task done, all he had was time. He pulled out his phone for something to do and opened up his Instagram. Sophia's name came up at the top left of the screen in the story section. Spencer had followed her profile on his walk home from her apartment when it became clear that Elizabeth wasn't going to accept his request. Sure, Sophia had said that she wouldn't give him updates on how Elizabeth was doing, but technically he was doing nothing wrong by keeping an eye on her from a distance. Social media was useful for something, at least.

He clicked on the story and his forehead creased. It was a video of Elizabeth in her pajamas, eyes looking huge and sexy, all covered in some brown shimmery powder, chugging a full glass of wine at their apartment. Wine, cheese, and various types of makeup and brushes littered the already small table. Since when were girls nights so rowdy? Whenever Grace had friends over they had the occasional drink with their movie but this looked like it was getting a bit out of hand. Who guzzled wine? Weren't you meant to enjoy that shit? And what was with that ratio of two bottles for two women? That tiny plate of cheese didn't count as a meal either.

His fingers hovered over the keys to type exactly that to Sophia, but he stopped himself. It wasn't his business what they got up to on their night in. If it was cheering her up, it was a good move.

With a resigned sigh he felt through his whole body, Spencer put down his phone and pulled his computer over onto the bed next to him. He put on the latest *Mission Impossible* and settled down. He loved a good action movie and he hadn't had a chance to catch this one when it was in cinemas. It would be the perfect distraction.

TWENTY MINUTES LATER SPENCER WAS CURSING. THE FUCKING movie was set in Paris. *Paris.* How the hell was he supposed to not think of Elizabeth when every two seconds there was a shot of a building she had pointed out to them on their boat tour, or a cobblestoned street that looked exactly like the one outside her apartment?

But this shouldn't bother him. He shouldn't be this obsessed with her. It just wasn't normal. He had *never* been like this with a girl. Maybe it was mix of that crazy attraction and some residual fraternal feelings, imagining it was Grace who had gone through a breakup like that. Yeah, the Seb connection was bringing out his protectiveness—that had to be it. The alternative was too frightening to imagine.

Tom Cruise was fighting with some guy in the bathroom of a party when Spencer's eyes first strayed to his phone. Eventually he took a breath and renewed his focus on the movie. Now some woman was beating up the guy. They were pretty damn lucky no partygoers decided they needed a piss, otherwise they would have some serious explaining to do.

During the next scene, without consciously thinking about it, Spencer picked up his phone and flicked it open. His thumb circled over the Instagram app for a few seconds before he finally gave in. Sophia had a new story.

The video started playing. This time it was from a bit more of distance and Spencer finally got a good look at what Elizabeth was wearing.

What. The. Fuck.

It was barely a dress. The tips of her boobs were spilling out of the top and his cock immediately woke up and decided to pay attention. He could see a generous amount of thigh, and damn it was hot. But more importantly, who the fuck was she trying to impress?

Elizabeth was quite clearly drunk and yelling out something that sounded like 'summertime sadness' along with a heavy beat in the background. She moved her hips around while she did it and fuck. Spencer groaned. This was not helping.

Once again he put the phone down and concentrated on the movie. Surprisingly, he got through it all without picking it up again. Seems like all that self-talk had finally paid off. At least something was working out for him.

It was closer to midnight when he put away his laptop and started to get ready for bed. Spencer showered, brushed his teeth, and made sure the majority of his stuff was packed away and ready to go before he allowed himself one final look at his phone. Sophia had a new story. Go figure.

Except when he saw this one, his stomach dropped.

The girls were no longer at the apartment. They were drinking what looked like tequila shots in the courtyard of a club and Elizabeth was wearing that damn dress. In the background he could see a number of guys leering at them.

Girls night, his ass.

He typed out a message to Sophia, jaw clenched.

Spencer: *Where are you guys? Do you really think a club is the best place for her right now??*

Sophia: *We're at Arc! It's so cool, you can see the arc de TRIUMPH!!!!*

Spencer: *You're both stupid drunk. You should just head home.*

Sophia: *Noooooo, boo! Fun police!!*

Spencer was clenching and unclenching his fists, trying to calm down a little before he responded when the next message came through.

Sophia: *Lizzard needs to get SLIZZARD for her rebound.*

Rebound? *Rebound?*

Fuck being calm.

Spencer's fists were balled so tight his nails cut into his palm. They were going out to get laid. One fucking week after her breakup. Yeah that was a fan-fucking-tastic idea. What sort of friend was Sophia anyway? The last thing Elizabeth needed was some sleazy shithead at a club using her, as well. The thought of it alone made Spencer sick.

Minutes later Spencer was flinging open his neatly packed duffel and pulling out a pair of jeans and his nicest shirt. He would bet good money the French clubs had a strict dress code. Of course, they had let Elizabeth in while she was wearing a dress short enough to be a top but she looked damn incredible so that made sense.

He was only going over there to keep an eye on her. If Seb was here, he'd be doing the same thing. Actually, Seb wouldn't have let her out of the house without putting on at least three more layers, but that was beside the point. Spencer figured he could go over, hang out on the edge of the crowd, and make sure no French fuckers were getting any ideas about taking advantage of her.

That was all.

Elizabeth wouldn't even know he had been there at all. He'd make sure he saw her get safely into a cab home, then tomorrow he would fly back to the States and be done with it. Maybe he would check in with Seb from time to time to see how she was doing and that was it.

AFTER PAYING AN EXORBITANT ENTRY FEE AND WAITING IN THE LINE for what seemed like hours, Spencer was inside. Every minute of the ride over there felt like hell. He constantly checked Instagram to see if Sophia had put anything else up but it seemed she was off her phone for the night. She hadn't replied to any of his messages either. It sure seemed like she was trying to drive him insane on purpose.

The club had a massive dance floor in the middle, and around the outside were dozens of tables that went for thousands of euros a pop. It was ridiculous. Good-looking women in not much clothing were everywhere, and for every girl there seemed to be at least two seedy men hovering around.

It didn't take long for his eyes to catch on Elizabeth. It wasn't hard.

She was in the middle of the dance floor next to Sophia, the red of her dress immediately drawing attention. The way she was seductively rolling her hips around to the beat didn't help either.

Spencer's jaw clenched. She was throwing her hands above her head, laughing, and twirling around. It should be illegal to look that good. Every little move she did made him imagine what the exact same move would look like if she was naked on top of him. He blew out his cheeks and made his way over to the bar to get a drink. He fucking needed one.

By the time he glanced back at the dance floor, his hands tightened so much he thought he might break the glass. Sophia was now nowhere to be seen, and a tall, dark-haired man was pressed up behind Elizabeth. He looked like he spent his life at the gym, his arms and neck were bulging and covered in what looked like tribal tattoos. Classy. He had those arms wrapped around Elizabeth's little frame, his hands low on her hips. The guy had the audacity to lean down and kiss her neck.

Spencer. Saw. Red.

Chapter Fifteen
LIZZIE

Kanye West's *Fade* was playing in the background and it was fucking perfect.

Lizzie beamed, twisting her hips in time with the song. She shut her eyes and just enjoyed it.

She was in that happy place when you've had so much to drink you're perfectly buzzed, but not at the point where you start to feel like crap. The fourth tequila shot Sophia was right now getting for her would probably tip her over the edge, but she didn't care.

The throng of bodies around her added to the rush. Here she didn't need to think about Amaury's betrayal. She didn't need to spew over Spencer. She could just dance and laugh and spin around and around until nothing felt bad anymore.

The music was hypnotic, and with her eyes closed she could put her full focus on it. She felt the hum of it echo in her bloodstream, breathed in the smoky air, and watched her closed lids as the strobe lights made them flicker.

A body suddenly pushed up against her, quite obviously male by the way the rock-hard object pressing into her lower back felt. Big hands encircled her hips and she swallowed nervously.

He hadn't even spoken to her, yet he thought it was okay to rub his erection on her? Was this the new normal?

Lizzie had never really been into the club scene, but this seemed a bit extreme.

She shook herself a little and tried to push those thoughts aside. This was what she was here for, wasn't it? This could be her rebound. He certainly felt up for the task.

Lizzie turned her head to the side to try and speak to the hulk of a man behind her, but he took that as a sign to start kissing her neck.

Those shots she'd drunk decided to start doing a tap dance in the pit of her stomach. This didn't feel right. His hands pulled at her hips, pressing her even farther into him, and he gave her neck a hard bite.

Lizzie tried to tell him to stop but the music was so loud he didn't hear her. She grabbed at his hands and attempted to pry them off, but he took that as a sign to grab them tighter and swivel their hips around. Did he think she was trying to *dance*?

"Stop. STOP."

The music she had loved so much before was now taunting her, painfully loud and echoing around in her head as she attempted to communicate to the oaf.

She turned her head to the side again, trying to get right into his ear so he would get the fucking message, and he took that opportunity to raise one hand and hold her head there while he stuck his tongue down her throat. He tasted like stale beer and cigarettes. His tongue moved around furiously, as if it were trying to audition for the role of a freaking washing machine.

Lizzie tried her best to move away from him, but he was holding her so tightly, her efforts made little difference.

Suddenly he was no longer at her back.

"She told you to stop, you fuck!" The voice of the man who had wrenched away the creep rang out. He pulled his fist back to deliver a punch and Lizzie realized it was Spencer.

Spencer. Fucking. Tate.

What the hell was he doing here?

She had never seen his face so furious. His eyes were glinting dangerously, and his jaw was hard. His chest rose and fell with rapid breaths as he leaned down to the man now on the ground below him. The crowd was so thick no one had seemed to notice there was a fight taking place.

"You're lucky I didn't break your fucking nose. When a woman tells you no, it means no." Spencer spat at the ground next to him. "Fucking asshole."

Before she knew it, those ice-cold blue eyes were on her and the fury hadn't faded one bit. "You."

Lizzie was still quite intoxicated and not really computing why the hell he was angry with her. Spencer grabbed her arm and started dragging her away from the dance floor.

"Hey. Hey!" Lizzie struggled to keep up in her heels. "Where are you going!"

"*We* are going home," Spencer replied without even looking at her, still holding her arm tightly.

"What? No!" Lizzie tried to put on the brakes to no avail. "I can't leave yet—I haven't—"

Spencer cut her off with a harsh laugh. "Found a rebound? Yeah, you won't be doing that."

How did he know that's what she had been doing? Surely Sophia wouldn't have told him her plan. *Hang on.* "But Sophia! She's still there!"

"I've already told her I'm taking you home." The low, hard voice he had been using all night suddenly softened. "Be careful on these steps."

Lizzie glanced down to the exit of the club and the twelve steps between her and the cab rank. They were an intimidating sight from where she was looking, on top of five-inch heels, a bottle and a half of wine, and three shots down.

She looked back at Spencer helplessly and, with a resigned sigh, he scooped her up into his arms. Lizzie allowed a few moments to soak in his delicious smell and the wonderful feeling of his arms around her before she let herself fully take in the situation.

Spencer was forcing her to leave the club. He'd literally torn her from a man's arms. Yes, that man had been a total jerk but still. Who the fuck did Spencer think he was, trying to control her like that? Lizzie was old enough to make her own decisions; she didn't need her brother's best friend taking it upon himself to shelter her from the world.

Lizzie tried a few more times to convince Spencer to let her stay but he was having none of it. Each refusal brought her anger to new levels. She spent the entire car ride back to her apartment fuming.

Lizzie pressed herself as far as she could to the door, leaving as much space between her and Spencer as possible. She turned the full force of her glare to his face, and she could tell he was feeling it because a vein in his temple was throbbing.

Spencer jammed his fists into his front pocket and started to grind his teeth. Yeah, he was mad.

But what right did he have to be pissed off anyway?

Lizzie folded her arms across her chest and turned her cheek to the window, deciding to focus instead on watching the landmarks whiz past.

She wasn't a baby, she was twenty-four for crying out loud. Spencer had no right to decide she was too drunk, or too fresh from a breakup to be out. The worst part was she knew none of it stemmed from jealousy. He was just being way too thorough in his favor to her brothers. Hell, he was probably angry right now because she was making his task frustratingly hard.

Lizzie gave a mirthless laugh, biding her time until they left the cab. Spencer was going to get a piece of her mind, but she would wait until they had some privacy. That way she could yell as loud as she wanted with no regrets.

By the time they actually made it to her apartment, her fury had built up so much she felt it in every inch of her body. Her face was hot and most likely red under all her makeup, her hands were balled into fists, and she liked to think she looked something like a lioness crouching right before she sprung.

They were standing at her door when she unleashed.

"What the *fuck* was that?" Lizzie demanded, turning her back to the door to face him, rage emanating from every single word.

Spencer's eyes sparked with a matching fire when he narrowed them at her. "That was me stopping you from making a fucking dumb decision."

"You're not the boss of me."

"Someone has to be when you're being an idiot. That guy was two seconds away from pulling you into a back room."

That vein in Spencer's temple was twitching again and his breaths had quickened.

It just wasn't fair that he still looked so good. The blue button-down he was wearing made his eyes even brighter, highlighting his perfectly clear complexion. The light sheen of sweat covering him only made him sexier. So did the lock of golden hair falling haphazardly over his brow.

"What if I wanted to go into a back room with him?" Lizzie was now panting, as well. Of course, she would never have done that. But Spencer didn't know that. And he deserved a bit of stress for everything he had put her through. She hadn't forgotten how much he had played her the week before, pretending to care.

Spencer let out a harsh breath and raked his hands through his hair. "Dressed like that you sure look like you wanted to."

That did it.

Lizzie surged forward so her nose was almost at his chest. She poked him hard, trying not to notice the pleasant way her body tingled when it came into contact with his. A glare took over her face as she spat out, "I already have three brothers, you know; I don't need another."

Spencer swore softly. Closed his eyes and took a long breath.

He opened them again and this time they were burning with something different from before.

"I don't want to be your fucking brother."

Suddenly, he crashed his lips against hers and all rational thought for Lizzie pretty much exited stage right.

The force of him against her pushed her backward until her shoulders were pressed against the door. Spencer caged his arms around her, pinning her body to his, while his tongue demanded entry to her mouth.

Lizzie's entire body lit up. She was on fire. Every single place where he was touching her sparked. She tilted her head up to give him more access and he took it greedily, using one hand to cup her cheek while he deepened their kiss.

His lips were soft. So soft. And the way they meshed against hers felt like absolute heaven. Lizzie's nipples hardened against the thin material of her dress and he must have felt it because he groaned and pushed his hips in closer against hers. He was all hard planes of muscle and between those dense thighs, she felt a thick length press against her stomach.

Now Lizzie was groaning, and she felt sparks of lust flare up deep inside her.

It was when she reached up to run her hands along his chest that Spencer abruptly jerked away.

The contrast in warmth from where his huge body had been covering hers to the frigid air of the hallway was painful. Lizzie blinked, eyes still hooded.

"What's the matter, Spence?"

"I-I can't." His brows drew together, and his nostrils flared. "This was a mistake. It can't happen again."

The flickering light of the hallway emphasized the hard set of his face and Lizzie knew he had made up his mind. She was a mistake. Of course she was. It didn't matter that the kiss had been the best one she had ever had. It clearly wasn't the same way for him. For Spencer it was just a slip in judgment, a regret he wouldn't care about later. Seb would murder him if he ever tried to pursue her, and obviously she wasn't worth fighting for.

She swallowed and felt her eyes flood with tears.

And Spencer? His blank face didn't change one bit.

"Goodbye, Elizabeth."

Humiliated three times in a week. This had to be a new record.

She waited until he had walked away before she let the tears fall.

Chapter Sixteen
LIZZIE

"**A**re we going to talk about the blond elephant in the room?" Sophia smirked. "Or should I say the *hallway*?"

Lizzie groaned and readjusted her sunglasses. They were doing their ritual Sunday walk around *Champ de Mars*, and this was the fourth time Sophia had brought up the Spencer Incident.

Sophia had left the club a few moments after they had the night before, arriving at their apartment just in time to witness Spencer making out with her. Like a good friend, she had tactfully made herself scarce in the stairwell, hoping to give them time to fumble their way inside. But of course, less than two minutes later Sophia had the honor of witnessing, first-hand, Spencer's abrupt departure. He couldn't get away from Lizzie fast enough.

Lizzie gave a dismissive wave of her hand. "It was nothing."

At that moment a grinning golden retriever came into her path and she busied herself petting it. The weather in Paris was just starting to warm up, and today was the first really fine day in a while. Their favorite park was the one at the base of the Eiffel Tower, and the sunshine had brought out even more people than usual. The bonus? More dogs.

While she told her new four-legged friend what a good boy he was, Lizzie glanced at Sophia out of the corner of her eye. So far, her attempts to dodge an explanation had gone pretty well, but looking at the expression on her best friend's face, she knew she couldn't get out of it this time.

"So, will I be seeing more of the lovely Spencer Tate doing 'nothing' at our apartment? Maybe a few 'nothings' in your bedroom?" There was a knowing glint to Sophia's eyes and the fact her thoughts were so far from the truth killed Lizzie a little inside.

"You won't be seeing him again. Ever." Lizzie got to her feet and strode forward, continuing along the path. "I won't be either." Okay, maybe it was a slight exaggeration, but Lizzie enjoyed the dramatic effect.

Sophia's brows knitted. "The kiss was that bad?"

"For him, apparently." The sharpness of her tone gave away her hurt.

"Oh honey, I'm sure you're just reading into things. That boy seemed crazy about you when he came over."

Lizzie grimaced. *Yeah, right.*

"He told me the kiss was a mistake."

That stopped Sophia dead in her tracks and the group of runners behind them almost barreled into them.

"He did *not*!" She exclaimed, hands on hips. "I'll kill the bastard."

Lizzie gave a half-shrug and pulled on her friend's arm, forcing her forward. "I don't even know where it came from. One minute he was telling me off for going out, the next he was giving me the best kiss of my life, then he just runs off."

"Best kiss of your life, huh? What about Amaury?"

Lizzie scowled. "I already told you we don't say his name."

"Why does Spencer get an exception?"

That was a good point. Lizzie bit her lip, considering for a moment, as they passed the base of the giant wrought-iron monument. They couldn't speak for a while as they maneuvered their way through busloads of tourists and street vendors selling crappy little keyrings. The noise died down as they reached the end of the throng and finally, they could talk clearly again.

"Okay, we can call him Microwave Meal."

Sophia arched a brow.

"Because he's hot *and* cold."

That had them both cracking up for a few solid minutes, drawing a number of confused stares from their fellow park-goers.

"But yes,"—Lizzie decided to tell Sophia the whole truth —"with him, it felt different. Better."

"Why was it so much better? You were obsessed with... Mr Nameless." Sophia's expression had turned serious, concern evident in her amber eyes.

"Nameless was really skilled. He obviously knew his way around a woman and it felt amazing." Lizzie sighed. "But last night...I didn't need any of that. With him, the slightest brush of his fingers gives me tingles, so when he put the full force of that on me?" She let out a breath and her shoulders sagged. "Yeah, it felt good."

It had been better than good. Lizzie finally understood what all those romance novels were always going on about. The kiss had just felt...inevitable. She was the moon, he was gravity. Like every interaction they had ever had with each other had been building to that one moment.

That was the heartbreaking part of it. For Lizzie, kissing Spencer had been something she'd dreamt of since she was a teenager. She couldn't count the number of times she had fantasized about him one day noticing her, falling in love... Inwardly she rolled her eyes, but that sort of history doesn't just disappear. Especially when the man himself shows up years later, charming as hell without even trying, and burrows his way further into your heart. Teenage crush met adult passion and created an inferno.

For Spencer though, it was nothing but a regret. He had never secretly pined for her, and he wouldn't be starting now. She was a lapse in judgment. A blip in the radar of what she assumed to be a long list of lovers.

A mistake, as he had so helpfully let her know.

"Is there any chance of you two fixing things?" Sophia's bleak expression mirrored her own.

"There isn't anything to fix. I'm nothing to him but a favor for my brother." Lizzie threw up a hand helplessly. "More importantly, how am I meant to find a rebound who can kiss like that? Maybe I should just invest in a rechargeable vibrator."

"Much less drama, you know."

"Better talkers than most men too." They shared a snicker.

"You know," Sophia began as she re-adjusted her ponytail, "Microwave Meal's one redeeming feature—aside from all those DVDs he left at our place—is he made you forget about Nameless."

Even though the thought disturbed her a little, Lizzie agreed. If it hadn't been for Spencer, she doubted she would have been able to leave the house all week. She liked to think she was a strong person, but there was something about heartbreak that ruined even the toughest of the tough. If you had asked her on the cab ride home from Amaury's whether she would be dreaming about someone else in less than a week, she would have laugh-cried in your face. A part of her wanted to believe her draw to Spencer was just a reflection of the accumulation of silly teenage yearnings, but she knew it was more.

She pushed those thoughts aside and plastered on a wry grin when she responded, "Have you *seen* Spencer? You'd be forgetting too."

"I tell you what, if he hadn't almost knocked our door down in demanding to see you, I would've tried my luck on him too." There was a wicked glint to Sophia's eyes and the playful punch Lizzie threw to her arm only made it shine brighter.

"Back off, skank." Lizzie tried to put on a threatening tone, but the fact her shoulders were shaking with the effort of restraining her laughter kind of ruined the effect.

As the girls ambled over to their favorite crêpe stand for breakfast, Lizzie took a moment to appreciate her friend. Just having Sophia here with her made her feel ten times lighter. She hadn't realized how much she was missing her best friend until she returned home and noticed the difference. Men would come and go, but she knew Sophia would always have her back. She would be maid of honor at her wedding, party organizer for her divorce, cool aunty to her kids. Whatever support Lizzie needed in life, Sophia was her girl.

She was so unlike some of the kids Lizzie had grown up with, spoiled by wealth and privilege. Sophia was down-to-earth, hilarious, and she cut through the shit. She didn't give a rat's ass that Lizzie's trust fund had more money in it than either of them could ever possibly spend. She wasn't a user. She was just…Sophia.

The woman in question was now sucking on the straw of her orange juice, making a loud slurping noise that was making the well-to-do French locals sitting around them turn up their noses. Lizzie chuckled.

She was going to be okay.

Chapter Seventeen
SPENCER

The only sound that rang out in the empty hotel gym was the pounding of Spencer's feet against the treadmill. Exercise always calmed him down. No matter how stressed he was or how complex a problem he was dealing with, Spencer was a firm believer that an hour-long sweat session was usually the answer.

Usually being the key word.

Because Spencer had been running flat-out for almost ninety minutes, his most motivational playlist his only companion, and his thoughts were still full of Elizabeth. Every step he took just seemed to make her run through his mind faster. Hell, the poor woman had probably done fifty circuits of his brain at this point.

The image that kept circulating?

That kiss. That damn kiss.

Even now his hands were curling in, imagining the feel of her cheek cupped in his, the other palming her tiny waist. He hadn't been prepared for her taste. It was as sweet as it was intoxicating, and despite his shower, he could still feel a ghost of that delicious flavor on his tongue, smell that mix of petals and sugar on his skin that just screamed Elizabeth. It was driving him insane.

Spencer upped his speed.

Idiot that he was, he had canceled his flight. Elizabeth hated him even more now; he had the perfect out. But he couldn't leave without mending things between them.

He had wanted to go back into that apartment with her last night. God he had wanted to. But she was drunk. Spencer wouldn't be able to live with himself if she woke up regretting being with him. Hell, he had been trying to save her from someone who wanted to take advantage of her; what did it say about him that the second they were alone he was backing her up against a wall? He had been a split second from taking her right there.

But then the head between his shoulders decided to take back the reins and he realized what an utter disaster the whole situation was. They would never work. He owed a duty to Seb not to go there. Ever.

Spencer started his cooldown and picked up his towel to wipe the sweat from his brow. Now, away from Elizabeth, he could step back and look at the situation more clearly. He had made the right decision. She would realize that, eventually.

That didn't mean that he couldn't go and make nice with her. She was his best friend's sister—they were always going to be a part of each other's lives, and no woman wanted to hear the word 'mistake'. He knew he'd fucked up with that one.

But he also knew how much Elizabeth liked her pastry.

SPENCER HAD HIS HAND RAISED TO KNOCK ON ELIZABETH'S DOOR when it swung open, revealing a smug Sophia.

"Look who's come crawling back!" she called over her shoulder into the apartment.

Sophia turned back to Spencer, eyes twinkling. "You better not fuck up again, blondie," were her only parting words before she pushed past him and disappeared into the stairwell. She had an overnight bag hoisted over her shoulder, and Spencer vaguely remembered that she occasionally spent nights at the house where she nannied.

He felt his heart rate pick up at the idea of being alone with Elizabeth in the apartment, but he quickly shoved that thought aside. *Pull yourself together, idiot.*

And suddenly there she was. Hair pulled low at the nape of her neck, that mouth-watering body clad in a tank top and denim skirt. Crossed arms and a fearsome glare completed the look. Spencer swallowed. This was going to be more difficult than he had anticipated.

"Don't worry, I come bearing apology gifts."

Her eyes narrowed. "Have at it, then."

Spencer picked up the bag at his feet. "Do presents at least get me past the threshold?"

"I suppose so." Elizabeth raised a dismissive hand to signal he should follow her inside.

As Spencer began pulling out the bottle of red wine, baguette, and selection of cheeses, he could see he was making headway. Sure, her expression was still cold as stone, but those gorgeous eyes were softening.

Time for the *pièce-de-resistance*. (See? He was a master at groveling.)

He knew the moment she smelled the *kouign-amanns*. With the amount of sugar inside the fuckers you didn't need to be a sniffer dog to pick them up a mile away.

"You really *are* sorry." Was that the hint of a smile?

"Yeah, I am."

"But what are you sorry for?"

Elizabeth was leaning against the kitchen counter, one hand crossed over her chest as she toyed with a strand of her hair. Her chocolate eyes seemed bigger than usual as she turned an expression toward him that was so honest and vulnerable he felt a pang in his chest.

Spencer poured them both a glass of wine and rested his back against the bench. He owed her a straightforward answer, at least.

Finally, he spoke, voice soft. "You know we can't do this."

"Because of Seb? Or?" Elizabeth's voice trailed off and she bowed her head, not meeting his eyes.

"Yeah, because of Seb. Why else would you think?"

Elizabeth took a long swig from the glass in her hand before she answered, "Maybe you're just not feeling the same,"—she paused, twirling the stem between her fingers—"pull, that I am."

A sharp laugh escaped his lips. He couldn't help it. "Princess, I've been feeling it since the moment you jumped into my arms."

"Then why did you wait until last night to kiss me?" Elizabeth replied, voice heavy with skepticism.

"It was the idea of you sleeping with a stranger." Now Spencer was the one gulping down wine. "You're worth more than that."

"But I don't want to go searching for another relationship. All I need is a rebound. I can't have him be my last, I just can't."

Elizabeth was gesturing with her glass, driving the point home, but Spencer didn't really see it. All his attention was focused on *I need a rebound,* playing on repeat like a refrain in his head. Image after image of Elizabeth tangled up in the arms of that wanker from the club were on a loop. Some other man dancing with her, kissing her, pulling her on top of him in bed… It was sickening. Wrong.

It's not like Seb would prefer that creep with his sister. It may as well be Spencer. He would treat her right at least.

Fuck it.

"Okay."

"Okay what?"

"I'll do it. I'll be your rebound."

"But why? You just said—"

"I've changed my mind."

Elizabeth's eyes went round as Spencer carefully put down his glass, then reached out his hand to take care of hers. He placed it down on the counter. Slowly.

"But you're leaving tomorrow."

Eyes never leaving hers, Spencer took a step toward her. Then another. He lowered his voice.

"Not anymore."

"But—"

He cut her off with a kiss.

She hesitated a moment, still in shock, but then her body responded. And fuck, it was magical.

Elizabeth moaned low in her throat, reaching a hand out to grab the front of Spencer's shirt and pull him closer. She tasted like red wine and springtime and every flick of her tongue against his had his cock throbbing.

Spencer grabbed that little waist and hoisted her up onto the counter, spreading her legs so he could stand between them. She made quick work of wrapping them around him and he couldn't help thinking this is what they should've done that very first night.

They were now eye-to-eye and he had even greater access to her incredible body. He wasn't an idiot in this area at least. He made the most of it, raising a hand to palm her breast, not stopping the kiss for a moment.

She must've enjoyed it because a small whimper escaped her.

"You like that, princess?" Spencer was breathing hard, voice husky. Fuck, he could barely speak.

"I—*oh*."

Elizabeth's eyes went to the ceiling, her mouth popping open as he dipped his hand into the neckline of her shirt, fingers just grazing her nipple.

The way her head was tipped back drew his eyes to the pounding pulse in her throat and he couldn't resist bending down to bite it. He nibbled and sucked all over her neck to a chorus of moans. He hoped she got a damn hickey, high enough so anyone who saw would know that she was his.

Spencer would worry about what that possessiveness might mean later.

Right now, he had a woman to please.

Chapter Eighteen
LIZZIE

Is this a dream?

It had to be.

Spencer Tate was kissing her. Scratch that. He was *ravaging* her.

As Spencer's hot tongue burned a path down her neck, Lizzie knew she would be ruined for anyone else. Who the hell kissed like this?

Dimly she realized that Spencer had somehow managed to relieve her of her shirt. He unclasped her bra in a move so effortless, Lizzie had to stop herself from thinking about it too much. But when she felt his hot breath reach her nipple, she decided it didn't matter. Not when the prick of his teeth sent a cascade of shivers radiating across her entire body.

"How do you want to come, princess?"

Oh God. Oh dear God.

"My fingers?" He gave her nipple a sharp tug. "Or my tongue?"

That voice was *killing her*. Low and dangerous and so full of promise. And those words? Lizzie had never been much into dirty talk but coming from Spencer's mouth it was pure erotica.

"Anywhere," she breathed, "now. I don't care, just *do* it."

That was all the confirmation Spencer needed before he lowered one of those big hands and slipped it under her skirt, his mouth still on her breasts.

But the devil didn't rush, no—he went so slow it was almost painful. With the faintest brush he painstakingly began to inch his fingers up her thigh, and she felt herself grow more and more damp in response. He had barely even touched her and already she was on the brink. Her chest rose and fell with her short breaths and if he didn't relieve her soon, he was a dead man.

Without warning he pushed her panties aside and plunged two long fingers inside.

"*Jesus.*"

He chuckled, deep and throaty. "I already said you can just call me Spencer."

This man.

Spencer was better than she ever could have imagined, and she had barely even had a taste. Throughout all of her teenage fantasies she had pictured them together, sharing a kiss worthy of any Disney movie, fireworks and all. She had dreamed of seeing those gorgeous blue eyes twinkle when they looked at her, of their lips meeting, and them just *knowing* they were perfect for each other.

But she had never anticipated the reality.

Because the reality was *hot*.

There were no fireworks outside her small apartment window, but there was an entire arsenal of them putting on a show deep in her core. Each stroke of his fingers, each matching flick of his tongue set them off, and the effect kept building and building until she imagined she was lit up more than Sydney Harbor on New Year's Eve.

The blue eyes she had wanted to shine just for her didn't just spark, they were on fire, hooded and burning with a lust more passionate than anything she had ever seen. She hadn't been convinced when Spencer had confessed to wanting her, but she sure as hell believed him now.

Lizzie put her hands on the counter behind her, leaning back to give him more access to, well, everything. The move didn't come across as sexily as she had intended, however, when she ended up knocking one of the glasses right onto the skirt pushed up her hips. Red wine spilled over her thighs and down her legs.

Fuck. Her cheeks instantly reddened, and she opened her mouth to apologize when Spencer cut her off, biting his lip.

"Don't." He growled. "More fun for me."

What?

Suddenly he was on his knees, face pressed between her thighs, and she understood. Oh, she understood.

If she had thought his fingers were good, nothing could compare to his mouth. His tongue lapped up the wine dripping between her legs and her back arched in response. Lizzie let out a sharp breath that elicited a low groan from Spencer.

"Fuck, baby, you taste so good."

His lips were pressed so closely against her skin that she felt the vibration of his words deep inside. The combination of the cool wine and his hot tongue was mesmerizing. When he moved it to circle around that magical bundle of nerve endings, Lizzie swore she could see stars.

Those blazing blue eyes met hers and she couldn't hold it off any longer.

"Spencer! Oh, *oh.*"

Lizzie wrapped her hands against the back of his head, threading her fingers through his hair as she came. Wave after wave of pure bliss coursed through her, and she bit her lip so hard it almost bled.

Spencer. Fucking. Tate.

It took a few long moments for Lizzie to collect herself. She could have been sitting there, head tipped back, hands in his hair for seconds, minutes, years. It was irrelevant. Eventually her breathing slowed and she released Spencer from the death grip she had on his head.

"Did I get the job?" he said as he got to his feet. A smug grin covered his face and yeah, he'd earned it.

Words were still a foreign language to Lizzie at this point. She glanced around in a daze, taking in the red wine all over her kitchen, the shards of glass scattered across the bench. Her eyes returned to the man in front of her, his soft lips glistening with the evidence of what they had just done. Lizzie's face grew hot at the realization.

Spencer had walked into the apartment approximately thirty minutes ago and she had let him go down on her in her freaking kitchen without a second thought. She had it *bad.*

"You'll do," she eventually responded, but her breathy tone gave her away.

When his only response was a smirk she continued, "Do you, ah, want me to return the favor?"

"Fuck yeah, I do." Spencer's eyes flashed. "But not tonight. We're taking things slow."

"*That* was slow?"

He laughed then cocked his head, voice husky. "Do you want it fast?"

Her stomach clenched. How the hell was she craving him again, already?

"Nope!" she squeaked.

Spencer only laughed some more.

LIZZIE SAT AT THE DINING ROOM TABLE AND TRIED HER BEST TO find the appetite for the copious amounts of food Spencer had brought with him. He was still cleaning up the mess in the kitchen, a mess which he gave himself full credit for because of his 'masterful' distraction skills. Lizzie just mumbled something in response.

The brief reprieve from his company gave her time to process what the fuck had just happened.

She had been so caught up in the moment, in finally giving in to the lust that had been driving her insane from the moment she had seen him standing there at her threshold, that she hadn't put one ounce of thought into the situation. Mortified was an understatement. What must Spencer think of her? She was barely a week post breakup and she let him do all those things to her in her kitchen, practically on a pile of broken glass.

Lizzie pinched the bridge of her nose. The dining chairs she had loved so much when she bought them last August now felt stiff and uncomfortable. The heat radiating from the light above her felt blinding and harsh, and the brief glimpse of herself she had caught in her living room mirror was nothing short of horrifying.

Her cheeks were beyond flushed, hair a mess. Dried red wine still caking her legs. Straight after she had come back down to earth, Spencer had given her his shirt to cover her bare chest. Somehow, even though she was now fully covered, Lizzie felt more naked than before.

What had he even meant by *rebound*? Was that it? One glorious encounter with his tongue and now they were back to being family friends?

"I can see those wheels in your head turning. Just come out and say it."

With a start Lizzie realized Spencer had come to sit next to her. He pulled his chair closer to hers, angling it so his knees brushed her thighs.

When she didn't respond he lifted a hand to cup her cheek. "Talk to me, princess."

Lizzie hated how much of a thrill his little pet names gave her. It just felt so damn desperate. She cursed her body for being that weak.

"What just happened, Spencer?"

Her head was hung and the words came out in a mumble. It was utterly ridiculous that she could be holding the man's head between her legs one moment and then be too shy to speak to him the next. Lizzie added another count to her mental tally of the many ways her body had betrayed her recently. Top of the list was of course allowing her to be too distracted by a nameless sexy Frenchman to realize he was the definition of asshole. Stupid, stupid ladybits.

"You need a rebound—I'm it. Simple as that."

Lizzie snorted. There was nothing simple about that.

"Isn't rebound sex just a one-night thing?"

"Honey, I'll need much more than one night for what I want to do to you."

When his hooded eyes met hers she had to deduct *another* point from her traitorous body.

"Aren't you meant to be heading home soon?"

Spencer made a face and shook his head. "I haven't booked a return flight yet, and all my work is online." He lowered his voice. "So I'm all yours."

Lizzie had picked up bits and pieces of Spencer's attraction to her over the past week. Yes, she had discounted most of them at the time, but looking back now she could see certain moments in a different light. Him looking at her a few seconds too long, the stolen touches, those hazy memories from that first night. But this was entirely different. That had been Spencer diluted, hesitant. The big body folded onto her living room chair, those high cheekbones and thick brows facing her way was a completely different creature. It was like he had flicked a switch and the force of his *want* for was hypnotic. She could practically see it pouring from those sky-blue orbs. If she wasn't careful, she was going to lose her head.

"Okay, but I think we need some ground rules, so we know where we stand."

Spencer leaned back, folding his arms. "Like what?"

Lizzie had read countless books where the main characters had flings. Sure, the bulk of them had been romance novels where the protagonists ending up falling in love, despite their casual relationships, but the premise seemed good enough. And they all had rules. Very important rules. If they were going to do this, she needed to protect the broken shards of her heart.

"Number one: no spending the night."

"Fuck that." Spencer grabbed her hand, which had been fiddling with her cutlery, and put it between his. "I'm a cuddler."

The twinkle in Spencer's eyes was going a long way to ease her nerves, as was the image of him spooning her. But she couldn't let him distract her from this.

"Right. Well, uh, obviously it doesn't need to be exclusive."

Spencer cut her off with a growl. "Yeah, it does. I don't share."

Okay. This was going super well. What the hell was she getting herself into?

"Will you at least agree that we can't tell my brother?"

Those baby blues clouded with guilt for a split second before Spencer winked. "As it turns out, I'm quite fond of my balls, so I'll let you have that one."

Spencer suddenly pulled out her chair, wrapping one arm under her knees and the other behind her back, before standing, taking her with him. "Enough rules, Beth. I'm taking you to bed."

Well. How could she argue with that?

Chapter Nineteen
SPENCER

Spencer woke up to something scratching his nose that smelled absolutely delicious. It was all honey and coconuts and transported him back to a holiday he'd taken in Mexico last year. Pure summer. A soft, warm weight was cradled in his arms, and behind his closed lids he could feel the hint of morning light. He cracked open an eye and realized it was Elizabeth's thick, chocolate hair in his face and her body against his chest.

His cock decided to take that moment to wake up, as well. *Funny that.*

Elizabeth must have sensed it, because she squirmed in her sleep, wriggling her ass against him before settling back in his arms. *Well, fuck.*

Even though it was pure torture, Spencer remained still. He wanted her to have a proper sleep-in. And despite her talk of a rebound, he didn't think she was ready for what he wanted to do to her yet. She needed some time to adjust to the idea.

Spencer remembered the uncertainty on her face last night, the embarrassment clearly evident on those lovely cheeks. He had no intentions of being the rebound she had planned with that fucker from the club. She was still Seb's sister, still one of the most brilliant women he knew. He would never give Elizabeth the meaningless sex he had given to so many before her. It just didn't feel right.

He didn't regret his actions one little bit. Spencer wasn't the sort of person to go back on a decision once it was made. Knowing that Elizabeth was planning to get what she needed from someone else had sealed the deal. Why not him? Yeah, they were going to keep it casual, which was technically breaking the Bro Code, but at least he would treat her well. Spencer's jaw clenched at the thought of some douche nailing her then bailing. He would take her on dates, bring that light back into her eyes. He would fuck her much better than anyone else ever had. Then she would move on and—yeah, he didn't want to think too much about that right now.

Besides, news of it never had to get back home. *What happens in Paris stays in Paris, right?*

And judging by last night, *a lot* would happen. His cock twitched at the memory of the taste of that wine dripping down her pussy, as if agreeing with him. There was nothing hotter than how responsive her body had been to his touch last night, like she had been stuck wandering a desert and he was her one glass of water.

As carefully as he could, Spencer lifted a hand to brush some of her hair behind her neck, and she started mumbling, "Set the taco trap."

His shoulders started to shake with the force of his repressed laughter. Elizabeth was a sleep talker. Fucking. Adorable.

Spencer's eyes explored her room. It was so Elizabeth. She had a fluffy, white comforter, wooden floorboards, and one of those fancy French balconies off her window. There was an old fireplace that couldn't be used anymore, but Elizabeth had filled it to the brim with books. Paperback after paperback, Spencer could practically see her slowly building up her collection from the carts near the Notre Dame. The ceiling was white and ornate, and along the walls she had stuck Polaroids and postcards. Spencer noted a few blank spaces where it was clear pictures had been removed, and his gut twisted at the reminder of the French fuck.

Elizabeth's voice soon brought back his good mood.

"Burrito," she said, barely above a whisper.

Spencer chuckled some more, put his lips to that sweet spot behind her ear, and softly kissed her, pulling her tighter against him.

Elizabeth moved her ass around some more, taunting him from her subconsciousness. The witch. He wasn't sure how much more of this he could take.

"Rise and shine, princess," he whispered into the shell of her ear.

Elizabeth woke with a start, flinging her body to the side so she was now completely facing him. "What—oh, Spencer." She ducked her head and gave a shy smile. "Hi."

"Hi."

Spencer darted his eyes back and forth between her eyes and lips, enough times for her to start laughing.

"Smooth."

"Then why aren't you kissing me yet?"

With a spark in those big eyes, Elizabeth leaned forward and pressed her lips to his.

Spencer looped an arm around her waist and pulled her closer so her whole body was pressed against his, as well, her nipples brushing against his chest. What a fucking glorious way to wake up. He would pay good money to start every morning like this.

Elizabeth raised a knee, lifting her leg over his hip, erasing even more distance between them.

"Is it time to finish what we started last night?" she breathed into his neck.

Yeah, that shyness had disappeared faster than a bottle of vodka at a frat house. This woman would be the end of him.

"Not today, princess."

As much as he wanted to take her right now, Elizabeth wasn't some casual hookup. He wasn't going to make their first time a quickie because he had morning wood. Last night was a write-off considering how blinded by lust he had been, but next time Spencer would make it special. After the way that French fuck had ripped her heart out, there was no way he was going to jump right into sex. She had to want it as desperately as he did. Want it enough that she would start to forget the French guy had ever existed.

Elizabeth pouted. "Isn't the point of having a rebound that I get laid?" She emphasized that last point with a slow grind of her hips and Spencer groaned.

"Tempting as you are, I'm not rushing into this." Spencer detached that gorgeous leg from his body before he went against his better judgment. "Besides, I've got things to do today."

"Better be life or death."

Elizabeth was clearly not a morning person. But she still looked damn cute, trying to maintain a frown while her lips were twitching for a smile.

"I've decided to open a gym here. For real this time."

Elizabeth picked up the pillow next to her and promptly began to beat him up with it. "Hope," *hit* "you," *hit* "have," *hit* "proof, beefcake. I'm still not over that."

Her laughter begged to differ, but Spencer didn't press the issue. He was enjoying the sight of her tits bouncing up and down as she attacked him way too much.

"What changed your mind?" she finally said once she had all the pillow-fighting out of her system.

Spencer stretched his arms out, managing to hook one around her shoulders and bring her back to him. He couldn't get over how good she felt in his arms. "I need something to keep me busy over here. Don't want to get bored."

Elizabeth arched a brow. "You think you'll get bored?"

Spencer let his eyes travel along her body, petite with curves that fit his hands perfectly. Clad only in a pair of panties and a tank top, the outline of her breasts was very visible. Her gorgeous hair had that messy just-fucked look, and her fresh face, those big eyes blinking up at him under thick lashes, was the stuff of fantasy.

He bit his lip. "Not with you around, honey."

～

A FEW HOURS LATER, SPENCER WAS ON THE PHONE TO HIS PA, Anna, trying desperately to cancel on his biggest client.

He had called her initially to start organizing what they would need to start a gym here. Spencer was good with the content, not the logistics. That's why he hired geniuses like Anna to do it for him. Technically he didn't really need to be in Paris to oversee the project, but it would be nice to play a bigger role in it.

That's when Anna had, very unhelpfully, reminded him about his calendar.

"Spencer. This is Cole Decker we're talking about. He specifically requested you. *Months* ago."

Anna wasn't one to mince words. Spencer had hired her when he had first started years ago. They met in college, friendship blossoming from a mutually beneficial relationship: she had given him her notes, he had introduced her to the men's football team. When the business had taken off, she was the first person who came to mind when he needed to find someone he trusted to handle his affairs.

"Anna-banana," Spencer whined, "I have things to do here."

"Why do I suspect these *things* are female?" Anna's voice deadpanned on the other line.

"Because you know me?" Spencer started halfheartedly packing his duffel, tossing his clothes in without his usual care. "And it's just the one thing. A special thing."

"I'm sure your lady of the week will understand coming second fiddle to the biggest movie star in the world at the moment."

Cole Decker was Hollywood's current heartthrob, playing the hero in the latest comic-book franchise that was hitting cinemas next year. Spencer had been training him on and off for a few years now. Whenever Cole needed to really beef up for a role, he gave Spencer a call.

"Can we just move it to next week?"

"*Spencer Tate*," Anna barked, "They are filming his shirtless battle scene in *two weeks*. There is *no* flexibility."

Spencer's only response was a grunt. He knew he'd lost this fight.

One day Anna was going to make a great mom—she already had that discipline voice down pat. Spencer loved her but the woman could be scary as hell.

"I've booked your transport to London for tomorrow afternoon. You'll be back in Paris a week later."

"Tell fucking Cole that he owes me."

Spencer wished his iPhone was one of those old-fashioned handsets with cords because it would be satisfying as hell to hang up with a slam right now.

Chapter Twenty

LIZZIE

Spencer was leaving Paris in less than six hours and he wanted to do a freaking *walking tour*. He had to be kidding.

"What? You may be a local but I'm still a tourist."

"This is a cruel and unusual punishment."

She narrowed her eyes at Spencer. He was leaning against the wall in blue jeans, a white shirt, and a black leather jacket. His hair was mussed, his five o'clock shadow darker than usual, lips curved into a devilish grin. The man just oozed sex appeal. They were standing in one of the old streets in *Le Marais,* waiting for the rest of the group to arrive. It was overcast and the wind chilly, the perfect day to say, spend in bed.

Spencer reached forward and hooked his hands around her waist, pulling her flush against him. When he ducked his head, the height difference resulted in his lips being almost perfectly in line with the shell of her ear, which he took full advantage of.

"Is there somewhere else you'd rather be, Beth baby?"

Beth. No one had ever called her that before. Coming from Spencer's lips it felt like the sweetest of secrets, a gentle caress meant just for her. Beth was *theirs*. It made them feel like an *us*, sending a delightful shiver up Lizzie's spine that she quickly repressed. Casual. They were casual. She was perfectly fine with that.

And she could hit back with some torture of her own.

Lizzie went up onto the balls of her feet, brought her lips right next to his. Licked them. "On top of you sounds pretty good right now."

Spencer's eyes went round and he let out a choked breath. He opened his mouth to say something, but before he could get out a word, a large, accented voice boomed out behind them.

"Excellent! Everyone is here, let us *commencer!*" A short man crammed into a hi-vis vest was clapping his hands together, beaming. Surrounding him were around twelve people, a mix of college kids, families, and couples. A few of the old couples were shooting frowns their way. Lizzie suddenly became conscious of the fact she was practically wrapped around the hulking blond man beside her, and she took a step away. Spencer just smirked. Bastard.

"You are standing on a piece of history. History!" Lizzie hadn't thought it was possible for the man's voice to become any more high-pitched but he proved her wrong. "Jean Baptiste Joseph Delambre lived in *this very street.*" Every word out of his mouth was emphasized. Lizzie had a feeling that he had been the sort of student to highlight every single word in his textbooks because everything was just. So. Important.

She turned her gaze to Spencer, her sardonic expression wordlessly communicating what she wasn't saying.

Her feet moved along with the group as they went from a *super exciting* eight-hundred-year-old tower to a museum that had been under construction for the past few years. Lizzie loved culture as much as the next bookworm, but no one in their right mind would choose to spend a day walking around their city when they could spend said day rolling around the sheets with Spencer Tate. *No one.*

Lizzie was working to keep her face in a polite, interested mask as the guide gushed about the *Musée Carnavalet* when she felt it. The lightest brush of a finger against her lower back.

She was wearing tights and a gray sweater dress that dipped low in the back, leaving a good part of her spine completely exposed.

Somehow Spencer had managed to sneak up behind her. And it was clear he liked her outfit.

Lizzie's eyes flicked to his. He was wearing that same polite mask, as if he wasn't touching her at all. Her eyes darted to the rest of the group, all of whom were listening to tales of Paris during the Roman empire, wide-eyed with the occasional nod.

Meanwhile, that damn finger was moving.

It trailed up from just above her tailbone to the small of her back, tracing a slow, ever-so-soft path. Every inch of contact with it sent frissons traveling along her spine, and she felt it deep inside her.

Now she could barely make out what the tour guide was saying. All her focus was zeroed in on that fingertip. Lizzie's mouth popped open slightly and she bit her lip when it circled around her waist and started to climb higher. When it came in contact with the under-side of her breast, she could barely contain a gasp.

Lust hit her like a train on the tracks. It radiated out from that one point of contact until it took over, her entire being now tuned in to Spencer's slightest whim. Her eyes took in the crowd in front of them. How could they not notice? She felt like she was naked.

"I couldn't be alone with you today, princess." Spencer's husky voice was at her ear, his hot breath the best kind of contrast against the brisk air. The finger moved higher. "I knew I wouldn't be able to resist."

"What's wrong with giving in?" Her voice came out barely above a whisper.

"When I have you,"—Spencer's touch rose, teasing just below her nipple—"I'll be taking my time."

The space where his body had been was suddenly empty, and she felt the loss like an ache.

Her heartbeat was tap dancing in her chest. Her breaths were uneven. Hell, her eyes were probably glazed over, for all she knew.

"You. Fucking. Tease."

"Shh," Spencer said with a frown, gesturing to the guide, "it's rude to talk during the tour."

THE TOUR WRAPPED UP A FEW HOURS LATER AT *PLACES DES VOSGES,* an ornate, fenced park. Parisian-style buildings surrounded it, with arches at street level that housed a variety of boutiques and artisanal shops. The sounds of footsteps on cobblestones combined with the sweet scent of French pastry, echoed around the area.

Lying down on Spencer's jacket, near the fountain in the middle of the park, Lizzie felt like she had traveled back in time. The architecture was so pristine, so conserved, and the streets here were mostly too narrow for cars. With the foot traffic and street vendors, it could easily have been the previous century.

Spencer was lying next to her, his head on her lap, listing all the reasons why Cole Decker could kiss his ass, when Lizzie's phone rang.

She picked it up without bothering to check who it was.

"Lizzie girl!" Seb's voice rang out on the other line and her stomach dropped.

"Seb!" It came out a little too high-pitched. "To what do I owe this pleasure?"

At her words Spencer sat up with a start and moved away from her, a guilty expression on his face.

"Can't I check in with my baby sis?" Seb was laughing.

"Can you feel my eyes rolling all the way over there?"

Seb laughed some more then went on, "Hey, is Spencer still over there? He treating you well? Haven't heard much from him lately."

Yeah, that could be because he's been busy with his head between your sister's legs.

"Spencer?" Lizzie gulped. "Yep. I've seen him once or twice."

Spencer's eyes went wide and he jerked his head back and forth, raising his hand in a gesture that mimicked slitting his throat.

Well, maybe he should have considered when he might need a favor before he decided to tease her so mercilessly during the tour. Lizzie smirked. Payback time.

"He's uh, here now actually."

"What!" The excitement was evident in Seb's tone. "Put the fucker on!"

With a glare, Spencer took the phone from her and plastered on a smile. "Seb man, what's going on?"

The longer the call went on, the further Spencer moved from her. It was like he was suddenly afraid to touch her.

"We just did a walking tour." A pause. "Yeah, I'm planning to stay for a few weeks—open up a Tate's here."

Lizzie reached a hand out to touch his arm but he jerked it away, eyes going dark.

"Uh, nope, no French guys in the picture that I know of." Spencer attempted a chuckle, but it came out a little choked. "Yeah, happy to scare them away for you. Why don't we just send her to a nunnery—Ow! Beth!"

He shot a petulant look her way as he rubbed the spot on his shoulder where Lizzie had delivered her punch. There was no way the bastard could send her to a nunnery after the way he'd worked her up that morning. That would be a new kind of hell.

"Really? I thought that was what everyone called her... Guess she's just not bothering to correct me."

An uncomfortable feeling sank into her gut. How many lies had they told in a five-minute phone conversation? It all seemed so simple when they were here alone, miles away from anyone they knew. It made it easier to forget how hurt Seb would be if he ever found out.

With a sigh, Lizzie forced herself to put a stop to that train of thought. Her brothers had controlled her enough. What she and Spencer did was really none of their business.

All the same, after they ended the call, Spencer and Lizzie sat in silence for the next half hour, wrapped in each other's arms and their own thoughts.

Chapter Twenty-One
SPENCER

"Add another twenty pounds and do ten more reps."

Cole groaned. "Fuck, man, are you trying to kill me on purpose?"

They were staying at the Savoy in London, and the entire gym had been blocked off for their use for four hours each day—two in the morning, two at night. Spencer had arranged for a few extra pieces to be brought in for them. Your typical hotel gym didn't have ropes, sleds or a chin-up bar, but thanks to Cole Decker's name, you could get pretty much anything.

"You're the one who took the role of a fucking superhero. Do it again, slower this time. Focus on activation." Spencer's lips curved into a wicked grin at the sight of Cole drenched in sweat, limbs shaking as he did another chest press. Cole had been working hard on his form for the past few months, but these last two weeks were always the most important. The poor fucker's diet at this point was basically boiled chicken, greens, and protein shakes. Now Spencer was making him do high-intensity resistance training, which was basically the bane of Cole's existence.

"Why are you so evil today?"

"Less talking, more lifting, asswipe."

Yeah, Spencer probably shouldn't be talking to his highest-profile client like that. But he needed an outlet for his frustration. Besides, he had known Cole for a long time and had a feeling he liked that Spencer didn't put on airs around him. It was hard to be impressed by the movie star when his best friend's family was one of the richest in the United States. He'd seen it all before.

Spencer's phone buzzed and his heart leapt in his chest. He frowned inwardly, scolding his heart for acting like such a pussy. Nevertheless, when he picked it up and saw a text from Elizabeth, he couldn't help but beam.

Elizabeth: *Just finished that J. R. Lonie book you bought me. It was sooo good, I have chills!*

Spencer chuckled. Only Elizabeth would be this excited over a book. He had no idea which one she was talking about. When he had gone to the store last week, he had just grabbed the fifteen newest releases in fiction. Still, this warm feeling rattled in his chest, ecstatic that he had pleased her.

Spencer: *There are other ways I can give you chills...*

"Oh, I get it. This is about pussy."

Spencer turned his gaze to the sweaty movie star, eyes flashing. "What are you talking about?"

Cole sat up on the bench and snapped his fingers in the direction of Spencer's phone, "You look like a love-sick puppy. It's a little pathetic."

"Fuck off."

Usually Spencer could handle a bit of crap from Cole. He was one of the most arrogant guys he'd ever met. And why wouldn't he be? The man could melt panties with a smile and had more money and fame than he knew what to do with. Hell, Cole had turned down the role of Superman. *Superman.* They had ended up giving it to Henry Cavill, who looked a bit like the older, home-brand version of Cole. Cockiness was to be expected. But not today. Not when Cole was the reason Spencer didn't have Elizabeth on top of him right now.

Cole leaned back, linking his hands behind his head with a smirk. "She that hot? Got any photos?"

"Don't talk about her," Spencer growled, striding over to the sled and adding two hundred pounds to it. "Get over here—I'm adding another station to your circuit."

Cole turned his eyes heavenward, as if cursing Spencer's existence. As he should.

What followed was probably the hardest training session Spencer had ever put him through. He decided to add a set of sprints to the end. Nothing that would get Cole injured, but just enough that every time he walked up stairs or tried to lift his arms the next day, he would feel it. He deserved it.

Cole was making the special lemon-ginger-water mix he drank religiously for his voice when Elizabeth finally responded to Spencer's message.

Elizabeth: *The memory of you just did. ;)*

Did she just...? Spencer blew out his cheeks. How the hell was he meant to go another five days without her.

"Oh man, you're in deep." Cole smirked, twisting the cap off his bottle and taking a long swig.

"I'm not—it's nothing."

"Sure doesn't look like nothing. Who is she?"

Spencer's face must have shown his guilt because Cole pressed on, "Oh man, now I've gotta know."

He sighed. It's not like he could talk to many other people about this. His best friend was obviously out of the question. Elizabeth's other brothers were also among his close friends. The other guys he hung out with back home would hear him out, but it wasn't the sort of thing you put in a text.

"My best friend's little sister."

There was silence for a beat, then a wild laugh escaped Cole's chest. It seemed to go on forever. "Oh—man—you—are —*screwed*." Each word was punctuated with an intake of breath and fresh peals of laughter. Spencer swore he could see the beginnings of tears in the corner of Cole's eyes.

"It's not that bad." Yeah, Spencer wasn't even convincing himself with that line.

"Uh yeah, it is."

"He's not going to find out, it's just a temporary thing."

"Your face lights up like a fucking firework from a text message." Cole half-shrugged, raising his hands as if to say *don't shoot the messenger.* He strode over to the mat to start his stretches. "Your head thinks it's temporary, but does the rest of you?"

Spencer just grunted in response, grabbing a few bands to help him cool down.

They worked in silence for a few minutes, Spencer helping to push back Cole's shoulders so he could get in a deeper stretch. The constant movement helped anchor his thoughts. This *was* temporary. It was going to be the hottest fling of his life, yeah, but that's all it would be. All it could be. Elizabeth needed someone to get over that fuckwit, and he didn't trust anyway else for the job. Afterward—well, that didn't matter.

"What are you going to do?" Cole's voice was quieter now, serious.

Spencer didn't want a heart-to-heart right now.

"I'm going to keep pummeling your ass for the next week because you're the only reason I'm not screwing her right now."

Cole groaned and put his face in his palms, "You fucking suck, man."

Chapter Twenty-Two
LIZZIE

The sky was as blue as Spencer's eyes, it was just warm enough to get away with shorts, and there wasn't a cloud in sight. A faint breeze ruffled the hair that had fallen out of her ponytail, but Lizzie didn't mind. She was on her third and final student of the day, and today they were doing their session at the park just off the Eiffel Tower. It wasn't the main one, which was always clogged with tourists, but a little garden set high on a hill, so the view was uninterrupted and magnificent.

"Try reading it again but this time do it aloud—tell me if it still makes sense to you."

Valentin stood up, in the little garden where writers across the ages had come to debate, learn, and be inspired. Being here just felt a little magical; it had this timeless atmosphere.

"I wouldn't do this for just anyone," the teen said with a wink as he began to recite the short story he had written. The kid was just shy of eighteen and was harboring a pretty strong crush on her. With high cheekbones and dark, messy hair he had the potential to be a real looker when he grew up. Lizzie was sure he enjoyed breaking teenage hearts across Paris.

While Valentin read, his brow furrowed, and he began tapping his foot against the grass. Lizzie's lips quirked. Success.

"This makes no sense." His tone was self-reflective, accusatory, his frown deepening.

"Sometimes when you write something down, it works in your head." Lizzie knew this better than anyone. "When you take a step back, it helps. It happens with artists all the time. After being so close to the canvas, it's only when they take a few steps back can they really see the piece for what it is."

Something glinted in Valentin's eyes and he began nodding along as she spoke. Lizzie knew she was making progress. Valentin was a smart kid, but his course included creative writing, which he hated. He was more analytical; he wanted some sort of formula he could just apply and would succeed with, like he had for math. Sometimes Lizzie wished for a magic formula, as well.

"When you get home today I want you to read out loud, then go back through and highlight all the bits that didn't make sense, or sounded forced. Once you know the areas you need to improve on, we can work on what we should replace them with."

Valentin's shoulders relaxed and he let out a breath. "Okay. I will do that and then we can fix it. Step by step." The kid looked like she had just told him Christmas was coming early.

Teenagers these days had so much pressure put on them at school. Lizzie saw the circles under their eyes, the energy drinks they guzzled, the binge-eating or even lack of appetite. These kids were stressed out of their minds, with years and years of schooling built up to one set of marks. For them, the weight of the world rested on one test, one essay, one story. It was ridiculous.

Lizzie loved being the one to show them not all hope was lost. English was a tricky subject for many of them; there were no easy answers. But Lizzie could give them solid strategies. And their work improved before their eyes.

"See? We can nail this." Lizzie sent a warm smile Valentin's way which he returned way too earnestly.

"I will see you next week, yes?" His English was usually pretty perfect, but occasionally his phrasing slipped and it became obvious it was his second language. His face was bright and he looked like he was holding his breath, waiting for her answer.

"I've got you in for Thursday afternoon during your free period. Any questions before then, just send me an email."

"How about a text?" He flashed his teeth, the spark in his eye now roguish.

Lizzie rolled her eyes. "Nice try, Romeo. Email is fine."

Valentin held a hand to his heart. "You wound me, Lizzie."

"*Goodbye,* Valentin."

With an exaggerated sigh, Valentin packed up his bags and began walking away, sending a wink her way as he left. Lizzie chuckled to herself as she watched his figure retreat into the distance.

She raised her face to the sky and felt the warm brush of the sun against her skin. She had the whole afternoon to herself now, but she didn't feel like leaving this spot anytime soon. Lizzie opened up her bag and pulled out a rug so she could lay down. Her Kindle came out, as well.

Lizzie glanced around a few times before she opened up the ebook reader. While her bookshelf was stocked with the classics, the literary prize winners, her Kindle was a little...different. This was where her guilty treats lived, and the shirtless men on the covers gave away exactly what they were.

It's not that she was ashamed, exactly. Most people just didn't understand. Once, her brother Josh had found her reading one on a family holiday and had made fun of her "mommy porn" for weeks and weeks.

Personally, Lizzie thought highly of romance novels and erotica. For one, there was an exploration of female sexuality and power that you just didn't see in other aspects of society. How many movies have you seen where a guy goes down on a woman instead of the other way around?

Above all of that though, they were an escape, a grown-up

fantasy. Lizzie didn't read them to educate herself or have new material to brag about. She read them to be sucked into a story that was so captivating she found herself still glued to it, hours later. To have a world where even on her shittiest day she could be entertained. To keep her hope alive that love was real even after Amaury had stomped all over her heart.

You don't get that with *War and Peace*.

But still, she didn't need any little old ladies walking their dogs to glance over her shoulder and read about the billionaire hero laying his intern down over his desk and fucking her from behind.

Surely there was a happy medium.

So, she settled down with her back to a tree trunk, a spot where no unwanted eyes would happen to come across her guilty pleasure.

Her latest indulgence was *Scandalous* by L.J. Shen and soon she lost herself in the book, sitting there for what could have been a few minutes or an hour. It wasn't until her phone sounded with a message that she blinked, realizing how stiff her limbs were from being in the same position so long.

Her lips curved into a smile at the name on the screen.

Spencer: *What are you up to, princess?*

They had been messaging near constantly. Once they had given in to those pent-up feelings, it was as if a floodgate had been opened. Lizzie felt like she was just a walking, talking bundle of lust since she had kissed him goodbye at the train station.

Cole Decker was her celebrity crush, but now she found herself cursing him. She needed to get laid. Bad. Who knew Hollywood's biggest heartthrob would be such a cockblock?

Lizzie: *I'm enjoying my afternoon off. Reading at my favorite spot.*

Spencer: *Is that the one you mentioned, by that big old tower everyone is so obsessed with?*

Warmth tingled at her cheeks and she had to work hard to resist a smile at the fact he had remembered a tiny detail she had told him only once. Before she had the chance to reply, another message came through.

Spencer: *Reading anything good?*

Lizzie bit her lip. He was the reason she was in this mess, unsatisfied and horny as hell. Spencer should have checked his schedule before he decided to be her rebound.

Without allowing herself much time to think on it, she took a photo of the page she was reading and sent it through to him.

A minute or so later, the screen lit up with those three little dots that showed he was typing. They disappeared. Reappeared. Disappeared again.

Her shoulders shook with the force of her laughter.

The page she sent him was a pretty explicit sex scene. The first line of dialogue was *deep throating is a requirement, not an option*, so you get the picture.

Finally her phone sounded again.

Spencer: *I thought you were into Shakespeare and stuff??*

Spencer: *What WAS that?*

Spencer: *Shit, are they doing it in a printing room? This man isn't playing.*

Elizabeth: *I'm just doing some...research. For when you get back.*

Spencer: *You are fucking killing me.*

Lizzie leaned back down on her blanket, bringing her book with her. She was still smiling when the next message came through.

Spencer: *Fuck, if you'd told me shit like that existed when I was in high school, I'd be a fucking bookworm now too.*

Chapter Twenty-Three

SPENCER

S pencer hadn't thought it was possible for a week to have gone so. Fucking. Slowly. Being apart from Elizabeth, when he'd barely had a taste of her was pure torture.

He spoke to her near constantly, sent her photos of London, called her once a day. It still wasn't enough. They hadn't even had actual sex yet and already he craved her like a drug.

But finally he was back in Paris, and he had plans.

Once again he found himself at Elizabeth's door, but this time he came empty-handed.

When it opened, Elizabeth's eyes widened and she let out a long breath. "You look… Wow."

Her eyes traced his face then quickly moved down to take in the rest of his body. A blush crept over her cheeks as her eyes lingered a bit *too* long below the belt. Spencer smirked. He knew he scrubbed up alright, but today he was putting in a real effort. He had a navy suit on, white shirt, no tie. Even his hair was brushed back.

"Ready for your first official rebound date?"

For a split second it looked like her face fell but just as quickly her lips curved into a smile, and he convinced himself he had imagined it.

"When were you planning on telling me how dressy you were going to look?" She had her hands on her hips and looked adorable as hell.

Spencer made a big show of holding his hands out and looking down at his outfit. "This old thing? You think it's too much for the pub?"

Elizabeth rolled her eyes and held up a finger. "Gimme one second."

Five minutes later, Spencer was absorbed in reading an email on his phone when he happened to glance up and promptly forgot how to breathe.

She was a vision. A fantasy. The most beautiful thing he had ever seen.

Olive-green silk, that just begged to be touched, clung to her frame in all the right places. It had to be magic the way the dress bunched in at her waist but still managed to artfully fall and highlight every single curve. The color brought out the rich chocolate and gold in her hair and eyes, and she had added some sort of shimmery bronze stuff to her cheeks and collar-bones that made her look like a fucking Greek goddess. Spencer could understand why Orlando Bloom in *Troy* had started a war with Sparta over a woman. With Elizabeth looking as she did now, Spencer would pretty much jump through fire for a kiss.

His eyes held hers for a long moment before he thought *fuck it* and stepped forward to claim that kiss. Spencer raised one hand to grasp the back of her head while the other reached down and cupped her ass. Those soft lips parted for his and his tongue took full advantage, until he wasn't sure where he ended, and she began. His lips were singing to her, saying tonight she was all his.

Spencer stepped back, breathing heavy.

Elizabeth cocked her head and did a little twirl. "I gather you like the outfit?"

She tried to hide it behind humor, but Spencer didn't miss the flush that had crept over her neck and cheeks, or those hard points on her chest he could see poking at the soft silk.

Spencer took her hand. "Come on, princess, we've got places to be."

THE LOOK ON ELIZABETH'S FACE WHEN HE OPENED THE DOOR, TO the suite he had booked at the Shangri-La, was worth every penny he had spent on the room. And that had been *a lot*.

But Elizabeth was worth it. And he wanted their first time together to be the best she'd ever had.

The suite was exactly what he imagined Paris would be. The wooden floorboards, ornate white ceilings, gold outlines on all the furniture. In the center of the room was a giant, four-poster bed covered in enough pillows to make any woman giddy. But the real hero was the balcony. It was only small, but there was a marble table set up with champagne and cheese. The view? The giant Eiffel Tower lit up against the night sky, so close that its gold twinkle was reflected in the window pane.

Elizabeth held a hand to her mouth, eyes wide and circling the room, as if not believing it was real. Gaze locked on the view, she ambled over to the balcony. They were on the highest floor, so the view was pretty damn impressive. Her hand drifted down and traced the edge of the chair absentmindedly before she twisted back to face him, eyes searching his.

"Spence. This is..." She shook her head and released a breath. "Why?"

Spencer crossed the room in three long strides. He cupped her cheek. "I'm going to make you forget he ever existed."

The pupils in those big, brown eyes dilated.

"Now," he breathed, "do you want your dinner first, or dessert?"

Elizabeth answered by crashing her lips against his, one hand reaching out to clutch his shirt and pull him closer. Her need for him was a bigger turn-on than anything else she could have done. Feeling her chest pressed against his; the way she got as high as she could, right up onto the balls of her feet, so she could deepen the kiss. Yeah, it didn't get much hotter.

Spencer ran his hand through her hair, pulling it down with a sharp tug to expose her neck. He layered kiss after kiss against that soft skin, rewarding her with a bite every time she moaned. The other hand moved up and down the silky dress, tracing her hourglass figure from hip to waist, and back again. It felt so fucking good.

He pulled back, chest rising and falling rapidly with his ragged breaths, and locked eyes with Elizabeth. "I need to see you."

Spencer took her hand and led her to the edge of the balcony, pushing her hips against the railing. He came up behind her, pressing his lips to the back of her neck as he worked on her dress. It was almost completely backless, with a series of silk ties holding it together. He undid ribbon after ribbon, being rewarded with another inch of fabric slipping down each time. When it finally reached her hips, his cock throbbed. She wasn't wearing any underwear. *Fuck.*

Spencer placed a hand on either side and yanked it down, leaving Elizabeth leaning there in nothing but a pair of heels.

He stepped back, hands laced behind his head as he took in the view.

They were hundreds of feet above Paris, the lights of the city like a sea of candles below them. Her legs were long and lean, her ass small and perky and the perfect fit for his hands. Chocolate hair cascaded down her back to frame her tiny waist. She was magnificent.

As he stared at her, the tower behind them lit up with its hourly show, the golden sparkles flickering against her skin as if a halo surrounded her entire body. Spencer wasn't much into religion, but when Elizabeth turned her head to lock eyes with him over her shoulder, he could've sworn he saw an angel. With the bedroom as their church, he would happily worship her all night long.

Spencer closed the distance between them, moving her hair from the nape of her neck so he could brush his cheek against hers. He felt like Aladdin, that moment where he sneaks up to Jasmine's balcony against all odds and gets a glimpse of her, looking like the most precious jewel in the world.

"Keep your eyes on the view, princess."

Elizabeth let out something between a sigh and moan as he raised a hand to her chest, using a light touch that he knew would drive her crazy. He moved his other hand to the place where her legs met and let out a groan at what he found. She was so wet, so ready for him.

He pressed up against her so she could feel what she did to him, how he was ready for her too. She just moaned some more.

Spencer was still fully clothed and she completely naked. It felt fucking incredible. Like she was completely at his mercy. Completely *his*.

He circled a finger around her nipple in time to the one that was moving lazily across her clit.

"*Spencer.*"

He moved his hands faster, pinching her nipple between his fingers. His lips moved to the shell of her ear. "You need something, baby?"

Elizabeth rubbed her ass against the bulge in his pants. "You. Now."

"Say the words, princess."

He needed her to want this as much as he did. The drive to be with her was so alien. He had never craved someone like this before. If he didn't sink into her soon, he would self-destruct.

Elizabeth turned her head around to face him, lust turning those brown eyes almost black. "Fuck. I want you to fuck me. Is that what you wanted to hear?"

That was all the cue he needed. Spencer unbuckled his pants, rolled on a condom, and plunged inside her.

She was so fucking tight it was almost painful, but in the best of ways. He wrapped an arm around her, bringing her back up to touch his chest while he sank deeper into her.

"Fuck, Beth, you feel *good*." He could barely get the words out; his voice was huskier than he'd ever heard it. It felt like she was made just for him.

Elizabeth's only response was to pull her hips forward then push them back again, forcing him even deeper.

"Harder." She moaned, and it drove him wild.

He hadn't meant for their first time to be this rushed, this frenzied, but their attraction was animalistic. They were clawing at each other, desperate. It was chaotic and beautiful, and when he leaned over her shoulder and saw the entire city below them, the tower sparkling in time with his thrusts, Spencer didn't think he had ever experienced a moment so perfect.

There would be time to savor every inch of her later.

"Come for me. *Now*." He moved a hand to between her legs and pinched that spot he knew would send her over the edge.

When Spencer felt her clench around him, screaming his name for all of Paris to hear, he let go, as well. She was so warm and clutching him so tightly it made his cock pulse in time to her orgasm. She was amazing.

Oh fucking hell. This woman.

Being inside her took their connection to an entirely new level. Before, he had wanted her so much it hurt, but this, this was different. It felt perfect. It felt like both their lives had been working up to this one moment, where the only thing in the world they cared about was melting their bodies together against the sparkling night sky.

Spencer felt his heart racing in his chest, and when he came, his eyes seemed to roll back into his head. It went on forever, and he knew that feeling of filling her up would never get old. He wanted to turn her around and come on her tits as well, take her on her back, in the shower, against a wall. In this moment she was the sun, and he was just the planet lucky enough to be in her orbit.

Finally, he released the breath he had been holding and pulled out of her.

Elizabeth turned around to face him, her hair wild, eyes wide. That damn dress was still pooled at her feet. He inched closer, touching his forehead to hers, not yet ready for words.

The same however, could not be said for Elizabeth.

She licked her lips. "So, when do I get to see those abs?"

Chapter Twenty-Four
LIZZIE

Sophia was grinning like a Cheshire cat when Lizzie walked through the door.

She was sitting on the couch, two cups of coffee set in front of her on the table, patting the cushion beside her. It was around midday, and she must have known Lizzie needed to come back before her teaching session later that afternoon. Couldn't get anything past her.

"Where do you think you're going?" Sophia said with pursued lips as Lizzie walked toward her bedroom to change out of last night's notably crinkled dress.

Lizzie ignored her, striding toward her wardrobe to find a pair of yoga pants and a shirt. She could get dressed for tutoring later. Right now, she needed comfort. She was *sore*. Delightfully so.

"Hey! I'm talking to you." Sophia was hot on her heels, barging into the room without any regard for the fact that Lizzie was currently half-naked.

"Is that a hickey on your *boob*?"

"Great to see you too, yes, I'm well, thanks so much for asking." Lizzie bounced her head side to side, putting on a high-pitched voice as she held up Seb's old T-shirt, giving it a little sniff before half-shrugging and pulling it on.

"I don't have time for pleasantries." Sophia threw her hands into the air before collapsing onto the bed. "I need *details*. Now."

Lizzie sighed, shoulders sagging, as she joined her friend.

"Alright then, you win. What do you want to know?"

Sophia narrowed her eyes, as if Lizzie was the most unintelligent human on the planet. "Uh, everything. Where did you go? Did you have sex with him? Well, obviously you did considering you left last night at seven and now it's like eighteen hours later. So how was he? Can we talk size? Is that allowed?"

Jesus. Sophia must have lungs of steel because she hadn't taken one breath during that interrogation.

"The Shangri-La. Yes, we slept together. He was..." Her voice trailed off. How could she put it into words?

She thought back to last night—the exhilaration she had felt looking out at the sky, the cool railing pressing into her front while Spencer's warmth pushed into her back. God, that suit he had been wearing, when he took her for the first time, was hot, but he looked even better when she stripped it off him not long after. Since she was already naked, it put them on even ground. Then she had put him on the *actual* ground when she climbed on top of him for another taste. Lizzie smiled wryly at the memory.

After they'd wrapped up round two, they had put on those silly hotel robes and slippers, sipped champagne, and ordered room service. They went back and forth for hours, sharing anything and everything that came to mind. Somehow, the joining of their bodies had sparked an even deeper connection between them. She had never felt so comfortable with another person before, not even Sophia, not even her family. Spencer's soul just called to hers.

It was scary as hell.

"Well?" Sophia's impatient voice snapped Lizzie out of her musings. Good thing too, considering the path they had been on.

Lizzie carefully studied her fingernails, refusing to meet Sophia's eyes. "I guess he was the best I've ever had."

Sophia's jaw dropped. "Are you serious?"

"Unfortunately, yes."

"And what the hell is unfortunate about that?"

Lizzie clutched a pillow to her chest, sighing. "Because he's my rebound."

"So? Isn't the whole point of a rebound having hot sex?"

"Yes, but what if I need a rebound from *him*?"

Sophia waved a hand dismissively, raising her coffee to her lips. "I wouldn't stress about it. You're probably just building him up in your head after the horror of he-who-shall-not-be-named."

Lizzie rolled her eyes. "I don't think I can just imagine four orgasms."

Sophia spat out the sip she had taken, eyes bulging. "Bullshit."

A smirk pulled at Lizzie's lips.

"Don't worry, we made it to the bed by the third."

Sophia threw a pillow at her, amber eyes flashing. "You bitch. How dare you have more sex in one night than I've had in months."

"That sounds like a 'you' problem."

For some reason, Sophia had decided to swear off men when she moved to Paris. Lizzie didn't really get it; for her, the idea of a lover was part of the whole experience of being here. In fairness, Sophia had dated some real tools before, never for more than a few weeks. She seemed to attract all the wrong guys and it didn't often turn out well.

Sophia sniffed, taking the pillow from Lizzie's arms and placing it behind her head. "That's beside the point. What's wrong with Spencer being more than rebound?"

"Everything!" Lizzie threw up her hands. "My brother being the obvious reason."

"Would he really care *that* much?"

Lizzie groaned. "Have you met my brother?"

"Good point." Sophia laughed. "Hey, do you remember that time he and Josh broke into the dorm of that jock?"

Lizzie gritted her teeth. "Yes."

How could she forget? Daniel Summers, hottest guy on campus, had been into her. She had accidentally told her mom, who told the boys. The next time Seb visited, he and Josh broke into Daniel's dorm and replaced all his shoelaces with shorter ones. They left a handy Post-It note that said *Stay away from Elizabeth Hastings*.

Daniel had been annoyed but laughed it off. That was until the next time, when the boys replaced his laces with bright pink ones. Eventually he had gotten over that, as well. But when he woke up one morning to find that one of each pair of shoes he owned had been taken, he had dumped her. Via text.

"This is his best friend, Soph. They're practically brothers." Lizzie scrunched her nose. "Well, okay, that sounds gross considering recent developments."

"May as well just call you Cersei Lannister now," Sophia said, voice dry.

"Ew, Soph, don't go there."

"In all seriousness though, what are you going to do?"

Lizzie sat up a bit, squaring her shoulders. "I'm going to keep it casual."

"Really?"

"Yes. It will be fine. Fun, even." Lizzie was nodding; this was the perfect plan. "I can totally do casual."

"Keep telling yourself that, honey."

Chapter Twenty-Five

SPENCER

Spencer finally booked an apartment to stay in. As much as he would've liked to just camp out at Elizabeth's, he figured that would freak her out a little at this early stage. He was happy to just take this slow and see where it went.

Well. Kind of.

Maybe he had gone a bit overboard with the whole fancy-hotel thing the night before. But he had all week to plan how he would have her that first time, and he wanted her to feel cherished. After what that bastard had done to her, she deserved to be treated like a queen. She deserved it anyway.

The apartment he was now standing in was a convenient five-minute walk from Elizabeth's place. It was nothing special, but it had a big bed and bathroom. Spencer had clear priorities, i.e. shower sex.

His computer was set up on a little corner desk by the window. Throughout the afternoon he had done a video meeting with his team back home, as well as a few online training sessions with clients. So, when his computer sounded with a Skype call, he assumed it was Anna again.

An uncomfortable feeling took over his gut when he saw Seb's name on the screen. Spencer had been avoiding him for the past few days. It just didn't seem right to be sexting Elizabeth in one message, then be catching up with her brother in the next. He felt like the world's biggest jerk.

Spencer sat down at the desk and reached out to accept the call before he second-guessed himself.

"Seb. What's up?" He schooled his face into as neutral an expression as he could muster.

"Just checking in. How are things going with the new Tate's? Who knew my brilliant cover for you would turn into reality?" Seb's laugh rang out on the other line. It looked like he was in his lunch break at work, judging by the way the New York skyline was lit up behind him.

"Yeah, pretty good, man; it's still in the early stages." Spencer rubbed his temple. "We're looking at a location near the Bastille; there's a good space for rent."

"That's great." Seb's enthusiasm felt like a knife to the gut. He was always so supportive of him, and here he was betraying him. "What made you decide to stay?"

Spencer sort of choked. He tried to hide it behind a cough, but Seb's eyes were narrowed in suspicion.

"Well, I was going on all these runs and kept seeing people everywhere exercising." Spencer's eyes were taking in the ceiling, the flaking wood on the desk, and basically anywhere that wasn't his best friend's eyes. "It just seemed like a good market."

"You did so much research before the London move and now you're picking cities based on the vibe?" Seb was the more logical and strategic of the pair. Spencer was more about his passions. He just focused on what felt right and let it take him where it wanted.

"Yeah, seems a bit stupid now." Spencer attempted a laugh but it fell flat.

"Are you sure this is the right move?"

"I've got cash to spare, even if it tanks, I'll be fine."

Seb smirked. "You could do so much more with it, you know. I could help."

Spencer waved him off. "I never thought I'd make over a million in my life. I'm happy. I don't need all the fancy crap you love."

They shared a bit more banter back and forth before the inevitable happened.

"How's little Lizzie girl doing? You still keeping an eye on her?"

Well, if keeping an eye on her extended to ogling her naked body, Spencer figured he was doing a pretty good job.

"Yeah, I've seen her here and there. She's fine, honestly."

A frown creased Seb's brow. "That's what I'm worried about. She seems *too* good. You know how she was the day everything went down with that fucker."

Spencer cleared his throat, keeping his expression neutral. "She's stronger than you think Seb. She's not some little girl."

"That may be true, but she'll always be my baby sister." Seb beamed, looking over his computer at what Spencer knew was a photo of him and Elizabeth. Even though Josh was closer in age with her, it was she and Seb who always had the tightest bond.

Seb went on. "Anyway—has she mentioned any guys recently?"

Spencer stifled a groan. When would this conversation fucking end? He had never been more uncomfortable during a chat with his best friend in his entire life.

"Do you honestly think she'd talk to me about that crap?"

"Why not?" Seb's brown eyes clouded with confusion. "You went on that whole tour thing the other day. You must have talked. I have Sophia on Instagram; I know they've been going out."

A muscle in Spencer's jaw started to twitch at the memory of Elizabeth dancing that night. Although retrospectively, a small part of him wanted to thank the guy— without him he probably would never had made a move on her to begin with. He'd been ready to pack up and leave the next day, dammit.

"Is it really that big a deal if she's seeing someone?" Grace had never brought a boyfriend home, so Spencer hadn't had the chance to test out if he would be as crazy as the Hastings boys, but somehow, he doubted it. Sure, he was protective of Grace but he really just wanted to see her happy. If some guy did that for her, he was all for it. If that same guy broke her heart? Yeah, that would be a little different. But you can't just wrap them in cotton wool so it doesn't happen. Life doesn't work that way.

Seb slammed a fist on the table. "Uh yeah, it is. She just went through a breakup." He shook his head. "You know what men are like. What *we've* been like. If anyone is with her now, he is just taking advantage of her crushed ego."

Spencer's mouth snapped shut, and he swallowed before he could say something he regretted.

"Yeah, I guess so. Anyway, man, I've got to go. Chat later."

He hung up before Seb could even say goodbye.

Chapter Twenty-Six
SPENCER

The following weeks seemed to pass by in a blur. One minute they were having their first night together, the next they had been seeing each other for almost two months. Their days fell into a routine. They would wake up in each other's arms, spend the morning together—although they didn't often leave bed—then part ways for the afternoon. Elizabeth's students were usually all booked in for after midday, so that gave time for Spencer to oversee how Paris's first Tate's Training was shaping up. So far, his team had locked in a building and he was training new staff on the techniques. They still had a way to go in terms of getting all his preferred equipment there, but it was looking positive.

Spencer kept odd hours to keep up with his clients back home and had even made a few trips back to be there in person, so they didn't spend every night together. But when they did, it was pure perfection.

Sometimes they went out and explored the city. Spencer loved watching the way Elizabeth's face lit up when she showed off her favorite parts of Paris. Seeing it through her eyes was pretty amazing. He knew the experience would be completely different without her.

Other nights, like tonight, they stayed in and enjoyed each other's company. But they still had fun. They always had fun.

Being with her was like breathing. It was natural. Effortless.

He tried not to think about the possibility of drowning when he no longer had her.

Elizabeth moved her head from side to side on the cushion on his lap, wordlessly begging for a massage. Spencer chuckled and obliged.

"Someone's demanding today," he said with a wry smile.

Elizabeth batted her eyelashes at him. "I think I deserve it after the treatment you got this morning."

Spencer felt his jeans tighten at the memory. There was no better alarm clock than Elizabeth's hot, wet mouth. He thought he'd been dreaming, because let's be honest, she featured heavily in them more often than not. But to open his eyes and find her straddling him? Best. Feeling. Ever.

He sighed. "Is there anything better than great sex?"

The corners of Elizabeth's mouth quirked. "I can think of a few things."

Spencer threw his hand to his heart and let out a loud gasp. "Better than *me*? Impossible."

"Croissants."

"You'd take a buttery, flaky ticket to high cholesterol over a night with me?"

Elizabeth twisted around and raised a hand to caress his cheek. Her chocolate eyes were solemn when they met his. She held his gaze for so long he worried something was up... But then she whispered, "Every. Single. Time."

Spencer shoved her off his lap with a grumble. Peals of laughter erupted from Elizabeth, a mega-watt smile transforming her face. He shook his head. "You know, I might just have to replace you with one of those Instagram models who keep commenting on my photos."

Her eyes narrowed. "And why would you do that?"

"They would never betray me for a croissant." Spencer's lips twitched. "They're too busy guzzling down skinny tea."

"Fine." Elizabeth shrugged, but a hint of a smile remained. "You can keep your insta-whores and laxatives, I'll take my book boyfriends."

"Hey, how'd your writing go today?"

Elizabeth had mentioned she was taking the afternoon off to work on the plan for her big book. It was strange, she never really talked about it that much. Elizabeth was such a passionate person; her emotions were written in those big eyes of hers and they would spark whenever she mentioned a book she loved or a French delicacy she couldn't wait to try. He couldn't understand why her life's passion didn't come up in conversation.

Elizabeth's face transformed, mouth setting in a hard line. "It was fine."

"When do I get to hear about it?" Spencer grinned, nudging her. "Do you have a title chosen yet?"

It fell completely flat. For a few moments the only sound that accompanied them was the television in front of them. The violent noises of a spy movie were playing, and the blare only served to heighten the silence between them.

"No. I don't." She wouldn't meet his eyes. "What's with all the interest in it?"

Spencer's brows knitted. "What's wrong with me being interested?"

"Because we're not serious. We're sex." Elizabeth stood up and stalked to the kitchen.

The clanging of what sounded like the kettle and a few mugs filled the void where she had been. *What the fuck?*

The cold words were alien coming from Elizabeth's mouth. The delivery a punch to the gut.

In the back of his mind, Spencer knew he was the rebound. They had agreed early on to be casual. But what about all those dates? What about the nights tangled in the sheets, whispering words to each other they wouldn't dare say in the light of day? Since when was it her right to decide all meaningful topics were off-limits?

This is bullshit.

He stormed to the kitchen and took the mug from her hand, planting it firmly on the bench behind her before placing his hands on her shoulders and turning her to face him.

"What did I do?"

His mind frantically searched back over the conversation. Yeah, he'd mentioned Instagram girls but surely she knew he was only kidding? She seemed to find it funny at the time.

Her nostrils flared and she looked away. "Nothing. Drop it."

"Beth. Talk to me."

She still refused to meet his eyes. He took in her hunched shoulders, arms circling her chest. Her face was carefully expressionless, which was his first sign that this was serious.

Spencer sighed and stepped forward to take her little frame in his arms. "Princess, tell me. Please."

Elizabeth buried her face in his neck and they stood there together in silence for a long while. Finally, barely above a whisper, she said, "I can't do it."

"Do what, honey?"

"Write." Her lower lip was quivering and when she turned her gaze to meet his, he could see her eyes welling up.

Spencer scooped her up into his arms and took her to the bed. This was where the truths came out. When you're stripped down next to someone else after sharing so much together, that's when true intimacy begins. Almost every significant conversation between them had taken place in this queen-sized, pillow-covered space, usually in the early hours of the morning.

He bundled her up into the blankets and put his arms around her from the outside. "What can't you write?"

"Anything." The word seemed to choke out of her.

"Why do you think that is?"

"I don't know." Elizabeth slammed her first in the pillow. "I keep trying and trying. I moved countries, for crying out loud. And I just—can't." The last word came out as a sob.

Spencer pressed his lips to her hair. "Do you ever think you're putting too much pressure on yourself? Ever since we met you've said you wanted to be a writer. Even when you were just a kid."

"It makes sense." She sniffed against the covers. "I read so much. It's what I love. I'm smart. What else is there to it?"

"I don't know much about writing but I know a bit about doing what you love."

Her gaze turned to his, searching. "And?"

"And I've never heard you say you love writing."

Elizabeth's expression darkened, "That's—"

He cut her off. "You know what brings a smile to your face every time you talk about it?"

She shook her head.

"Teaching. Helping all those stressed-out kids."

Elizabeth frowned, pondering it. "But Spence, that's different, it's a..." She twisted her lips. "A hobby. It's just meant to give me some more real-world experience to help with writing."

Spencer had to suppress an eye roll. Sometimes Elizabeth seemed like the most cultured, down-to-earth person he'd ever met. Other times she sounded exactly like the sheltered heiress she had been raised as. He guessed it was hard to shake off a childhood where your family had more money than some developing countries.

"You enjoy it. Why not go back to school, become a teacher?"

Elizabeth sat up, mouth falling open. "It's not that simple."

"Why?"

"Because." She pinched the bridge of her nose. "My whole family is one giant success story. Josh and Seb will take over Hastings Properties, Dylan will end up partner at New York's biggest firm. How does teacher stack up against that?"

Looking at her pursed lips and flushed cheeks, Spencer knew she wasn't ready to hear this yet. He didn't give two shits what her career was; he just wanted to see her doing something she enjoyed. She was one of the few people in the world who didn't have to worry about money. Elizabeth could literally do anything she wanted, so why waste time sweating about her image?

But this wasn't the time for that conversation. And he wasn't sure how she would react to hearing it from him. He knew her earlier words were said in anger, but it didn't lessen the sting. His dad had always told him every lie had a seed of truth in it. Maybe she did just see him as sex. At this point he'd take her any way she would let him.

"I know something else that would make you smile, princess."

Elizabeth pouted. "And what is that?"

Spencer didn't respond. He just pulled the blanket over his head and started moving down her body. He looked up as he reached his favorite spot. She was beaming.

Chapter Twenty-Seven
LIZZIE

Cheap wine, cheese, and the Seine.

Was there anything so fundamentally Parisian?

Their legs dangled over the stone, the last rays of sunlight casting an orange glow over the water below them. Lizzie's favorite thing about the city was how everything blended together so seamlessly. The buildings weren't strangers, they were siblings. From the colors to the design, to the tiny illegal-looking extensions on the roofs.

A busker was set up twelve feet away from them. He had graying hair and a hunched back, but when she closed her eyes, his voice was full of youth, belting out French classics accompanied by his accordion.

Lizzie took a swig from the bottle and sighed. "I love this place."

Spencer's eyes met hers and the color was a perfect match for today's sky. "Do you come here often?"

Lizzie nodded, "Sometimes Sophia and I meet up here for lunch." She gazed out over the water to the people walking by on the other bank. "Other times I come alone. It helps me think."

Spencer cut up some of the brie and smeared it onto a bit of baguette. He raised it to her lips and took the bottle of wine in exchange.

"What are you thinking about now?"

She picked up the paper packaging at her side, twirling it between her fingers. "I get this sense that I've reached a turning point in life. I just don't quite know what it is."

They were onto their second bottle and the flow of wine helped the flow of conversation. There was something about red wine that drew out your deepest thoughts.

Spencer's face darkened. "You'll know when it happens." He took a long swig from the bottle.

"I take it you've had one?"

Something flashed in those eyes and he visibly swallowed. "When my mom died." Another sip.

"You never talk about her."

"There's not much to talk about. One day she was there, one day she wasn't."

"So, what was the big turning point?"

Spencer picked up her hand, the one that had been fiddling with the paper. He turned her palm up, tracing patterns on it absentmindedly while the busker's melody echoed in the background. His frown faded somewhat.

"I guess I stopped fucking around. Stopped being ungrateful." He flipped the hand over to start caressing the back. "Before…I was a little shit. Always annoyed that we didn't have much growing up. When she died, it all happened so quickly. It made me realize I could go out that quick, as well." Spencer released her hand with a heave of his shoulders. "I started just living for me, I guess."

"I don't want this to come out the wrong way but you don't seem really cut up about it."

When Spencer finally answered, Lizzie released the breath she had been holding. "It's my normal. It happened more than ten years ago. I know she wouldn't have wanted me to throw my life away because she no longer had one. Getting lost in my grief was just never an option."

Lizzie took him in, the golden afternoon light glinting off his hair as he raised the bottle to his lips. His high cheekbones were especially prominent today, and they only served to heighten the effect of those full lips and piercing eyes. Yes, the man was beautiful, but she hadn't realized until this very moment the strength that he exuded. No one had ever expected him to be where he was today. He defied odds with a nonchalance that was difficult to comprehend.

Teenage Lizzie had been obsessed with his looks, his smile. Freshly single Lizzie was caught up in what he could do to her body. But now. Now she really *saw* him. The man behind that beautiful exterior. And she liked him. A lot.

"You're pretty damn impressive, Spencer Tate." Her lips curved into a smile.

Spencer laughed it off. "Says one of the smartest people I know."

A shiver traveled up her spine hearing him talk about her like that. It felt so good, it had to be written all over her face.

"What about you, princess? Learned any life mantras in your time on earth?"

Her gaze turned back to the river as she mulled it over. A sickening feeling came over her gut at the first thing that came to mind. She had this image of Amaury, gray eyes sparking with what she had thought was love, walking hand in hand with her along the bank of this same river. A montage of night after night they spent together came to her: his whispered excuses, the pieces of jewelry he would buy her when he had been too busy with 'work' to see her. The worst part was that even though she could buy herself anything she wanted, when it came from Amaury, she always got this thrill. Looking back now, it was just another sign she was caught under his spell. Learning that every one of those moments they shared together was a lie was soul-crushing.

It was Lizzie's turn to gulp down the wine. "Things aren't what they seem."

Spencer's arm came around her shoulders and he pushed a kiss to her temple. "Don't let one bad experience change the way you see life."

God. Why did he have to be so perfect all the time? Every time Spencer spoke it was like he was touching her soul. She needed to steer this conversation away from the deep and meaningful, stat.

"At least I'll always have Paris..." Lizzie waved the bottle in front of them. "And wine."

The corner of Spencer's mouth lifted. "Have you ever had a book drive you to drink?"

"Ugh, yes. *Heart of Darkness*. It didn't take that long to read but once I shut it, I was done with humanity. Love and kindness didn't exist. The whole world was just evil waiting to happen." Lizzie shuddered. "You?"

A sheepish grin greeted her. "Not much of a reader. But I did cry in *A Star is Born*."

"Anyone who didn't cry in that movie is a robot. Or one of those lizard men the YouTube conspiracy theorists think are going to take over the planet."

Spencer arched a brow. "Do I even want to know?"

"I get into some dark YouTube holes sometimes. Don't ask."

He gave a lopsided grin. "What about characters? Any you just hate?"

"You know, a sign of a good book is how much it can make you hate the villain,"—she gestured across the river with her wine —"and a great book can make you love them. I was halfway through *Lolita* when I realized I was rooting for the freaking pedophile."

Spencer threw his head back and laughed.

"Names are a good one too," Lizzie continued. "Do you have any of those names you just detest because of someone who has it?"

The slightest of flushes crept across Spencer's cheeks and he bowed his head.

"Come on, spit it out."

"Amaury."

That had them both cracking up, especially because he had butchered the pronunciation in a big way. Lizzie's shoulders were shaking so much she was teetering dangerously close to falling off the edge of the bank into the Seine. But it was worth it.

"Off your baby name list then?"

"Oh definitely. It was top place before but what can you do?"

They only laughed harder.

Once the tears stopped leaking from her eyes, she searched her mind for another question. "Okay, how about this one—what's something you should do but probably won't?"

"Tell your brother about us." Spencer deadpanned. Another swig of wine. "You?"

"Stop caring what people think."

They were as bad as each other, but still somehow perfect together.

Part of her wanted to share this with Seb. Normally they could talk for hours; there were never secrets between them. But Spencer had just signed up to be her rebound. It's not like he ever expressed interest in taking things further. He was doing her a favor. A mutually beneficial one.

Soon he would be gone and they would have to go back to pretending they were family friends. She went to take another drink but the bottle was now empty. Figures.

"Do you have a favorite quote?" Spencer's soft voice brought her back.

"*Vivre jusqu'aux larmes.* Live to the point of tears. Albert Camus."

It summed up the whole reason she had moved here in the first place. It explained so many of her life choices up until this point. Money can't buy you experiences. The only way to collect them was to truly *live*.

Spencer nodded, understanding.

"Describe your perfect day," she said, eyes tracing the way the light danced across the water.

Spencer reached up and brushed away a strand of hair that had fallen into her face. Lust and something she couldn't quite name glowed in his eyes.

"Here. Now." He inched closer, eyes never leaving hers. "The details don't matter much to me, but every time I imagine where I want to be, I picture your face."

Then his lips met hers.

Well, fuck.

How on earth was she meant to not fall in love with this guy?

Chapter Twenty-Eight
LIZZIE

"Three free tables and the chain-smokers chose the one right next to us. Typical." Sophia shot a dirty look at the couple who had just sat down next to them.

"You moved to Paris. What did you expect?"

"I don't know! Human decency maybe?" Sophia tossed her hair over her shoulder with a sniff.

"Come on, it adds to the atmosphere."

"Tell that to your lungs when they get second-hand cancer." She emphasized her point with a fist to the table, shooting another not-so-subtle look the couple's way.

Lizzie rolled her eyes. "Shut up and eat your baguette."

They were sitting at one of their favorite haunts in Saint-Germain. It wasn't as pricey as some of the cafés on the main boulevard, but the people-watching was much better here. Nestled between a bookstore and a patisserie on a foot-traffic-only street, there was always someone interesting passing by.

Sophia huffed out a breath but complied, shoving the remaining half of her sandwich into her mouth while glaring at their fellow café-goers out of the corner of her eye.

Having grown up with three brothers, mealtimes were akin to survival of the fittest for Lizzie. She had learnt how to quickly throw back her food from a young age, so she had long since finished her lunch.

Lizzie pulled out her phone to pass the time and saw Spencer's name on the screen. Warmth immediately rushed through her at the thought of him. Without fully realizing what she was doing, she began to twirl her spoon around her coffee, lips curved into a small smile.

"How *is* lover boy, anyway?" Sophia's knowing amber eyes drilled into her.

Lizzie shook her head with a start. "I wasn't thinking about him."

"Oh, please. Don't insult my intelligence." Sophia snorted, waving her hand in front of Lizzie. "It's written all over your sappy face."

"It's not like that with us."

"You're not even convincing yourself with that line."

"He's fine. Might see him later tonight. No definite plans." Lizzie shrugged nonchalantly.

"And how are the plans going with your relationship?"

Lizzie raised her eyes to meet Sophia's and she knew hope of avoiding this conversation was futile. Her best friend had a way of wheedling out information from her, no matter the subject.

Although, if the direction of her thoughts about Spencer was as obvious as Sophia was implying, she shouldn't even need to voice it. Suddenly a startling notion crossed her mind: What if *Spencer* realized, as well? Oh God. That would be a new kind of hell. He was probably rehearsing the let-her-down easy speech already. How mortifying.

"What do you want me to say? That I have feelings for him?"

"Uh, yeah." Sophia was looking at her like she was crazy. She planted her hands firmly on the table, never losing eye contact. "Admitting it is always the first step."

"That doesn't help anything." Lizzie ducked her head, looking anywhere but her best friend. Why couldn't she just let it be?

"Why don't you do this properly? You're practically dating anyway."

Lizzie turned her gaze over the street, as if this wasn't the tenth time she had mulled over this idea. She watched a young couple walking toward the bookstore. The woman's arm was linked with the man's, their smiles matching, laughter contagious. You could see the flash of a ring on her finger. It looked uncomplicated. Perfect.

Lizzie sighed.

"It's not that simple." She responded to Sophia, rubbing her temples. "You're the only person who even knows we're together."

Sophia shrugged, sipping her coffee. "So tell people. It's really not that big a deal."

Lizzie started counting her fingers. "One: It is a huge deal. Seb would kill both of us. Two: Spencer literally signed up for casual sex. That's it. Yes we go on the odd date, but he also knows no one else in this city." Sophia opened her mouth to speak but Lizzie cut her off, "And before you say it, three: The only reason we're exclusive is because he's possessive."

"Possessiveness is a good sign, though."

"It's not because he likes me; it's because he doesn't share."

"Just *talk* to him."

Lizzie ignored her. "We don't even live in the same country."

"Sure seems like you do."

"Plus I just got out of a relationship. I shouldn't go into another one so soon."

Sophia snorted. "What, now you're putting some arbitrary time limit on your heartbreak?"

Yes. That was a great idea. A perfect one, in fact. Any sort of guideline would be helpful right now.

"Well, I was with him for six months. So, six months is a good time to be single. To,"—Lizzie's brow furrowed as she searched for the word—"balance it." She nodded.

Sophia put her face in her hands. "That is literally the worst idea I've ever heard. And I work with kids."

When Lizzie didn't deign that with a response, Sophia continued, "And are you really defining yourself as single right now?"

"Not single," Lizzie clarified, frowning to herself, "unattached."

"You sure seemed pretty *attached* to one another when I got home early the other night."

Sophia smirked and Lizzie's cheeks flushed scarlet. Movie night had turned a little heated from the moment they decided to share a blanket. To be honest, it wasn't difficult for the most innocent of situations to become X-rated with Spencer. Come on. She was only human. The man could charm the pants off a nun, for God's sake.

"That's the only kind of attached we'll be. And right now it's working out well for both of us." Lizzie took a final sip of her drink, finishing it. "If it ain't broke, right?"

"Right."

Sophia didn't sound convinced.

Chapter Twenty-Nine
SPENCER

Spencer was having the best dream. Ever.

A warm, wet tongue was flicking over the head of his cock. Back and forth. Slowly. He groaned, thrusting his hips forward. He could recognize Elizabeth's lips even in his subconscious.

Who the hell would ever want to wake up?

The tongue darted out again, taking in drops of precum while it traced around the tip. Spencer felt his heart rate start to quicken. The thought of Elizabeth on him was the biggest rush.

"Rise and shine, baby."

Huh?

He cracked an eyelid and did a double take.

The covers of Elizabeth's bed had been completely swept aside and she was kneeling between his legs, fully naked. She had one hand grasping the base of his cock, the other holding herself up. He could feel her hot breath on his tip, she was that close.

Elizabeth met his gaze, eyes flashing. She bit her lip.

Fuck. Me.

Spencer didn't know what the hell he had done to deserve this, but he sent a quick thanks to whatever higher power was sitting in the big chair up above. He would donate to charity more, he decided —maybe do some volunteer coaching work for kids. Anything to increase the odds of this happening again.

GABRIELLE ASHTON

Elizabeth got back to work, tracing a path from head to shaft. The little witch was teasing him in the best of ways. Every time she gave a little flick he felt his balls tingle.

Fucking hell. Not going to last long.

Without warning she opened wide and took him all the way in. Feeling her all warm and wet with no barriers between them was his kind of paradise. The sensation was almost indescribable. Some people have this idea blow jobs are degrading to women, but holy fucking hell, it was Elizabeth who had all the power right now. Spencer was completely at her mercy.

He began to move his hips in time to her long drags on his cock, and the frenzy inside him just built higher and higher. He swore he could see stars.

Spencer reached out a hand to palm the chocolate veil over her shoulders and pushed himself farther in.

"Take it all, princess."

Elizabeth shut her eyes and moaned as he touched the back of her throat. Spencer felt the vibration along his whole cock and it was fucking incredible.

Now, she needed no further encouragement. Elizabeth worked him harder and faster, seeming to know exactly what he needed and when. She was beyond good at this. Spencer pushed aside the thought of how she had developed that particular skillset. That should be none of his business, and besides, he had other priorities right now.

His hips moved faster of their own accord. There was something about being inside her like this, the idea of claiming her that just got to him. He fucked her mouth more roughly.

"Beth baby, I'm going to come."

She only sucked him harder, wordlessly answering his unasked question.

Oh fuck.

Before he knew it Spencer was exploding into her, the warm

172

liquid trickling right down the back of her throat. Her eyes were open and locked with his the entire time. It was beyond sexy. Eventually she swallowed then licked her lips.

"Good morning." The corners of her mouth twitched.

Spencer hadn't yet mastered the ability to speak. He blinked a few times, realizing that this had definitely not been a dream. Since when was his reality better than anything he could have imagined?

"Fucking hell, Beth, are you trying to kill me?"

She laughed, this light tinkling sound that warmed him up inside almost as much as the blow job.

"I wanted to wake you, and I figured that would be a better alarm clock." She blinked up at him from under those long lashes, all false innocence.

Spencer looped an arm around her middle, throwing her over his shoulder while he stood up. Time to return the favor.

"You, Elizabeth Hastings, have been a very dirty girl." Spencer strode over to the shower, giving a little spank to her bare ass. "Time to clean you up."

AFTER A MUCH LONGER THAN NECESSARY JOINT SHOWER, SPENCER wrapped a towel around himself and made his way to Elizabeth's kitchen. He had this big, stupid smile plastered on his face. It was Sunday so they both had the whole day free and it was already shaping up to be the best one of the week.

Morning light drifted in through the white, gauzy blinds and it made the whole apartment seem softer. They had it all to themselves today because Sophia was nannying, and judging by how they had spent the early hours, it wasn't looking like they would be leaving this sanctuary any time soon.

Spencer hummed to himself while he padded around the kitchen, turning the kettle on. He had been here so much, it felt like his own apartment.

"Beth?" He ducked his head out of the door, calling out across the hallway, "You want some tea?"

"You know it," she said, coming out of the bedroom wearing nothing but his shirt. It was one of his work ones so it had *Tate's Training* in big letters across the chest. He raked his eyes over it with a smirk. There was something so damn satisfying about seeing your woman in your shirt.

Inwardly he cringed. He needed to stop calling her his.

Elizabeth stood on her toes to plant a kiss against his cheek. "I might stay in bed and read for a bit."

Spencer brushed a lock of hair away from her face. "Is that code for 'Spencer please make me breakfast in bed'?"

Elizabeth shrugged. "Read into it what you will…" she said, turning on her heel with a giggle.

"Yeah, yeah princess." Spencer waved her off but deep down he loved it. Loved making her feel special.

He was in the middle of putting the bread in the toaster when he heard a knock on the door. Spencer slammed the plate he had been holding onto the counter. Who the hell would be popping over at eight in the morning on a Sunday?

It's probably someone lost looking for one of her neighbors, he told himself as he strode over. He didn't bother putting on something more than a towel. If they wanted to intrude on his Sunday, they deserved to cop an eyeful.

Spencer wrenched open the door, "Yes?"

The words died in his mouth.

Oh fuck. Fuck. *FUCK.*

"Spencer?" Seb's brow was furrowed. "What are you…"

His voice drifted off, eyes tracing a path from Spencer's head to the towel slung across his hips. Seb's jaw clenched.

Spencer opened his mouth, no fucking idea how he could explain this, when Elizabeth's voice drifted over to them.

"Sophia, you bitch," she yelled from the bedroom, "just because you're not getting laid doesn't mean you can come home early and cockblock me."

Spencer met Seb's gaze, eyes bulging. "Seb, it's not—"

Seb's fist slamming into his face cut him off. White-hot pain lashed at his cheekbone and his eyes watered. Spencer hunched over, clutching onto the towel. He swallowed, tasting blood.

"Seb—"

"Get. Out." His best friend jerked a thumb to the door. Seb's face was hard, lips pressed into a thin line, and his voice was like a bucket of ice pouring over Spencer's head.

Spencer found himself nodding even as Elizabeth ran into the room, screaming at her brother.

"Seb, what the *fuck*?"

"I'll deal with you later, Lizzie. Right now this bastard needs to get out of my sight."

Spencer held up his hands. "I'm sorry, man, I—"

"Save it. Just leave."

He had never seen his friend look so furious. It was like a mask had come over his face and it made him a completely different person. His hands were balled into tight fists, his jaw clenched. And his eyes were like cold marbles, the color almost black with rage.

Spencer turned to meet Elizabeth's horrified gaze. He gave a small shake of his head. There would be no reasoning with Seb right now.

So, with his head hung low and cheek throbbing, Spencer left.

Chapter Thirty
LIZZIE

Seb had been pacing for so long, it was looking likely he would wear down a groove in the floor. Every few steps he would stop, take a breath, and open his mouth as if to speak, before snapping it shut.

Her brother Joshua was all passion, Dylan either felt everything or nothing but Seb... He was usually the calming force out of the four siblings. That didn't stop him becoming angry, but Lizzie had rarely ever seen a real outburst of emotion. He bottled it all up, locked down his expression, and gave nothing away. Seb could be falling apart on the inside and that outer façade would never crack, his voice would never raise. It's what made him so ruthless in business.

But seeing him now?

Lizzie shook her head. He wasn't just pissed. He was *furious*.

Each step he took back and forth felt like the wick of a bomb slowly shortening, inch by terrifying inch. But the really scary part was she wasn't sure what she would get on the other side. She had never seen him like this.

"Seb," she whispered softly, desperate to get through to him.

He ignored her, running a shaky hand through his hair.

With a sigh Lizzie ambled over to the couch, the tea Spencer had made her still sitting on the coffee table. At least the whole disaster had killed enough time for it to be at a drinkable temperature. You've got to think of the positives, right?

The image of her brother punching her...boyfriend? Lover? She wasn't sure what to call Spencer but that was beside the point. She cared for him. A lot. Picturing Seb's fist slamming into his face, making him double over in pain, fucking sucked. She loved Seb to bits. She would do anything for him. But now she felt like she was in the middle of a tug-a-war, her loyalty split between the two men. There was no point denying the way Spencer made her feel. And yeah, hiding everything from Seb wasn't great, but Spencer didn't deserve his best friend turning on him.

It was all such a mess.

After what seemed like an age, Seb stopped in front of her.

His eyes, the same ones she saw in the mirror every day, bored into hers.

He opened his mouth. Closed it. Balled his hands into fists. "How could you?"

The words were cold as ice, sharp as stalactites driving into her spine.

Lizzie blew out her cheeks. Where to even start?

"How could I do it in the first place? Or hide it from you?".

"Both."

Right. Well then. Guess she was starting from the beginning.

"You know I've always been into him."

Seb scrunched up his face. "That was different. You were a kid."

"It started when I was a kid but the attraction never stopped." Lizzie realized belatedly that she was finally admitting that point to herself. "That kind of stuff doesn't just disappear."

"Why now?" Seb sat down next to her, the old couch groaning in protest. He maintained more of a distance between them than he ever would have before. Each extra bit of space felt like a tiny pinprick driving into her skin.

Lizzie threw her head back against the couch. "A week after he arrived, he saw me with this other guy, about to make a really bad decision. He was so angry and we were arguing and then suddenly we were kissing..." She gave a half-shrug.

Seb's brows snapped together, eyes flashing. "That was *months* ago."

Oh shit. She had assumed he'd figured out the whole picture. God she sucked at this. She felt like every sentence she got out just drove another nail into her coffin.

Lizzie opened her mouth but no words came out.

Unfortunately for her, Seb had very much regained his powers of articulation.

"You're telling me my best friend has been sneaking around screwing my baby sister behind my back since May?"

"Uh..."

"The same sister that I sent him to Paris to check up on, because some fuckwit had just broken her heart?"

Part of Lizzie wanted to rebuke him but hey, he wasn't technically wrong. He was just kind of taking loose facts and painting a much worse, yet somehow correct narrative, Daily-Mail-style.

"The sister who was such a mess she was half crying, half drinking on Skype."

"Hey! That makes me sound horrible."

Seb leveled her with a look. "You were. And in no fucking state for any guy to be messing with you."

"It wasn't like that, Seb; he was good to me."

His eyes darkened. "Oh, I bet he was."

Lizzie punched him in the shoulder. "That's not what I meant. You know how devastated I was. He made me smile."

Seb threw up his hands. "Yeah, great—but why did he have to fuck you to do it?"

She didn't think she had ever had a conversation that made her feel so uncomfortable. For one, talking about sex to her brother was freaking gross. And two, the guilt she had relentlessly been shoving down into a box somewhere in the back of her mind was leaking out. Fast.

"Seb," she bit out slowly, enunciating every word, "he's made me really happy."

"So why hide it?"

Lizzie's eyes went round and she gestured a hand at her brother. "Exhibit A."

When Seb only narrowed his eyes further she gave in with a sigh.

"Fine. Look, this thing with me and Spence is just casual. He's here doing his gym; I'm here doing my writing. He didn't want me rebounding my way through the city." She folded her arms, looking everywhere but at her brother so he couldn't see the hurt under her skin. "It'll last a few more months then we'll move on and never speak about it again. There was no point in telling you and going through all this mess for something that wasn't serious."

There was silence for a few long moments then Seb said softly, "You could have had anyone. Why did you have to take my best friend?"

She pinched the bridge of her nose. "I'm not taking him. He's still your best friend."

"Do you honestly think we can go back after what he did?" Seb's voice was hard and low and he was gritting his teeth.

"Come on Seb, don't be dramatic."

"You don't get it." Seb started tapping his foot against the floor, but Lizzie didn't dare tell him off. "Sisters are off-limits. He knew that. He *chose* this."

Lizzie had known Seb wouldn't react well if he ever found out about her and Spencer, but she hadn't expected this level of hurt. Anger she anticipated, but betrayal? That was on another level.

"Will you ever forgive either of us?"

Seb let out a long breath. "You, yes. I'm pissed off but you were in a vulnerable state; you used to crush on him. I get it. Him? Never."

Lizzie had to stifle a gasp. The last bit was said without an ounce of hesitation. It scared the crap out of her.

This was getting beyond ridiculous.

"You can't just end your friendship because of this."

She and Sophia would never let something like this get between them. It would be weird as anything for Soph to start dating one of her brothers, and sure, Lizzie would be pissed if they lied to her, but she would get over it quick.

But Seb? He jerked back as if offended. "I'm not the one ending it! He did the moment he went after you."

This was going nowhere fast.

"Okay, new plan." Lizzie stood up, grabbing her brother by the hand. "Come look at our takeaway menus. Let's get some food, watch a few movies, forget about this. You can cool off and we'll revisit this conversation in the morning."

Seb's brows were still tightly knitted together but he allowed her to pull him up.

"Fine."

He paused.

"Do any Michelin star restaurants do home delivery around here?"

Lizzie rolled her eyes. There was the brother she knew and loved.

Chapter Thirty-One
SPENCER

Spencer checked his phone for what felt like the thousandth time since Seb had arrived in Paris. His best friend had been in the city for a few days now and had yet to respond to any of his calls. Eventually they had stopped going through and it was pretty obvious he had blocked Spencer's number. Fucking hell. What a mess.

His muscles ached in protest when he stood up. He hadn't been able to see Elizabeth yet because she was spending most days catching up with Seb, so he had filled in his time at the gym. While it helped distract his mind, his body was not as thankful for it.

The worst part was Seb had flown to Paris to surprise both of them. Spencer should be with them right now. It would have been a little awkward at first because him and Elizabeth were a secret, but once he got over that, having his best friend and his girl together would have been perfection. And he hadn't seen Seb for weeks. He missed him. Plain and simple.

Since the day they met, when they found out they were college roomies, they had instantly clicked. Seb felt like the brother he had never had. Despite their wildly different backgrounds they just worked well together. Even as they both got older and more involved in their respective careers, they still saw each other a few times each week. Most mornings they would meet at the Tate's

Training near Hastings Property and work out together. Ten years of friendship and not one real rift. Until now.

Spencer strode over to the bathroom and splashed water onto his face. He took in his appearance. His eyes just looked so flat, lifeless. There were dark circles under them because he could never sleep when his mind was constantly ticking over, stressing. Even a stranger would be able to tell something was up.

Spencer shaved and tried to make himself look a little more respectable. Like the kind of guy you would be happy dating your sister. A snort escaped him at the thought. Seb had seen him with so many one-night stands over the years, he doubted all those memories could be erased by running a comb through his hair and getting rid of his five o'clock shadow.

He had spoken to Elizabeth on the phone this morning and she told him Seb was leaving tomorrow. She had students this afternoon so it was likely Seb would be free. He was staying right in the middle of the city at one of the big fancy hotels, and Spencer would bet good money he had booked the penthouse. Elizabeth liked to escape from her upbringing, always avoiding the spotlight and high life. Most people wouldn't even recognize her. But Seb? He flaunted it.

Just get it over with, Spencer told himself as he left his apartment and hailed a cab to take him to Seb. He would just have to hope the guy was there. Considering he had taken a few days out of the office and the man lived and breathed his job, Spencer figured he was probably doing some work from his hotel room.

On the way over he instructed the driver to pull over outside of *La Maison du Whisky* and picked up the most expensive bottle of single-malt scotch they had in stock. It was almost eight thousand dollars but Seb had expensive taste, and Spencer had some serious groveling to do.

Ten minutes later he was in the lobby, trying to think of a way to get up to the penthouse. He had tried to convince the receptionist to let him in but she understandably declined. Spencer was about to head to the bar to try and wait Seb out when he spotted Dimitri, one of his security guys.

"Dimitri, what's doing?" Spencer plastered on a smile as he greeted him. The six foot seven man-monster had been working for Seb for a few years now. He was the most intimidating guy he had ever met. Russian, ice blue eyes, dark hair. Dimitri was silent most of the time, that shrewd gaze taking in every possible vulnerability in a room. It wasn't a good idea to get on his bad side, that was for sure.

"Mr. Hastings didn't tell me you were coming."

Straight to the point. No surprise there. Dimitri scanned Spencer head to toe. Jesus. Why couldn't it be Joe in the lobby today? At least he was friendly.

"It's a surprise." Spencer said with a smile, raising the bottle of whiskey in his hand. "I come bearing gifts."

The Russian paused for a few moments, eyes narrowed, before finally he nodded and escorted Spencer to the lift, and hopped inside with him.

Spencer suppressed a gulp. This was going to be interesting.

When they made it to the door, Dimitri spoke into a headpiece to the team inside.

The door swung open and Seb's hard face greeted him.

"What do you think you're doing here?"

"Seb. Please. We need to talk." Spencer looked at his best friend, trying to communicate in one look the hell he had been through the past few days.

Seb shut his eyes and sighed. "Fine. You have ten minutes before Dimitri drags you out."

They sat down on enormous armchairs that looked over the city, a marble coffee table in between them. Spencer set down the scotch and two glasses, shooting a side glance at the security team standing

GABRIELLE ASHTON

a few feet away. Seb caught his look and signaled for Dimitri and Joe to back off.

And then it was just the two of them. The amber liquid trickling into the crystal glasses was the only sound in the room.

"How could you?"

Seb's jaw was set and his face was carefully expressionless. Spencer knew a half-answer wouldn't cut it.

Spencer sat back and took in the view below him, trying to think of what he could possibly say. How he could express what was going on inside his head?

Why was she worth giving up his best friend?

He thought of how Elizabeth's laughter never failed to brighten his mood, the way her touch could set him on fire, how amazed he was when he saw her brilliant mind at work. Those big, chocolate eyes always lit up when she was excited, whether it be about some book she was reading or a student who was suddenly acing their work. Sometimes her breathing would get a little quicker, her cheeks a bit pink. He fucking adored it. Every. Single. Time.

She made him lose his mind. She was a streak of color amidst the gray. A current coursing through his fucking soul. He knew runner's high. He knew endorphin rushes. But this? It was on a whole new level. And the worst part was he hadn't even realized what he was missing until that first time her lips met his.

Knowing that, knowing *her*, the whole world just seemed different.

He had never put much stock into the whole relationship thing; he didn't get how people could lose themselves so completely in someone else, but maybe it was just because he had never met a person worth giving himself to.

And just like that, it hit him.

"I love her."

Seb's eyes bulged. It was usually so hard to shock him.

"Since when?"

"Since she opened the door with tears streaking down her face and I wanted to murder a man I've never met." Spencer sipped his drink, letting the burn of the scotch linger in his throat. "I just didn't know it then."

Seb's scrutinizing gaze met his. "Then why is she telling me you're just fuck buddies?"

It was like a punch to the gut.

"She *said* that?"

"Not in those exact words." It was the first time Seb's lips looked like they might smile. Seemed like he was enjoying torturing him. Fucking fantastic.

"The timing was all wrong. She just got out of something; she kept talking about how she needed a rebound lay and it fucking killed me." Spencer let out a harsh breath. "I didn't really plan it but once I started, I couldn't stop. She's just..." He raised his head, "Everything, man. She's it. We were inevitable."

For a few long moments Seb simply stared at him, gulping down his drink. Even though they were the same shade of brown, unlike Elizabeth's eyes, Seb's never gave anything away. The ten minutes were almost up and Spencer mentally prepared himself to be thrown out of his best friend's life. He hung his head, staring at his glass.

"So what are you going to do about it?"

Spencer jerked his head up. "What?"

"You love her, my sister. She isn't anyone's casual fuck. When are you fixing that?"

A giant smile broke out on Spencer's face and he burst out of the chair. He just couldn't contain his excitement. "Well, eventually I'm going to propose and all that, but I thought first I should ask her to be my girlfriend."

Seb rolled his eyes, standing up to join him. "Good strategy, Romeo."

"So… Are we good?" Spencer didn't think he had ever looked so hopeful.

Taking a step forward, Seb pointed a finger at Spencer's chest, face hard.

"No talking about my sister and sex together. Ever."

"Okay, no brainer there."

"And treat her like royalty."

"Done."

Seb loomed even closer, his eyes now cold and boring a hole in Spencer's head.

"Break her heart and I'll kill you. I've got enough money to get away with it, you know."

That wasn't an exaggeration.

Spencer reached a hand out to grasp Seb's shoulder. "I would never."

Seb let out a long breath and shook his head, pulling Spencer in for a hug. "Sit back down, you bastard. This scotch isn't going to drink itself."

Chapter Thirty-Two
SPENCER

"So you're doing it today?"

Spencer beamed at his best friend. "Yep. I've got it all planned out."

They were standing just outside the First Class lounge at the airport, around ninety minutes before Seb's plane was set to take off. Elizabeth was working this morning so she hadn't been able to come out to say goodbye. Last night, though heavily intoxicated, Spencer and Seb had met up with her for dinner. Spencer had been careful not to be too touchy with her. Although Drunk Spencer did have some difficulties being receptive to Rational Spencer telling him to stay away from his girl. Especially when he had just accepted that he loved her.

Every brush of their shoulders had earned him a kick to the shin from Seb.

But hey, baby steps, right?

Seb made a face, waving him off. "Enough. I don't need the gory details."

Spencer just laughed. "I meant I'm getting her flowers, you fucker."

"Just flowers?" Seb's eyebrows rose and he folded his arms.

"No! That's just the start." Spencer held up his hands defensively. "I'm going to set up the apartment with romantic candles and all that crap, and I'll cook her a meal. Pasta. *By hand.*"

Seb cocked his head to the side. "That's a good start."

"A start? *A start?*" Spencer reeled back. "Dinner is going to take me three fucking hours to cook. I have a bouquet of blue roses on the way. I researched *flower meanings*. What more do you want?"

You can't find blue roses in nature; you have to create them. They represent the mysterious, the unattainable. Something you shouldn't have but you so desperately want, you can't help yourself.

Elizabeth. To a fucking tee.

"I want you to be the best thing that's ever happened to my sister." Seb shrugged, his lips twitching as if he was trying to repress a smile.

"Yeah, sure. A really small ask." Spencer narrowed his eyes at his best friend, folding his arms across his chest.

"You saying she's not worth it?"

Spencer groaned. "Are you ever going to let up on this?"

"Nope!" With a grin Seb turned on his heel and strutted through the entry to the lounge.

Well then.

Spencer laughed to himself as he strode over to where his car was waiting. Seb had insisted on traveling to the airport with a chauffeur instead of just letting Spencer drive him in his hire car. Joe had traveled with them while Dimitri had been in a car behind 'just in case'. Spencer didn't envy Seb's fame. Being the heir to a multi-billion dollar company, as well as an attractive bachelor, had its drawbacks. He was so glad Elizabeth hated the limelight and had nothing to do with the family company. Spencer wouldn't be able to take it if she was constantly in danger.

It was stinking hot outside, the July weather hitting Paris hard. But not even the stifling heat could put a damper on Spencer's mood on the drive home. He put the windows right down and stuck his head outside so he could feel the wind on his face. The romantic atmosphere of Paris was really getting to him.

Everywhere he looked he could see people on the streets; there seemed to be some sort of jazz festival going on. It was impossible not to be caught up in the mood. Everything about the city screamed love. Every couple he saw wandering the streets together made him think of Elizabeth. Hell, every flower, or leaf, or baguette reminding him of her. At this point, his brain would take any connection, albeit loose, to turn his thoughts back to her.

The warm breeze caressed his cheeks and he couldn't wait until he saw her again. Last night had been so brief. And fucking Seb had made sure to escort both him and Elizabeth back to their separate residences. The little shit. Even off his face Seb knew what he was doing.

It had been days since he had seen her properly and he felt so fucking full of emotion for her, he couldn't wait to get it all out.

As the car pulled up outside his apartment, Spencer grabbed his phone and clicked on her name. It was just midday so he knew she would be having a break now. Elizabeth answered on the second ring.

"Hey, handsome."

The warmth of her voice seemed to reach out and touch him. This woman.

"Princess, we've got plans tonight."

"Do we? Have you consulted my assistant? My agenda is pretty full." Her tone was teasing, and it felt like foreplay. He would take whatever he could get right now.

"I'm making gnocchi. Any chance that will clear it up?"

"Keep talking…"

"It's going to be super dirty. *Dripping* with cheese."

"Oh *Spencer!* Don't tempt me—I'm at work."

He could practically see her stifling her laughter on the other end of the line. He pictured her sitting at a desk in her favorite library, hair up in a messy ponytail, legs clad in those tiny shorts that drove him insane. Tonight couldn't come soon enough.

"Be at my place at eight. Sharp."

"What if I'm running late?"

"I'll have to punish you."

He heard her sharp intake of breath on the line. Spencer bet she was remembering the other night when he had tied her up. The thought of it alone was making him ready for a repeat performance.

"In that case, I'll show up at nine."

"Yeah, yeah."

Fat chance of that. Elizabeth was always on time. You wouldn't really expect it with the scatterbrained-writer image but she was a stickler for schedules. She was the sort of person who wouldn't just look at what time she had to leave; she would factor in the three-minute walk to her car park and the two-minute lift ride, as well.

"Can't wait," she whispered as she hung up.

Neither could he.

Chapter Thirty-Three
LIZZIE

Lizzie locked her phone with a smile. Last night seemed to go pretty well. She had never expected Sebastian to come around to the idea of them so soon, but Spencer must have gotten through to him. Being the only sober one at dinner had certainly been an entertaining experience, with the two men in her life alternating between bantering back and forth and fighting because Spencer was allegedly touching her too much.

She was smiling to herself when a voice that sent chills down her spine rang out behind her.

"Lizzie, *cherie*, I've been looking for you."

She looked over her shoulder and her gaze met two familiar piercing, gray eyes. Dark brown hair, light beard, thin lips, and high cheekbones. Amaury wasn't as tall as Spencer but she still had to look up to lock eyes with him.

His brows were drawn together and those eyes were shining. A suit clung to his well-built frame and his hands were clutching a single red rose.

It was like her ability to speak had been completely sucked away. She felt like crying, like running into his arms, like throwing up. Her pulse was beating erratically and a part of her was convinced this was all some illusion.

Amaury inched closer, holding a hand to his chest. "*Cherie*, I have thought of nothing but you for weeks. What happened with us,"—he paused, wincing—"I deeply regret it."

Lizzie blinked. What on earth?

Musicians were playing softly in the background and the weather was peak Parisian summer. The light sundress she was wearing was stuck to her like a second skin and the heat seemed to pound in her temples. This couldn't be real. It just couldn't.

Meanwhile, the Amaury illusion was still speaking.

"You never responded to my calls."

Lizzie's vision cleared. "I blocked you."

Amaury nodded, gaze clouding over. "I understand, Lizzie, I do."

He licked his lips and held out the rose. "More than anything I would love to talk to you. Please." Those eyes were like lasers boring into her soul. "Have lunch with me. Let's talk about this together, like adults."

Adults. She was an adult. Amaury thought she was mature; of course he would think she would agree to lunch. Still in a daze, she somehow found herself nodding along with him, allowing him to take her hand and lead her to a nearby restaurant.

His eyes were hypnotic. Every time that shade of light gray came into her line of sight, it was as if she was transported to every date they had ever been on together. His grand declarations of love against the backdrop of the most beautiful city in the world. The way his accent would come on stronger when he was feeling emotional. How he was most himself when he let his beard grow out because it meant he wasn't so caught up in his work. Those weekends away in Bordeaux.

As Lizzie held onto that clichéd red rose and clutched the hand that felt alien yet still so familiar, she realized she had never really processed everything between them. Spencer had swept into her life like a hurricane, knocking aside every one of her tears. She had been so captivated by him suddenly appearing that she had forgone basic closure of her failed relationship.

Lizzie exhaled, long and slow. This was good. It was obvious she needed to talk to him to move on. What harm could one lunch do?

FIFTEEN MINUTES LATER THEY HAD ORDERED THEIR ENTREES, AND Lizzie was sipping on a much-needed glass of wine. He still looked so good. It wasn't fair. Some hidden part of her had been hoping he would be run down, looking like a haggard mess with his life in pieces.

But Amaury was his usual polished self, sitting there, napkin perfectly folded in his lap. He had been raised in the high-society of Paris, with all the old money and old etiquette. No matter how much her family had in the bank, they would never be on the same level of class. Her parents were not ones for pomp and ceremony; they preferred a casual barbeque to a sit-down dinner. But Amaury was all about the show. Every time she was with him, she felt like a big bumbling fool.

Her voice, her opinions… They were just gone.

Amaury leaned forward and took her hand between his palms. He had this way of looking at you like you were the only person in the whole world. The universe, even.

"Elizabeth Rose Hastings." His eyes glistened. "I am hopelessly in love with you."

What. The. Fuck.

Her silence didn't bother Amaury; it never had. He just continued with his declaration.

"I had a family, a duty. But I wanted to have it all. I acknowledge how despicable that was, how *détestable*." His face clouded over as if he was in real pain. "After you and I ended, I tried to feel for my wife. I tried so hard. But in the back of my mind there was always you."

His thumb stroked up and down her palm while she stared at him, mute.

"Despite my best efforts, I love you. Hopelessly, recklessly. You make me careless, make me disregard everyone else in the world."

Amaury had always spoken like some sort of Hallmark card. She wasn't sure if it was the accent or the high-brow English, but everything he said just seemed to have this profound echo to it. She had always loved fantasy books as a kid, and if sirens ever existed in real life, he was it. Some people have a charisma that seems to weave a spell over you.

Then, he really went for it.

"I divorced her. For you."

Oh. Dear. God.

Lizzie felt her face heat up and her pulse race even further. This wasn't happening. This *couldn't* be happening.

She shook her head and felt a shiver echo through her shoulders and flow down into the rest of her body.

"What are you saying?"

That hand grasped hers tighter.

"I want you back. Let's do this properly. Nothing between us."

"I—"

Amaury held up a hand, effectively silencing her. "Don't give me an answer yet, *cherie*. Sit, enjoy your lunch. Sleep on it."

He flashed a mega-watt smile in her direction and she found herself smiling in return.

"Okay." Lizzie nodded. "I'll think about it."

What the fuck was she doing? It was like an out-of-body experience. The rational side of her was floating above her reality, watching in horror as every aspect of her personality she was proud of was squashed.

"I knew you would understand." The corner of his eyes crinkled. "A love like ours cannot end like that."

So Lizzie put Spencer to the back of her mind and made small talk with Amaury for another hour, allowing him to pay for the overpriced meal. She couldn't even remember what she had ordered, much less what it tasted like.

She was just caught up in his gaze. It was like her mind reacted on autopilot to the charm she knew so well.

Soon she found herself kissing him goodbye on the cheek, unblocking his number from her phone, and promising to let him know what she decided.

Chapter Thirty-Four
LIZZIE

When Lizzie sunk down into her lounge-room couch, the breath that she had been holding came out in a big whoosh.

She palmed her head in her hands.

What a clusterfuck.

Her stomach felt like the inside of a washing machine with a mix of thoughts, feelings, and fears swirling through it. On high speed. With a scalding-hot temperature and home-brand soap.

Amaury still loved her.

Amaury divorced his wife.

Amaury wanted her back.

How the hell was she even meant to process that?

"Sophia," she groaned, tipping sideways so she was lying down. "SO-PHI-A," Lizzie yelled louder, emphasizing every single syllable.

Her best friend stomped out from her bedroom. "What?"

When Lizzie didn't respond, Sophia approached with a huff. But when she caught sight of her, she stopped dead.

"Why do you look like you've seen a ghost?"

"Because I have?" Her voice was so small she couldn't believe it was coming from her own mouth.

"What kind?" Sophia joined her with a sigh. "Are we talking a metaphorical ghost like Lindsay Lohan's career or a real dead person?"

"Worse. Amaury."

Sophia's eyes widened. "In the *flesh*?"

"Yup." Lizzie sunk her face into the pillow, fully succumbing to her rapidly deteriorating mood.

"You can't just drop that and give me no details! When? Where? What did he say?"

She scrunched her eyes shut. "He said he loves me so much he divorced his wife. He gave me a rose." Lizzie gestured halfheartedly to the wilting flower on the ground next to her bag.

"And you believe him?"

"That's the problem!" she spat out. God, her head hurt. "You know what he's like. I could barely get a word in. It's like I become a little kid in his presence. He seemed genuine." Her voice sounded uncertain even to her.

"How long did you talk?"

"About us? Around fifteen minutes. Then we had lunch and just kind of avoided the topic in general. He's doing really well at work."

Sophia snorted. "Of course he got in how good his billable hours have been this month. You seriously went on a date with him? What about Spencer?"

"It wasn't a *date* date. It was just somewhere to talk." Lizzie rolled onto her back and rubbed her throbbing temples. "Spencer and I aren't even really together. He's never mentioned being anything more than casual."

"He doesn't have to. It's written all over his face. Both of your faces." Sophia added, shaking her head.

"What do I do about Amaury? What do I say to Spencer?" Lizzie's lower lip was trembling and she hated herself for it.

Sophia scooted over so she was right next to her. "Let's just deal with one guy at a time."

The thought of that alone set a pang of guilt straight to her gut. She had no idea where she even stood with Spencer. They had been seeing each other for what seemed like forever but in reality it had only been a couple months. The only time they had ever talked about their relationship was right at the start when they had agreed to not sleep with other people. She had just been going with the flow and living in blissful ignorance until this point. Deep down she knew he wouldn't be happy she had spoken to Amaury.

Then again, he didn't really have a right. The fact he had re-entered her life had been a big contributor to the reason why months later she still hadn't had any closure about the whole thing. Fuck, even now, after speaking with Amaury for over an hour, they had never really *talked*. He never explained why he lied to her, how long it went on for, when he and his wife separated. Why he was so, so cruel at the very end.

The sound that came from her mouth was half-wail, half-moan. "Forget Spencer for now. Let's deal with Amaury." Lizzie met Sophia's amber gaze. "He didn't actually give me an explanation."

"I kind of feel like we should have a whiteboard and start marking out for-and-against points." Sophia's lip jutted out as if she was seriously considering that idea. She cocked her head. "Amaury would be on like minus ten at the moment, by the way."

"I know, I know. But I invested so much into that relationship. Maybe he deserves a chance?"

"A chance!" Sophia's voice was horrified and her mouth dropped open. She lifted her palm to rest against Lizzie's forehead. "Did he drug you?"

"I just meant that I arrived at his door and made a lot of assumptions then left. I never let him explain anything."

"Okay, yeah, we definitely need a whiteboard. Do you know what I would write in bold at the top?" Sophia dragged Lizzie into a seated position, placed her hands on her shoulders and gave her a little shake with every word. "He. Threatened. To. File. A. Restraining. Order. Against. You."

Oh yeah. That.

An uncomfortable feeling twisted inside her. Lizzie had done her best to erase most of that night from her mind. What was the point of dwelling on the worst day of your life? But Sophia had wormed out all the details early on and that woman could hold a grudge like nobody's business.

"The French are very passionate. I don't think he meant it." She gave a half-shrug. "I'm not saying I want to date him but he deserves to be heard out."

"Fine," Sophia said, "but I want the record to show that I think this is a horrible idea."

"Duly noted."

"I have conditions." Sophia held up a finger. "Phone call only. I don't trust you to stick to your guns if he's pulling out the puppy-dog eyes on you."

"I'm not that bad."

Sophia arched a brow. "*Soph, you should see his eyes they are sooooo pretty.*" She had scrunched up her nose and put on a high-pitched voice. "*The color is so unique. They're so mesmerizing.*"

"Shut up! I don't sound like that."

"You did when you were in love with him."

Lizzie huffed out a breath. "What? They *are* nice eyes, you have to admit."

"Spencer's are nicer."

There was that pang in her stomach again. Spencer's *were* pretty damn gorgeous. They didn't have the mystery of Amaury's gray ones, but the light blue color transported her to summer. To perfect days and even better weather. It was impossible to look into them and not feel at home.

"What am I going to do?" she groaned.

Sophia started to pull her dark blond hair to the top of her head. "Tonight you're going to put them both out of your mind. We're going to put on face masks, eat takeout food, and talk shit until you feel better. May even throw a Ryan Gosling movie into the mix."

"Sign me the fuck up."

Chapter Thirty-Five
SPENCER

Spencer readjusted the plates he had set out. Again.

The white tablecloth was still in the same position it had been two hours ago. The dusty-pink plates were placed in the exact spot a YouTube video on table setting had instructed him to place them. There was a decanter full of pinot noir and a crystal carafe filled with water sitting next to it.

He had spent the afternoon hand-making gnocchi. It was a dish his mom had always loved to make on Sundays. She would force him and Grace to join in. Most of the time they ended up with more flour on each other than in the mixing bowl, but it was so much fun. The sauce he made was simple: mostly just oil, basil, and slow-roasted cherry tomatoes. But his mom was a big fan of the idea that a few ingredients done well made for the best dishes.

The dish in question was currently wrapped in foil, sitting in the still-warm oven so it didn't get too cold. The sunset he had planned to coincide with the meal had passed and he still hadn't heard a word from Elizabeth.

Spencer ran his sweaty palms against his jeans, fingers twitching to call her one more time. The last two times he'd tried, there had been no answer.

Minutes passed. He tapped his foot against the wooden floorboards. Readjusted the cutlery. Checked to make sure the flowers still had water in that little foam base. They had come wrapped, looking like a birthday present, and were arranged in a way he had no hope of replicating, so he was reluctant to take them out and move them to a vase before she saw them.

His fingers itched again.

Finally he gave into the urge and brought up her number. So many rings went by, he thought he would be met with her voicemail again, but then he heard her voice.

"Hey, Spencer."

He breathed a sigh of relief. It was completely irrational but when he hadn't been able to get in touch with her, a small part of his brain got pretty creative thinking of different things that could have happened to her. God, he was getting clingy.

"When you said you would show up at nine, I thought you were joking." Spencer kept his tone light. It was disappointing she was late, but he was sure she would have a good reason.

"Huh?"

The grin he had been wearing at the sound of her voice morphed into a frown. "Are you on your way?"

There was a pause. "On my way?"

"To my place. For dinner."

This better be a joke. She had seemed so excited on the phone earlier. Spencer found himself jiggling his foot again.

"Oh! Spencer, I'm so sorry, I completely forgot." Her voice sounded…off. He couldn't put his finger on it but something about her tone didn't sound sincere.

"Are you okay?"

There seemed to be a muffled conversation on the other line and he thought he heard Sophia's voice.

"Yeah, I'm just not feeling well."

Spencer grabbed his keys and started walking toward the door. "I'll be there in five."

"No—don't. Sophia's with me. I'm fine."

He dropped his keys. The sound echoed through the apartment, emphasizing its emptiness.

"You sure?"

"Yep."

She was being so damn short. Normally he struggled to get a word in. What was going on?

"Okay, then I'll see you tomorrow?"

"Sure. Sorry about dinner."

Yeah, he was sorry too. He hung up and turned around. If he had handed her his heart yesterday when he realized her loved her, today she crushed it in her fist.

Love was overrated as fuck.

It wasn't fair that one person could have such power over you. One minute the thought of her was turning him into a love-sick puppy, trying to make some big gesture to win her over. The next he felt like he had been slapped, and every sign of her in his apartment was a reminder of the rejection.

With a sigh Spencer walked over to the table and blew out the candles he had set up. He started packing away the plates and the wine, half tempted to throw them at the wall. She couldn't have known what he was doing today; it wasn't her fault she got sick, for God's sake. He shouldn't take out what he was feeling on her. It just hurt that she didn't want him there with her. That she forgot about him in the first place.

Maybe it was too early to be going around making declarations of love. Maybe she didn't feel the same way at all.

Spencer searched the room, trying to latch onto anything to avoid going down that particular rabbit hole.

But soon his eyes reached those damn blue flowers. He couldn't give them to her now. There was no point half doing it. His gut twisted. If she didn't love him back, they would look pretty damn pathetic. Almost as pathetic as him.

He pictured him giving them to her, her eyes going wide and

then settling in an awkward expression. Maybe she would take his hand, explain gently that it wasn't about him—she just wasn't ready for that now.

Spencer shook himself. He picked the bunch up and bent down to grab his keys, as well. Then he walked outside and knocked on the door of the old French woman who lived in the apartment opposite his.

Her name was Valerie. She couldn't speak much English and he couldn't speak much French but they always smiled at each other when they passed in the staircase. He helped her carry her groceries when she needed it, because the old French building was too archaic to have a lift.

He heard the sounds of her fumbling around with the lock for a few moments before the door swung open.

Spencer smiled sadly and held out the roses. "For you."

Her eyebrows, which looked like they were drawn on, rose. She waved him off. "Me old—give to girl."

Was it that obvious? Spencer slumped his shoulders and tried to ignore the memory of waking up to the sight of sleepy, brown eyes next to him the other day.

"Well, she's not here."

Valerie accepted the flowers with a small smile and a shake of her head. She gave him a long look. "*Il n'y a qu'un bonheur dans la vie, c'est d'aimer et d'être aimé.*"

"Yeah, you have a good night, as well."

Ten minutes later he was alone again, sitting in his bed, eating hand-made pasta out of a plastic container.

Chapter Thirty-Six
SPENCER

Three days.

Three fucking days.

That was how long it had been since he had seen Elizabeth.

It was becoming beyond ridiculous.

Every morning he called her to see how she was feeling, every afternoon he tried again. And every single time she brushed him off.

The first few times it had happened he had convinced himself she really was sick. He hadn't ever seen her unwell before but maybe she was self-conscious about not looking her best around him. Yeah, that sounded nothing like her, but girls were mysterious creatures. You could never fully predict what you were going to get.

But they hadn't had one meaningful conversation since before she had stood him up at dinner. That's what tipped him off. Even if Elizabeth was sick, she would never shut him out like that. Hell, she would probably be lying in bed at home bored out of her mind and desperate to talk.

That's how he found himself standing outside the library she normally tutored at. He hated himself a little for not trusting her, but he had to know. Sophia had been no help either; she had only given him cryptic responses to his attempts to get in touch.

It ticked over to one in the afternoon when she usually took her lunch break and his eyes frantically scanned the entryway. He really hoped he wouldn't see her. Ideally she wouldn't be here, he would breathe a sigh of relief, and she would never know he hadn't trusted her.

Ten minutes went by with no sign of her and he was just turning to leave, when he caught a glimpse of the mane of chocolate-brown hair. He focused his gaze and there she was, walking his way. Looking very healthy, he might add.

She hadn't seen him yet and was passing right by the wall he leaned against when he called her name.

Elizabeth jerked back. "Spencer? What are you doing here?"

"I wanted to see you." Spencer folded his arms across his chest and took in her guilt-clouded face. She looked genuinely surprised to see him there.

"Oh, yeah, about that." She bowed her head. "I'm really sorry, Spence. I've had a lot on my mind."

"What is it, princess?" He took a step toward her. "You know you can talk to me about anything."

Elizabeth's eyes darted to the pavement then back up to meet his gaze. "Let's go somewhere quieter to talk."

Well. That was never a fucking good sign, was it?

Spencer clenched his jaw as Elizabeth led them over to a bench at a nearby park. It was hot and the sky was completely cloudless. There was a faint breeze cool enough so as not to make the temperature unbearable. Little wildflowers dotted the park and he could literally hear birds chirping. The whole effect was so beautiful it seemed to be mocking him.

She bit her lip and looked away, then rushed out her words so quickly he had to strain to hear them properly. "I ran into Amaury."

Okay. That wasn't too bad. He lived in Paris. She lived in Paris. It was inevitable, really. Spencer nodded. He could deal with that.

He said, "That must have been hard," at the same time she said, "We had lunch."

"You *what?*"

Elizabeth had the decency to grimace. "I need closure, you know?"

Closure? What the fuck was closure? Sounded suspiciously like something women made up when they were trying to rationalize acting like an idiot.

"No, I don't know. How do you go from bumping into him to going on a date?"

Spencer tried to keep the tone of his voice even, reasonable. But it was fucking hard. Just the thought of her going out with Amaury killed him a little inside.

He'd given her his heart, but right now it felt like she was clutching it in a vice-like grip. Every word seemed to be accompanied with a squeeze.

"It wasn't a date!" Elizabeth's eyes were wide. She tucked a lock of hair behind her ear and sighed impatiently. "He wanted to talk to me. He seemed really sincere. I owed it to him."

"You don't owe him a fucking thing! He cheated on you!" He felt like shaking her. "In what world do guys like that get a second chance?"

Elizabeth was smart. She was beautiful. A catch in any world. Even without Spencer around she had absolutely no reason to be even entertaining the idea of letting Amaury back into her life.

"I know, I know. But he's divorced his wife. He's turning his life around, coming clean and all that."

"Divorced his wife? Oh, that's big of him. I wonder how many affairs he had after you?"

Spencer clenched his fists. He knew he was overreacting. He shouldn't be speaking to her like this. Sarcasm during arguments always came across crueler than anything else. But he just couldn't help it. He was seeing red.

"Spence." Elizabeth sighed and placed a hand over his. "Don't be like that."

He shook her off. "I can't believe you gave him the time of day."

Elizabeth stood up and ran her hands through her hair. She started pacing back and forth under the shade of the tree next to them. A light blue dress clung to her frame and it really wasn't fair that she looked so damn good right now. He hadn't seeing her for what seemed like forever and his body craved her like an addict craved their fix.

"He said he still loves me."

That stopped his thoughts short.

"Of course he does, you're amazing. But him being in love with you doesn't change anything."

Elizabeth paused and glanced down. "I've been thinking."

Thinking? *Thinking*? Spencer drew out a long breath and tried to calm the rage building inside him. He focused on the callouses on his palms and said in as even a voice as he could manage, "What's there to think about?"

She took a breath. Wrung her hands together. Still didn't meet his eyes.

"We spent six months together, Spencer. I loved him. It's a lot to process."

That was it.

Spencer couldn't take another second of this bullshit. What was so special about that fucker anyway? How do you cheat on your family, hide it from your girlfriend, be an absolute dick to her along the way, and still somehow get into her head when it was all over?

He thought back to that first kiss with Elizabeth, the way her body responded to his. To those few days before, all those moments where it felt like gravity was pulling them together. In front of the Eiffel Tower she had practically leaned into him and shut her eyes. What clearer sign was there?

There was no way someone who had been in love with another person could move on like that. He knew how he was feeling about

Elizabeth right now and he was fucking crushed just hearing about her with someone else. There was no way that in a few days he would be capable of flirting with a different person.

Spencer stood up and loomed in front of her. He made sure those big, brown eyes were locked with his so she could see that he was speaking the truth, harsh as it was. "You didn't love him, you loved the idea of him. Of moving to Paris, finding an older man. All of it." He gestured his hands around the park they were standing in.

Elizabeth's eyes flared with rage. "I did not. You don't know that. You don't know anything about why I came here."

What did she think he had been doing all these months? Ignoring every time she spoke? They had seen each other basically every day for almost ten weeks. He knew her pretty damn well at this point and that wasn't even counting the ten years since he had first met her.

Every second of this conversation was adding logs to the fire of fury burning underneath him. Some part of him was aware of the words leaving his lips, but the rational side of his brain had left a few minutes ago so it was pretty much a free-for-all.

"Yeah, I do. You came here to chase ideas and dreams and perceptions of how you want to be."

Elizabeth's shoulders moved up and down with the force of her rapid breaths. Her face started to go red but this time it was from anger.

"I came here to be a writer. That's who I am; it's not some fucking pipe dream!"

She waved her hand in the air to emphasize her point. There was a direct correlation between the amount of hand gestures and how quickly a conversation was deteriorating, and this one was going downhill. Fast.

For one of the smartest people he knew, Elizabeth could sure be damn obtuse.

"I've barely seen you write anything. You toss it all into the trash."

Her brows snapped together. "Just because it's a work in progress doesn't mean it's not happening."

"Okay tell me a name. A plot. Anything." Spencer held up his hands. "Fuck, I don't even know if you're doing fiction or non-fiction."

Elizabeth remained silent and her nostrils flared. But Spencer was on a roll.

"This whole writing thing—it's just some idealized version of who you want to be."

"Oh yeah?" She huffed. "And what does this idealized person want?"

Spencer folded his arms across his chest. "An older, cultured, French man apparently. No worries that he's an adulterer." He shrugged, face hard.

"You don't know anything about him. And he's not why I came here anyway. It's not some *idea* of who I want to be. I moved here to do it properly, to experience life, and be inspired. To change. You obviously know nothing about me if you didn't even pick up on that."

Elizabeth flicked her hair over her shoulder and Spencer laughed. "Honey, no amount of op-shop dresses and walks along the Seine can hide the fact you grew up in a mansion in Connecticut and haven't wanted for anything a single day in your fucking life."

"Oh what, so the fact you had working-class parents and your mom died suddenly makes you authentic?"

Ouch. Spencer pinched the bridge of his nose. This was spiraling out of control fast. "You know what's authentic? *We* were authentic. You can't make that stuff up."

Now Elizabeth was laughing. "Oh *honey*," she emphasized, mocking him, "you were a rebound. About as artificial as it gets."

Spencer blinked. He had no words.

Elizabeth's face hardened. "And I think you've served your purpose now."

With that she turned on her heel and stormed out of the park, leaving him standing there dumbly, wondering how the fuck that conversation had happened.

Chapter Thirty-Seven
LIZZIE

Forget *la vie en rose*, Lizzie was seeing life in red.

She stomped all the way back to her apartment. She could have taken the metro but she needed movement to anchor her fury. And hitting her feet against the pavement was just so damn satisfying.

A couple came into her path and her expression only became more murderous. They must have noticed it because they hastily stepped aside. So did all the other Parisians out enjoying the warm weather.

How dare he? How. Fucking. *Dare*. He.

She could understand that he would be mad about Amaury. She got it. But when did that morph into a personal attack? Had he thought she was a phony this whole time?

After what seemed like no time at all, she entered her apartment, slamming the door shut. Sophia was out today, *thank God*. She did not want to deal with her right now.

Lizzie threw her bag on the counter and stormed into her room, bending over to pick up a few books from where she kept them in the fireplace. After a few seconds she also grabbed her Kindle. She needed every reinforcement she could get today.

She collapsed onto her bed and shut her eyes, counting down in her head until her breathing finally slowed down, her pulse calmed, and that throbbing in her temples subsided.

She stared up at the ornate ceiling above her. The panels were intricate and beautiful but when you looked closer you could see the edges curling over and the cracks. A snort escaped her lips. It was probably how Spencer saw her writing dreams. Pretty from the outside but fundamentally flawed within.

Reaching out to the books laying around her, she picked one at random and tried to lose herself. It was *1984* by George Orwell, and maybe reading something set in a dystopic universe would make her feel a little better about her own.

Ten minutes later she shut it.

Every single page it felt like Spencer's baby blues were boring into her, judging her. She wasn't enjoying the book. Not really. Despite how much she wanted to, she just couldn't get into it right now.

With a grumble she threw it aside and picked up another. This one was newer. It had won the Man Booker prize that year and she hadn't yet read it. But after thirty pages the protagonist didn't even have a name. She groaned. Lizzie didn't have the mental stamina right now to have to *think* to read. She needed a distraction. An escape.

Her eyes lit up with an idea and she sprung out of bed. She grabbed a pen and her notebook and headed over to the little writing desk by the window in the living room.

Inside her was such a mix of emotions and thoughts it was perfect. She would write them down, use all this hurt in a productive way to create something amazing. Isn't that what she had wanted all along? To be inspired? To *feel*?

Lizzie chewed on her lip and tapped the pen against the paper. Where to even start? She could start with documenting what she was feeling right now. Or she could start from the beginning, from opening her front door in tears and seeing Spencer.

With his big frame, golden hair, and blue eyes, he looked the part of a white knight, a fairy-tale prince come to save her. He wasn't charming in the conventional way. Spencer didn't have the fancy phrases that Amaury could produce at the drop of a hat. But Spencer showed it with actions. By showing up to her house with her favorite food and movies. By holding her when she cried. By spending his day walking around the city with her, side-by-side.

Her grandparents had been together for seventy years now. They celebrated their anniversary last year and she had asked them their secret. Her grandpa had just smiled and said that love is a verb.

She couldn't help but think of Spencer—hang on. No. She was meant to be angry with him, not throwing around the word love.

Spencer didn't love her. He didn't respect her. He was nothing to her.

Nothing.

Lizzie's face fell. She had been pretty cruel, as well. Bringing up the fact his mom had died was way too far. But in that moment she had been blind with fury. Hurt had crashed into her like a train and all she wanted was for him to feel a little pain, as well.

She rubbed her forehead and stared down at the still-blank page.

If she started from the beginning she would just get swept up in Spencer again.

Lizzie groaned as she thought back to Spencer's face when she told him about Amaury. He had been so angry, so quick to jump to conclusions, and lash out. It's not like she had spent the last few nights in Amaury's arms. And she would have told Spencer that, if he had let her.

She hadn't even met up with Amaury again. They had only spoken a few times on the phone.

All she had really needed was some time away from Spencer to process everything Amaury had said. Her attraction to Spencer was so intense, she knew it would cloud her vision, and she needed a clear head.

So she had let Amaury say his piece. He had the whole story about how his wife had also been cheating and that it was a loveless marriage. They were trying to stay together on the outside, to make things easier on their son, but in the end it hadn't worked out. He had been so worried about his son, realizing when Lizzie had shown up that he had lashed out at her without thinking.

He was sorry. He loved her. He wanted to try again.

But she didn't want him. Not anymore.

Her thoughts were full of Spencer, and now that was over too.

Lizzie glanced at the clock and realized she had been sitting there, staring at a blank page for almost an hour. She almost laughed. It's not like any of her other writing sessions usually went better. If she couldn't find the perfect words to put down, she wouldn't write down anything at all.

But that mess of emotions was still inside her.

Whoever said writing was therapeutic was a liar. It only ever made Lizzie more stressed, more pressured to come up with something incredible.

Her chair made a loud scraping noise as she pushed it back and got to her feet. It was time to go back to reading.

As she walked into her room and saw the mess of books in her bed, she remembered her earlier struggles.

Her gaze flicked to her Kindle.

Lizzie bit her lip. No one would know. It's not like anyone was here watching that she was going to read a romance novel instead of a literary masterpiece.

She had a long, hot shower, changed into her pajamas, and crawled into bed.

And when she brought up the book, her guilty pleasure reading, she completely lost herself in the story.

Finally, she could breathe.

Chapter Thirty-Eight

SPENCER

Spencer packed up his duffel for the final time. As he walked out the door, he took a last glance around his now-empty apartment. Almost three months in this place had started to make it feel like home. It was smaller than what he was used to but that only seemed to make it cozier. Homey. Or maybe it was Elizabeth who had made it feel that way.

He had spent much of the afternoon collecting all the books, clothes, and trinkets she had left at his place. It was pretty fucking disheartening to see how much their lives had melded together in such a short time. He packed them all up into a box and dropped it over to Sophia when he knew Elizabeth wouldn't be home. Her forehead had creased, and she had given him a sad smile when he handed it over, but she didn't say much. What was there to say?

He and Elizabeth were over. And according to her, they had never really begun in the first place.

Fuck.

He closed the door softly and slipped a goodbye note under Valerie's door. One of the trainers at his gym had helped him translate it into French. He had tried knocking earlier but it seemed like she was out. There was no way he could hang around this space that reminded him so much of *her* any longer.

At least the gym worked out, he thought to himself as he heaved his bag down the stairs. Tate's Training, Paris had a great team of staff behind it now and being in the city had allowed Spencer to see to their training himself which was pretty cool. The building they had rented was impressive too; it was open-plan and huge with big windows looking out onto the city. Already they had over one hundred people on the waitlist to sign up. Most of them were French girls who followed him on Instagram, but it was a start.

Every second of the cab ride to the airport was torture because he saw her face in every part of this damn city.

They passed the Notre Dame and he remembered searching for that hair he loved so much. When he wound the window down to get some air, the scent of pastry wafted over, and he thought of her happy smile every time he had popped into one of her tutoring sessions to drop off a croissant. He eventually tried to concentrate on his phone, but the car was pulled up at the lights, and the sound of a busker took him back to that evening they spent watching the sun set over the Seine and drinking red wine.

Spencer shut his eyes and pinched the bridge of his nose. But in his mind, it was worse. Much worse.

Memory after memory of Elizabeth assaulted his brain. He thought of when people talked about having near-death experiences and how they had this moment where a highlight reel of their life flashed before their eyes. This was it for him. Except his life wasn't ending; his heart was just being torn in two.

His only consolation was that even though he had fucked it up, there was nothing to save anyway.

While he had been pining and planning ways to sweep her off her feet, Elizabeth had been using him for sex. Making the most of her rebound. And nothing more.

She didn't care; she didn't really want him. She needed him to get over a slump.

Spencer exhaled, long and loud.

And after all that, she was just going to run back into the arms of the man who had screwed her over. Spencer must be pretty damn unattractive if she would pick a man who lied to her for months, cheated on his family, and now came crawling back over him.

But she was a princess. Raised in a big castle with all the finest things.

Spencer was just a dumb kid who got a lucky break. He wasn't intellectual. He had no idea about those books she liked. He had money now, yeah, but that was just a drop in the ocean compared to what Elizabeth had.

The only thing he had worth giving her was his love, and that hadn't been enough anyway.

Finally, he made it to the airport and could sink into the meaninglessness of check-in procedures to distract him. Once he made it through he decided to give Grace a call. She answered on the second ring.

"Spence!"

He felt a pang of guilt at how little he had spoken to her these past few weeks. Back home they saw each other all the time, but over here on the other side of the world, it was easy to fall out of touch.

"Gracie, I've got good news for you."

"What!" Her excitement was evident even over the phone. She had always loved surprises when they were growing up.

"I'm coming home. Today."

"Why?"

Huh. She didn't sound happy at all. Wasn't exactly the reaction he was expecting.

"Wow, don't sound so happy to see me."

"Oh shush. Why are you coming home?"

"Gym is almost done; I'm ready to be back. It's just time, I guess."

Spencer was walking past all the shops on the way to the gate. A waft of something fruity and delicious and painfully familiar brushed past him. He spun on his heel, craning his neck to see if

Elizabeth was there but then he caught sight of a woman giving out free samples of her perfume. The smell he knew so well was suffocating. He felt like he was drowning in it.

"Well, Spencer?"

Belatedly he realized Grace had been talking. "Sorry?"

"Is Lizzie coming too?"

"No. Why would she?"

Right now, he wished he hadn't spilled the beans to Grace so early on. Since that first conversation they had about Elizabeth, she had weaseled out every detail on their non-relationship.

"Uh, because you're dating." Grace's tone was incredulous. And why wouldn't it be? He had told her everything short of his realization that he loved her.

"Yeah, that's over."

He heard the sound of crashing on the other line, then fumbling as Grace seemed to be picking up the phone.

"Tell me you didn't just say what I think you did."

"Unfortunately so, Sis. I've been dumped." Spencer sighed then added, "Well, actually not dumped since in her words I was just rebound sex, so there's not really a relationship to end."

"She *didn't*." There was a pause then she was back, more suspicious this time. "And what did you say to deserve that?"

Spencer rolled his eyes. This girl missed nothing.

"Oh, nothing major. Just crushed her dreams. You know, the normal stuff."

A few people standing at the gate gave him a weird look and he smiled awkwardly back at them. Fan-fucking-tastic.

"You big idiot. Why would you do that?"

"Why do you assume it's all my fault?"

He found a seat near the window to wait for the plane. His ticket was business class but he didn't like hanging out with all the wankers at the lounge. The chairs at the gate were fine by him.

Grace carried on with her accusations. "It sounds like it. And you've never really had a girlfriend before so I didn't expect things to run smoothly, round one."

"Thanks for the vote of confidence but no, this wasn't all me." Spencer settled back and folded a hand behind his head. "She went on a date with her ex, seemed to be thinking about getting back with him."

"The one who cheated on her?"

"Yep. That's the one. Great idea, right?"

"Oh, Spencer that's really bad."

"Don't I know it?"

He hated how pitying her voice sounded. It made him feel pathetic. Saying it out loud made the whole situation seem even worse. How could she pick that fucker over him?

"Is there any chance—"

Spencer cut her off. "No Grace, it's done. Completely."

He heard his sister sigh. "Okay, well, I'll cook you some of Mom's pasta when you get home to cheer you up."

Spencer winced. "Let's just get some takeout, Gracie."

Eventually they said their goodbyes and Spencer used his remaining time to check in with a few clients and let everyone know he was heading back home. At least the turn of events would make some people happy.

Soon enough the gate filled with the sound of the flight attendant announcing the plane was ready to board.

He waited to be the last in line. He didn't know why.

Scratch that. He knew exactly why. His eyes gave it away.

They kept flicking over to the gate behind him, hoping to see Elizabeth's face there. Sophia knew his flight details so she could easily have passed them on.

If this were a movie she would come running through, maybe purchase a last-minute ticket to be on the plane with him. She wouldn't have any bags, hell, maybe she would be in her pajamas, so desperate to catch him she didn't have time to change.

They would lock eyes and hers would fill with tears, and she would confess that she was sorry, she loved him, and could they start over?

He would answer her with a kiss and the crowd around them would cheer.

The final boarding call sounded.

Spencer looked out to the area behind the gate but it was empty.

She wasn't there. She never would be again.

He turned and walked on the plane, refusing to admit how much his eyes were stinging.

Chapter Thirty-Nine
LIZZIE

Lizzie was editing one of her student's essays when she heard the telltale buzz of her phone against the kitchen counter.

Her heart leapt and she found herself racing over to see who it was. Could it be—oh.

It was just Amaury again.

Her shoulders slumped and she went back to the work in front of her without really reading it.

Amaury had been messaging her a lot. Every day he would ask her if she had thought about it more, and every day she would say she wasn't ready.

But it was a lie.

She would never be ready.

Now that her head had cleared she saw the situation differently. Seeing Amaury again had thrown her off. She couldn't just erase months of feelings. There was no way that speaking to him would have no effect on her. It made sense that he had knocked her off-balance for a few days.

But despite everything he had done, even if it was at all forgivable, more than anything she realized that she didn't like the person she became when she was with him. He was so mature and worldly, she became intimidated. She lost her voice.

With Amaury she wasn't herself. She was a version of herself.

Just like Spencer said.

She sighed.

His words had hurt. No matter how much time passed, she couldn't get them out of her head. There was something about someone she cared about criticizing her that had a way of cutting right to the core. Other people she could have brushed aside, but coming from Spencer? No.

Lizzie shut the lid of her laptop when she realized she had read the same sentence three times now. Her mind was too active to focus.

She began to aimlessly clean the apartment. Anything to keep her hands busy.

Lizzie loved Sophia to death but she wasn't the cleanest of housemates. In fact, it didn't get much messier. As Lizzie walked through the living room to get out the vacuum, she spotted one of Sophia's shirts sitting in the middle of the room. Sure enough, as she followed the path of discarded clothes, they ended up in her bedroom.

Sophia was always going one hundred miles a minute, but sometimes she got so caught up in whatever excitement was ahead that she just left a trail of chaos behind her. Lizzie didn't get it. She couldn't relax until her environment was pristine.

But today she was thankful for it.

Lizzie had the entire day off and nothing to do but think. And reflect. And regret.

Just as she shut the lid of the washing machine, she heard her phone buzz again. Despite her best efforts, her stomach did an excited little flip. It had been two days since the fight with Spencer. She was still a little angry at what he'd said to her, but that didn't stop her from wishing things could be different.

Maybe he would fight for her. Convince her that they were worth a shot. Apologize for stomping all over her career choice.

But when she held up her phone it wasn't even a message. It

was a notification from Instagram. Sophia had tagged her in something.

Resigned, Lizzie opened the app, but the first thing that showed up in her feed was a video posted by Spencer.

He was shirtless and boxing with someone. Every time he moved, you could see the ripple of his muscles and it was doing funny things to her. All eight of his abs were on display, and she tried her hardest not to remember how they tasted but she failed. Miserably.

But that wasn't the worst part.

No, the worst part was that he had added a location. Tate's Training, New York.

New York.

Lizzie blinked, feeling her eyes sting.

He left.

He really left.

It was like the weight of the entire building came crashing down on her shoulders. Lizzie put her back to the counter and slowly sank down, bringing her knees to her chest.

Spencer had walked away from her. Just like that. He hadn't even tried to fight.

Her shoulders started heaving as the reality of the situation really hit.

Yes, the fight had been bad. But everyone had fights. No part of her had ever considered him truly gone. After every good moment they had shared together, how could it end with a few harsh words?

Fuck.

What had she done?

Warm, salty tears trickled down her cheeks, and she bit her lip to stop herself from crying out.

You don't know what you've got until it's gone. There was a reason clichés were so often repeated. They were true.

Lizzie wiped her eyes with the back of her hand and stood up.

She was having a breakdown in the fucking kitchen. It practically shouted pathetic.

She went into her bedroom and searched in her drawers for one of the big T-shirts she liked to wear to bed. But the first one she pulled out was Spencer's. Without realizing what she was doing, she brought it to her face and inhaled.

It smelled like cinnamon and soap and something deep and masculine that was just so Spencer. It smelled like home.

Lizzie balled it up and shoved it to the bottom of the drawer. She wasn't ready to get rid of it just yet but she couldn't have it in her face either. Turning on her heel, she strode over to her wardrobe to search for something different, and that's when she noticed the cardboard box sitting there.

With a frown she pulled it out and peered inside. A cry escaped her lips.

Spencer had packed up all her things. Every single one of his memories of her was neatly piled inside this square. Seeing their relationship reduced to nothing but a bunch of objects in a box just brought the tears on more.

What clearer sign of 'it's over' was there than giving back all her things?

Lizzie left the box where it was and stumbled over to the bathroom. She went to the sink and splashed her face with water. Her cheeks were still blotchy from crying but she didn't care at this point.

She needed to get out of this apartment, away from the memories of Spencer everywhere she looked.

Dark sunglasses on, Lizzie headed out the door and onto the streets.

She maneuvered around the tourists that clogged the streets of Saint-Germain and passed by all her favorite little stores. It seemed like every man and his dog was out and about in Paris today. Clouds dotted the sky but that didn't stop the sun from shining through.

She wandered down her usual route to the Seine and tried to feel something. Anything.

Maybe it was her bleak mood but it seemed like the city had lost a bit of its charm.

The words Spencer had said to her came rushing back. She was chasing a dream here, but was it her dream?

Lizzie trailed her hand along the edge of the sandstone railing leading down to the water. She closed her eyes and took everything in.

She loved being here. She really did.

But it wasn't for the reasons she had originally thought.

The writing process itself sucked. Nothing she wrote was good enough, and every moment she spent agonizing over it just stressed her out. She dreaded sitting down to write.

When she did get anything down, she over-analyzed it to the point where it no longer resembled the original message that inspired it.

Her feet led her to the edge of the bank and she sat down, swinging her legs over the side. She tried to shake herself from the path her mind had wandered down.

She shouldn't let him get to her. Her heart was in a fragile place right now. That was all this was.

Lizzie had always been sensitive to criticism and coming from him, it hurt even more. She was overthinking this as she did every-thing. There was nothing wrong with struggling with her writing dreams. How many of her favorite authors had setbacks along the way? J.K. Rowling had twelve publishers reject Harry Potter before she struck big.

She leaned back and allowed the sun to dry the lone tear still on her cheek.

Spencer had no idea what he was talking about.

That's what she told herself, anyway.

Chapter Forty
SPENCER

Seb flagged down the bartender. "I'll have a scotch. Whatever your best one is."

"Same for me." Spencer piped up, slumping down in his chair.

Spencer's dad, Frank, frowned at him. "I think you'd do better on beer tonight."

Spencer rolled his eyes but went with a beer in the end. His dad seemed to have a sixth sense for when Spencer wasn't doing too well. Frank probably suspected Spencer had been going in on the hard liquor most nights since he had landed.

The drinks arrived just in time for the game to start.

Yankees were playing the Red Sox, and they always came to the same shitty little bar to watch it. It was a ritual for Spencer and his dad to watch the games here, and Seb had eventually started joining in too. Sometimes Seb organized box seats for them all, but Spencer and his dad never really enjoyed it as much.

They drank mostly in silence as they watched. After a few hits, Boston scored a home run in the first innings. The second came around and Boston got a two-run homer. They were leading 3-0, going into the break, and no one in the bar was happy about it.

Innings break eventually arrived and Seb and his dad turned expectant gazes his way.

Spencer jerked his head. "What?"

"Spit it out then, boy," his father gruffly demanded.

Seb smirked and sipped his drink.

"What do you want me to say? We're playing shit out there?"

Frank narrowed his eyes. "That's not what I'm talking about and you know it."

Spencer brought his beer to his lips and downed it. He knew he looked like he was sulking but he didn't care.

"Had an interesting conversation with Gracie." His father went on, nonplussed. "Said there was a girl in Paris."

"Not just some girl," Seb growled with a frown, "my fucking sister."

"I didn't know it was Lizzie Hastings." His father was beaming. "She's a great girl."

Spencer dropped his shoulders. "Yeah, well, she's not mine so don't get too excited."

"Why the fuck not?" Seb's expression was hard. "I knew it seemed suspect when you arrived home so out-of-the-blue but she wouldn't tell me anything." He rose in his chair and leaned over. "What did you do to her?"

Spencer slammed his hands down onto the table. "I didn't do anything! She did."

"Yeah, blame it on her—real mature of you." Seb's eyes were flashing dangerously.

"Boys, boys. Settle down." Frank got between them, shaking his head. "Spencer. Normally I don't want to get involved in all this stuff but you've looked like crap since you got back. You're not happy, son."

That was possibly the longest sentence he had ever heard his father utter, and if only because of that, Spencer decided to tell him the truth.

Spencer steepled his fingers and let out a breath. "She had lunch with her ex."

"Which ex?" Seb's eyes narrowed.

"The one who had a wife and a kid and was lying to her the whole time."

"What!" Seb roared but Frank cut him off.

"What's the big deal with lunch?"

"She said she 'had a lot to think about'." Spencer made quotation marks with his hands.

"Is she getting back with him then?" Seb's face was going red. The exact same way it happened to Elizabeth. Noticing all the similarities between them only made him feel more like shit. He had risked his whole friendship over a girl who didn't even care about him.

"It seemed like it." Spencer took another long drag of his beer.

"And you just *left* her to do that?" Seb slammed his fist against the bar hard enough for a few of the guys around them to shoot looks their way.

"No. She told me it was over. That I was only a rebound to her."

Seb winced at the same time as his father finally spoke. "What the fuck is a rebound?"

Spencer groaned. "It's when someone has a breakup and uses someone else for sex to get over it."

"Hey!" Seb punched him in the arm. "I thought we agreed you were *never* to mention sex and my sister in the same sentence."

Spencer raised his hands. "I'm sorry, I'm sorry." When Seb looked away, he mouthed to his dad. "Not *that* sorry."

"I heard that, fuckwit."

Frank began to laugh at the same time as Spencer started rubbing his throbbing arm. Seb didn't pull his punches.

The game came back on and the conversation naturally went on hold. Yankees started to come back when one player landed an RBI double. There were a few sliders and some fouls but eventually they went into another break.

"So you love this girl?" His dad didn't sugarcoat things.

"He does," Seb confirmed.

When Frank and Spencer just stared at him, Seb shrugged. "What? He told me. He needed to say something good so I didn't beat the living crap out of him for seeing her."

"I don't know now," Spencer admitted, hanging his head.

He nursed the beer in front of him and thought of the past week. He had tried everything in the book to get her out of his head.

Almost three hours of every day he spent at the gym training. The rest of the day he made sure to book back-to-back clients so he wouldn't have time to think. His body wasn't thanking him for it. Every morning he woke up stiffer than the last. He knew he should take it easy and have a rest day, but it was easier not to dwell on the way Elizabeth's hair glinted gold in the sun when he was doing an HIIT session on the treadmill.

But in the moments of silence in between his mind inevitably wandered back to her. To every time he held her in his arms. To that smile. And to that last conversation they had where she took his heart and stomped on it.

Last night in desperation he had even gone to a club. He sat by the bar, sipping scotch on the rocks and looking as sad as he felt. Woman after woman approach him—the kind he would have gone home with without a second thought a few months ago. Every single time he turned them down. One he tried to talk to for a while but every second that went past, he felt this uncomfortable pang in his gut that reeked of guilt.

His body had decided he was hers. No matter how hard he tried to tell it differently.

Spencer wasn't perfect. He had as many faults as the next guy. But he was loyal. And while he was still in love with Elizabeth he wouldn't—he couldn't—touch anyone else.

"Well? You either do or you don't."

"Fine." Spencer's shoulders slumped. "I do."

His father gestured with his beer. "Then why did you come running back here with your tail tucked between your legs?"

"Dad. She's not into me. She dumped me. That's it."

Seb snorted and shook his head. "You're an idiot if you think that."

Spencer cocked his head. "What are you talking about?"

"She's obsessed with you." Seb waved his hand in the air dismissively. "She has a temper sometimes and says shit. So does everyone. But every time she spoke about you,"—he pointed at Spencer—"her whole face lit up. It was disgusting. I should've realized what was going on much sooner."

His dad shot Spencer a pointed look.

"What? It doesn't change anything. I'm here. She's there. It's done."

"I thought you loved her, man. You can't feel much for her if you're giving up that easily."

Spencer made a face and took a swig of his drink. This was feeling more and more like an intervention. "Since when were you so supportive of me and your sister anyway?"

Seb saluted him with his beer. "Congratulations, you are now the lesser of two evils."

"Gee, thanks."

Frank nudged him. "Stop fucking around, Spencer."

"What do you want me to do? Fly over there and beg her to take me back?"

Seb and Frank just stared at him, blinking.

"Uh yeah, that sounds like a good idea actually."

"Shouldn't I call her or something first?"

Seb shrugged. "Have you seen any movies? Women like a good, grand gesture."

"But what if I go all the way over there and she doesn't feel the same?"

His dad gave him a look. "What if you don't go and she does?"

The next innings began and Spencer had some time to think. Was he making the biggest mistake of his life?

He thought back to their conversation. She had only told him at the end that he was a rebound. After he had shat all over every single one of her dreams. He'd not respected her decision to speak to Amaury, then he had insulted her. Of course she would hit back at him.

And why wouldn't she go for where it hurt? He'd done the same to her.

The only reason he had said all that to her in the first place was because he was so damn pissed off that she was giving Amaury the time of day. Fights were just a vicious cycle of arguing where no one really won.

Spencer downed the last of his beer and stood up.

"I'm leaving. I'm going after her."

"Good idea, boy," his dad said, not taking his eyes off the game. Spencer understood. Baseball time was sacred time.

Seb waved him off, muttering, "Fucking finally, idiot."

Gotta love a support network.

Chapter Forty-One
LIZZIE

ONE DAY EARLIER...

She was in love with Spencer Tate.

The realization came to her slowly.

Every day away from him was meant to make her feel better but it had the opposite effect. It was like each passing of time physically increased the distance between them. She felt as if she was on one of those medieval torture machines, slowly being pulled in different directions.

Each morning that she woke up and noticed his scent fade a little more from the pillows, she was taking way too long to wash, crushed her. His memory in her life was waning away while her feelings ignited.

Lizzie was standing on her balcony, looking out over the bustling street below. Saint-Germain was nothing like it had been in the time of her big writing heroes.

Picasso wouldn't be caught dead at *Les Deux Magots* or *Café de Flore* nowadays. They were basically tourist traps.

But that hadn't stopped Lizzie from making them her local watering hole. And why was that? Did she really like the image of herself there more than the activity herself? Did that sum up her trip in general?

The more she thought about Spencer's words, the more she realized that they hurt so damn much because they were true. She *was* chasing a fantasy. An idealized version of reality.

Writing had always been a dream of hers. But she had never enjoyed it, not really. The act of writing stressed her out. And once she had something down and someone gave her criticism, it killed her a little inside.

She remembered when she was younger and such an obvious bookworm, every adult who ever saw her asked if she wanted to be a writer. Lizzie loved books so much, everyone just assumed she would go on to do that. And so she had.

She had money. She had freedom. She had the whole world at her feet. Why was she agonizing over something that she didn't enjoy?

Lizzie strode back into her apartment in a rush. She swiped her notepad off her desk and also grabbed a lighter from the kitchen. Holding the two items, she made her way over to the living room fireplace and set the paper inside.

A big, roaring fire would have been more satisfying, but it was the middle of summer and she wasn't that much of a sadist. Instead she ripped out piece by piece, set them alight, and threw them into the hearth.

Her face was expressionless as she watched the words she had slaved over disappear into ash. Every paper that went in felt like a load lifted off her shoulders. It was crazy how months and months of work could burn away in seconds.

She inhaled deeply and the smell assaulted her senses. It was clean and crisp. It wasn't producing much smoke and it made it all feel pure. Symbolic.

It was at that moment that Sophia walked in.

"Uh Lizzie, you doing okay?"

Lizzie beamed for the first time in over a week. "I'm better than ever."

"Okay." Sophia drew the word out and her tone made it clear

she was skeptical. "Care to tell me why you're suddenly into pyromania?"

Lizzie set her shoulders back and took a deep breath. "I'm not going to be a writer. I hate it and I'm not doing it."

"Am I allowed to ask what sparked this paradigm shift?" Sophia inched forward slowly as if approaching a wild beast. "Or do I just play along with the mad woman?"

"I'm serious, Soph, I'm done with it. It's not me."

Each time she said the words aloud she felt better about her decision. Pursuing writing was pure arrogance from her. She had wanted to excel at something no one could throw back in her face as coming from her upbringing. But how weak was that? Making an entire life decision off other people's perceptions. Vain to the core. And people were always going to talk. You didn't grow up in one of the country's richest families without picking up a few enemies.

The more she tossed the idea around in her mind, the more she felt like kicking herself for being such an idiot. Why had no one called her out?

Was Spencer the only one with the guts to say it to her face?

Sophia knelt down next to her. "So what are you going to do?"

Lizzie stared into the flames in front of her, searching for guidance. And just like that, Spencer's earlier words came back to her, from all those weeks ago.

Teaching.

He said her face lit up when she spoke about her students.

Lizzie turned the idea around in her head, mulling it over. Being such a bookworm made her the perfect editor, the perfect writing coach. When it wasn't her own work, she could see things more analytically. Being able to take a step back from the emotional investment allowed her to look at the bigger picture and help guide others to doing their best.

And what better feeling was there than when she brought a smile to a kid's face who had almost lost hope?

There was no rush.

She didn't need money. She was young. There were no excuses she could throw back to convince herself not to do it. What did she have to lose? Lizzie already had a degree in English and Creative Writing. Adding teaching to that wouldn't be much of a leap.

Lizzie's shoulders sagged but this time it was in relief. "Soph, I'm going to be a teacher."

Sophia's eyes brightened and she jumped up in excitement. "That's an amazing idea! You're already halfway there."

"Pretty much. I mean, it makes sense, right?" Lizzie found herself nodding.

"It just seems perfect. You'll be a great teacher."

Looking into her friend's eyes, Lizzie knew she was being sincere. Sophia wasn't one to avoid a tough conversation. She hadn't realized how important Sophia's reaction was to her until she let out the breath she had been holding.

Sophia opened her arms and crushed Lizzie into a hug. "I'm proud of you."

"I am too." A rush of warmth filled her. This just felt *right*.

"So will you do it over here?"

Lizzie pulled away and took a step back. "No, I'm going home."

"And why is that?" Sophia smirked.

Lizzie aimed a scowl her way. "You think you're so funny."

Sophia went on, unperturbed, "I'm sure it wouldn't have anything to do with a six foot four, golden-haired best friend of your brother, right?"

If Lizzie rolled her eyes any harder they would unscrew from her head. But her facial expression quickly fell. "I'm sure he hates me right now."

"Uh, from what I've seen it's far from hate."

She shook her head. "We both said some pretty bad stuff. I don't know if it's repairable."

Sophia grabbed her shoulders. "Honey, before he left, he

showed up at our place with all your stuff and I swear it looked like someone had kicked a puppy right in front of him. I think he was trying not to cry."

The tiniest flare of hope lit up inside her. "Do you think he would give me another chance?" Lizzie said in a small voice.

The look she received from her best friend made her feel like the dumbest person on the planet.

"Soph. Seriously."

"Do you love him?"

Lizzie bit her lip and nodded.

"Then what are you waiting for?"

FOUR HOURS LATER SHE WAS BOOKED ON THE NEXT FLIGHT TO NEW York. Lizzie had gone through the apartment and packed up as much as she could. She emailed all her students and said they could continue to send her work via email and that she was happy to do Skype sessions if they wanted to. They were all booked on a casual basis so she was lucky she had no loose ends to tie up in that department.

Sophia sat on her suitcase to hold it shut while Lizzie attempted to zip it closed. It was not the easiest of endeavors.

"Jesus, woman, what the hell do you have in here?" her best friend exclaimed, watching in horror as item after item spilled out from it.

Lizzie glowered and tugged on the zip harder. "Essentials."

"Can't you like, pay people to send this back for you?"

Another few tugs and the damn bag was finally closed. The process had been strangely exerting and Lizzie actually found herself puffing a little. "I'll do that for the other stuff." She gestured around the room dismissively. "These are just for when I first get home."

Sophia stood up and attempted to pick up the bag. She bent at the knees and made a big show of trying to lift it up as if she was a medieval knight trying to pull Excalibur out of a rock. "Did you put freaking *bricks* in here?"

A grin tugged at Lizzie's lips. "Getting warmer."

Sophia's eyes bulged and darted to the now-empty fireplace in her bedroom. "Are you telling me this is full of *books*?"

"I plead the fifth."

"Oh God. You're lucky he's head over heels because no one else would put up with you."

Lizzie grumbled but they worked together to get the bag out of the apartment and down the stairs. Soon enough they were standing outside the security door, getting ready to say their goodbyes.

"I'm gonna miss you, Soph." Lizzie found herself tearing up a little at the thought of no longer living with her best friend.

"Come visit me in a few weeks. I know you can afford it, rich bitch."

Lizzie laughed. "Fine. You're really twisting my leg but I guess I could fit in a little Paris trip."

They went in for another hug and Lizzie added, "By the way, I've paid for another year's rent so keep living the Parisian life."

Sophia jerked back, eyes wide. "*What* did you just say?"

"I said, enjoy yourself. Find a hot French man to break your drought and report back." Lizzie grinned. "As an investor in the Get Soph Laid Fund, I want results."

"Lizzie." Sophia was blinking back tears. "You didn't need to do—"

"I know. I wanted to."

They embraced one more time before Sophia stepped back, wiping her eyes with her palms. "Go!" She waved her off. "Get your man."

Chapter Forty-Two
SPENCER

The cab ride home passed by in a blur. Spencer's mind was going a million miles a minute, trying to come up with ways to fix things with Elizabeth.

It would have to be face to face. There was no way this conversation could happen over the phone. She had to know how serious he was.

Every street they passed on the drive made him more impatient. The traffic lights were even worse. It seemed like they were on red every damn time. He began to tap his foot against the floor. Now that he had made up his mind, every second was precious—it was another moment he could be with Elizabeth that he wasn't. In other words? Torture.

After the fifteen-minute trek, he threw a few notes at the driver and sprinted out of the cab and through the front gate of his building. He took the stairs instead of the lift because that bastard was not reliable. Spencer would not let his building's subpar maintenance guy be the reason he missed the last flight of the night. Plus, he needed some way to get rid of the pent-up energy bouncing around inside him.

When he finally burst through the entrance to his apartment, his first stop was his laptop. Spencer brought up the next available flight to Paris—three hours time—and selected a ticket. Even technology seemed to be against him today. When he made it through to the section, where he needed to put in that little code to prove he wasn't a robot, he kept fucking it up. He groaned at the screen but it didn't help matters. After four tries, the confirmation came through and he felt his heart race in his chest. He was doing this. He was really doing this.

Next stop was his bedroom and his good, old, trusty duffel. He had no idea what she would say when he arrived—if she would even take him back. He could be in Paris for three days, months, or years. What the hell to bring?

Spencer sat down on his bed and forced himself to inhale and exhale slowly, a few times. Was he rushing into this? Yes. Was she worth it? Fuck yes.

But what was he prepared to give up?

Did he really care about having New York as his base?

After a few moments he decided that no, it wasn't a big issue. Not when Elizabeth was the prize. His work was great. He loved being able to make money from his passion for sport. But Spencer had already overachieved in the field so much there weren't many milestones left to hit. Love, on the other hand, was a different story.

Elizabeth had this way of making his whole fucking world brighter. It was the sort of thing no material possession or achievement could ever give you. The woman made him happy. Pure and simple. There was no grand reason for it, just that he loved her. She completed him.

When he thought of it in those terms, it was a no-brainer. Spencer did most of his training online, so changing where he lived wouldn't affect his clients much. For the bigger names, he could travel, but there weren't too many of them that needed his presence at every session.

Mind made up, Spencer began throwing every conceivable form of outfit into his bag. It would suck if she laughed in his face, but if she didn't, he was prepared for any situation. After stuffing them all inside, he glanced at the mess and realized he would be showing up with a crinkled shirt. His mom would kill him from beyond the grave if she found out.

Spencer rushed into the back of his wardrobe and found a suit in one of those fancy garment bags. He ripped it out and put a nice shirt and pair of jeans inside. He could get changed on the plane, spray on some deodorant. Put his best foot forward.

He found himself rubbing his hands on his pants, they were getting so sweaty. Fucking hell. He was overthinking this for sure. Spencer had never been this nervous about a woman before. Did Elizabeth even realize the crazy effect she had on him?

As he packed, his eyes continually darted to the clock. He would need to leave in twenty or so minutes if he wanted to make check-in with no problem. It was late but you never know what can happen with traffic in New York.

Somehow, Spencer managed to fit in a shower. As the warm water caressed his body, he allowed himself to hope.

Hope that she loved him back. Or just agreed to date him. Finally he would be able to sleep again.

Lately the thought of her moving on with someone else was plaguing him. Just the idea of that slimy Amaury bastard was enough to make him see red, but over the past few days he had realized that wasn't the only issue. Last time Elizabeth had a breakup, she wanted a rebound. What if she decided she needed a rebound from *him*?

Spencer shuddered, somehow feeling cold despite the hot steam around him. He scrubbed himself a lot harder than usual, as if he could wipe himself clean of the image of the woman he loved with another man. It didn't work. If anything, it made him even more anxious to get the hell out of the country and onto that plane.

When he finished his shower, his eyes made their way back to the clock on his bedside table.

Fuck. He needed to leave in five. Where the hell did the time go?

Spencer dodged furniture as he raced to grab his bag from where he had left it in the hallway, opening up an app on his phone to order a ride to the airport while he did so. He eventually made it to the front door but not before realizing he had left his fucking passport in the study.

God, he was an absolute mess. Elizabeth pretty much had him wrapped around her little finger even when she wasn't here.

His legs pumped as he ran back up the staircase, almost slipping on the tiles as he went. His study was a bit of a mess. Spencer hadn't been in here much since he got back from Paris and he apparently hadn't had the foresight to stash his passport in its usual spot when he returned. No surprises there. He remembered the night he arrived home, flung his things to the ground, and spent the evening with a bottle of vodka and some lemonade. Guess organization hadn't been his top priority.

Curses flew from his lips as he flung open draws and upended piles of paper. Where could the thing have disappeared to in a week anyway? Knees bent, Spencer crouched down to look under the desk. *Bingo*. His travel wallet was laying there, zippers opened, and various documents scattered haphazardly around it. Must have been another casualty of his post-Elizabeth bag-throwing phase. Spencer reached his fingers forward to latch onto that small yet important square book.

Then he was back running down those damn stairs for what had to be at least the eighth time tonight.

He glanced at his watch again. Now he was a few minutes behind. Spencer groaned—a long, frustrated sound. He couldn't risk fucking this up, not again. And every minute that went by, he felt deep in his soul. He needed to be on that plane.

When he made it the front door, he flung it open, tossing his bag over his shoulders. Spencer was starting to race out when he almost ran into something.

He looked up, an annoyed expression plastered on his face, and his breath caught.

He literally lost his fucking breath.

Elizabeth was standing there, wide-eyed, hand raised to knock.

Chapter Forty-Three
LIZZIE

"Elizabeth?"

Spencer blinked a few times, a wondrous expression on his frazzled face as he stood at the threshold of his apartment. His chest was rapidly rising and falling, and a light sheen of sweat coated his skin. One hand was full of a bag and the other clutched what looked like a suit. It did nothing to detract from his beauty, though.

Lizzie felt something light up deep inside her at the sight of him. Those eyes she adored were wide but still so bright. The shirt he had on did little to disguise those bulging muscles and the way he was holding his bag made them pop out even more. After way too long without him in her bed, the pull to him was stronger than ever, but Lizzie was pretty proud of the way she forced her eyes not to drop to his crotch.

It was then that she really took in the sight of the bags in his hands. She threw a hand to her mouth. "Oh, I'm sorry. Is this a bad time?" Her voice came out croaky.

Spencer shook his head and exclaimed in one big breath. "No. It's a perfect time. Great actually."

He dropped everything he was holding to the ground and offered her a hand. "Come in. Are you hungry? I can order some-thing to eat. Do you want a drink?"

Lizzie just nodded dumbly. Being here and seeing him suddenly sent the doubts rushing straight to the surface. How desperate would he think she was to move her whole life back over here for him? Had he moved on? Where was he even going tonight?

She took his warm hand into hers and felt a spark in the exact spot where they touched. A little breath escaped her lips and when she met his gaze, his eyes blazed with passion.

They seemed to stand there, suspended in time, connected by that one point forever.

Lizzie shook herself a little to clear her head and glanced down. "Do you want help with your bags?"

Spencer blinked a couple of times as if he was just noticing them. "No, you just go inside—make yourself at home." He froze, eyes widening. "Not that you need to make it your home. I mean, if you want, you could, you know…"

His voice trailed off and the next thing she knew he had released her hand, picked up the bags, and rushed inside.

What on earth?

Lizzie dutifully followed him in, eyes raking around the apartment that was just so Spencer. Understated but beautiful. Everything was quality but not in-your-face expensive.

It was a giant loft, covered in dark timber floorboards. Big windows that almost stretched to the floor filled an entire wall showcasing an incredible view of the city. The fittings were all matte black, and the exposed brick blended in with them to create an effect that was sleek and modern. Twin staircases framed the doorway, leading up to what she could only assume to be bedrooms. Although, she wouldn't be surprised if he managed to sneak a gym in there, as well.

"Do you want to sit down?" Spencer gestured toward the dark gray L-shaped couch in the corner of the space.

"Sure. Okay."

Lizzie hated how awkward she felt. Before this moment she had all these grand ideas of bursting in, confessing her love, riding off into the sunset and all that. But now that the time was here, she found the words trapped in her throat, doubt holding them hostage.

Spencer settled down next to her on the couch, a good foot of space between them. He seemed…nervous.

"So what are you doing here?" Spencer asked, rubbing his palms on his pants.

This was it.

This was her moment to get it all out.

Lizzie took a deep breath. "I moved back."

Spencer swallowed and looked away. The silence that echoed between them seemed to stretch on for an age.

Finally, he spoke, a resolute expression on his face. "In that case, I have something you need to know."

Oh God.

He didn't look happy at all. In fact, he looked like he was about to throw up. Spencer always seemed so confident, so unflappable, so seeing him like this was weird as hell.

"I know it may not be something you want to hear, but if we're going to be seeing each other again I have to tell you." Spencer scratched the back of his neck, his voice coming out a little shaky. "It's not fair to keep it to myself."

Oh no. Please, please no.

He had met someone else. It was obvious. The way he looked so uncomfortable. How he thought he had to tell her, seeing as they might run into each other. Lizzie felt her face go hot, acid rising in her throat. She had expected rejection, had mentally prepared herself for him to tell her he didn't love her back. But to start dating someone new that quickly?

Fuck. She must have meant nothing to him.

"You can tell me, it's okay."

Spencer swallowed again, twisting his hands together. "I wanted to do this differently, to make it easier for you to understand."

Fucking hell. This boy needed to say his piece so she could get the hell out of here before she crashed and burned into a million pieces. Lizzie's temple throbbed with her pounding pulse. She was seconds away from a breakdown and she would *not* let him see her cry.

"Spencer." Her voice broke. "Just rip the Band-Aid off. I'm a big girl; I'll be fine."

Spencer took her hand in his. Those blue eyes bored into hers and there was so much raw emotion there she almost reeled back from the force of it.

"I love you."

Her eyes bulged. *What?* Was her mind so desperate now that it had become delusional?

Meanwhile, Spencer was still speaking.

"I've loved you for a long time now; you're like a current, a wave…" He shook his head, trying to find the words. "My gravity. It was inevitable. And I know I should have told you sooner but—"

She cut him off by crashing her mouth to his.

Those soft lips she had missed so much enveloped hers, the hesitancy in his earlier words nowhere to be found here. Lizzie wrapped her arms around his neck, half climbing onto his lap in the process.

There was nothing romantic about this. Nothing gentle. It was all animal, pure instinct, and unbridled lust. Their tongues battled together, neither of them wanting to come up for air anytime soon. He tasted like spice and beer and man, and she wanted *more*.

She threaded her fingers through his hair, bringing him even closer. Spencer's hands traced her curves and left a path of tingling need in their wake. She would never get enough of this man. It just wasn't possible.

"Beth, love," Spencer breathed, touching his forehead to hers, "I'm so glad you're home."

"I came back for you."

Sparks burned in his eyes and he drew back, scrutinizing her. "What did you just say?"

A smile broke out on her lips. "I wanted you to give me another chance. To have a shot at this for real. So I moved countries." Lizzie shrugged and red blossomed on her cheeks.

"For me?" Spencer clarified with his face still full of wonder.

"Because I love you."

And then they were kissing again, tangled up in each other for what could have been seconds, minutes, or hours. They didn't care.

Out of the blue, Spencer laughed. "Guess where I was going with all those bags?"

Lizzie frowned and remembered his earlier appearance. "I thought you were sleeping over at some girl's house."

That just made him laugh harder.

"I have a flight leaving for Paris in about an hour. I decided to move countries for you too."

This man.

It was amazing how her life could go from such doubt to this level of happiness in the blink of an eye.

"You were going to move your whole life for me?" Her tone was equal parts delighted and incredulous.

"Of course." Spencer reached a hand out to caress her cheek, his gaze burning with pure love. "You just did the same for me."

Lizzie shook her head. "No I didn't. You're my world, Spence. My life is wherever you are."

Epilogue
LIZZIE

"Spencer!" Lizzie squealed as he pushed her against the sandstone wall, "everyone can see us."

Spencer ignored her, nuzzling his face against her neck. His hands roamed between her hips and waist, and the thin, cotton fabric she was wearing was light enough that she could feel his warmth through it.

Lizzie tipped her head back and wrapped her arms around his neck. Everyone told her attraction faded over time but she didn't believe it. Every extra day she spent with her man, she just fell harder, and the pull became stronger. It was impossible to resist him.

"I'm being serious. We're in public."

"Don't care." He growled into her ear, "I wanted to do this to you here two years ago. I'm just making up for lost time."

Lizzie started to laugh but it turned into a moan as his lips found that spot behind her ear she loved.

They had arrived in Paris yesterday. It was their anniversary and Spencer was pulling out all the stops. He pretended to be all rough and manly but deep down he was a big romantic at heart. He'd flown her to Paris, for crying out loud. Now he wanted to retrace the steps of that first day they had spent together, when she had given him a tour of the city.

His hands started to skim under the hem of her dress and she pushed him back. "Spence. There are *religious* people near here."

"So? I want to do some worship of my own." His eyes melted as they raked from her head to feet and back again.

Lizzie put her hands on her hips and plastered a stern expression on her face. "I thought you wanted to walk around the city, not take me against a wall opposite the Notre Dame."

Spencer raised his hands, shrugging. "Why can't I have it both ways?"

"Come on, you big, horny bastard." Lizzie sighed, pulling on his hand and dragging him away from the side of the café she had been waiting for him at so long ago.

With a dramatic sigh, Spencer went along with her.

As they walked side-by-side, Lizzie tried to loop her hand around his waist and into his pocket in the way she often liked to do. This time though, he stopped her.

"Beth baby, it's way too hot for you to be doing that."

Lizzie frowned but played along. "You didn't seem to mind getting all hot and bothered a few minutes ago."

"I had better incentive then," Spencer replied with a wink, keeping a firm grip on her hand.

Lizzie shrugged it off. It *was* pretty hot out. Summer was in full swing in Paris. The pink flowers that had been in this spot that first time they were here were nowhere to be found now. It didn't do anything to detract from the atmosphere though. With all the tourists that loved this part of the city, there were people every-where. Buskers played their works at every corner, and when she turned her eyes to the river banks, it seemed like there were more book carts than ever.

"Can I go browse?" Lizzie tilted her head at Spencer and batted her eyelashes. "Pretty please?"

"Yes!" Spencer burst out with more enthusiasm than she expected. The glint in his eyes quickly went out as he made his face neutral. "I mean, that's a good idea. I can take some photos while you go be a big nerd."

A frown creased Lizzie's brow. Spencer had been so weird all day. It had started this morning when she rolled over in bed to find him getting dressed.

Where are you going? she had asked him. They were on vacation and had only arrived yesterday. Who the hell didn't have a sleep-in on the first day?

Nowhere, he had replied, *I'm just going to the gym. Want to see how Tate's is doing.*

Then he had burst out of the room in record speed, bringing his entire suitcase with him. It was the strangest thing.

At the time she had dismissed it as Spencer just still being in work mode. He had been putting in so many extra hours these past few months, and now actually had gyms all across Europe, as well. Paris's second Tate's Training had just opened a few weeks ago.

But looking at his wide-eyed gaze now, she knew something was up.

"Well?" Spencer said, "are you going to go look at the books?"

Lizzie nodded and ambled over to the first cart. She wasn't going to press the issue now. Later, when they were somewhere alone, she would ask him about it.

As she reached the stand, the tension seemed to leave her body. She had so many happy memories here, browsing her next great read. Lizzie loved the idea that someone else had read them—all the extra stories that could be attached. She always opened them up to see if there were any bookmarks or little notes left inside.

"I'm going to just wander around nearby, okay?" Spencer was talking but Lizzie just murmured back absentmindedly. This was her kind of heaven.

She trailed her fingers along the spines, waiting to see if one of them spoke to her.

The title *Romeo et Juliette* caught her eye and with a smile she realized this was a French version of the Shakespeare classic. She extracted it carefully from the pile, reading the blurb even though she had no need to.

The cover was beautiful; it was the balcony scene and it reminded her of her old Paris apartment.

She opened it up and saw a folded note in the front page that said *To my love.* Her heart gave an excited little leap as her mind began to rapidly concoct possible tales behind this one little message.

Lizzie unfolded it, eyes greedily devouring the words in front of her.

Elizabeth Rose Hastings,
My heart. My light. My love.
Will you marry me?

If her mouth dropped open farther it would hit the pavement. What a strange coincide. She twisted on her heels, ready to tell Spencer about the odd turn of events when she caught sight of him, kneeling on the ground behind her.

His blue eyes were shining with pure love, his hair was in that messy way she adored, and in his shaking hands was the most beautiful ring she had ever seen. It was gold with a huge, round, blue stone in the middle, circled by smaller white diamonds.

The world seemed to freeze around her as she locked gazes with Spencer, and she had never felt this happy in her entire life. This was the man she was going to marry. She pictured them spending the rest of their lives together, having a few kids, a dog. Growing old by each other's side. He was her wildest dream, her happiness, her future.

Tears sprung to her eyes and she raced forward to embrace him.

"You need to say yes first, princess." Spencer laughed and as she tried to join him on the ground, wrapping her arms around him, he stood up, taking her with him. Somehow she had ended up with her legs around his waist, arms around his neck, and clinging to him like a freaking monkey.

Lizzie peppered kisses across his face. "Yes. *Yes.* One million times, yes." She wasn't sure if she was laughing or crying but right now she didn't really care. The throng of tourists that had gathered around them cheered.

Spencer kissed her back a few times before he pulled away. "Are you going to let me put the ring on?"

Everyone laughed and Spencer put her down so he could slide the band around her finger.

Lizzie tilted her hand back and forth, mesmerized by the way the light glinted off that stunning blue stone. It was the exact color of Spencer's eyes.

"It's perfect, Spence." She sighed, still not taking her eyes off it.

"It's a blue diamond," Spencer said, laying a kiss against her fingers. "I saw it and knew it was for you."

Lizzie gasped. She knew how expensive that would have been. The white diamonds surrounding it weren't small either. "Spencer, this is too much—" she began to say but he cut her off.

"Beth love, nothing will ever be too much when it comes to you."

She beamed up at him, tears coming back to her eyes. Then, a thought crossed her mind. "How did you know that was the book I'd pick?" She frowned. "Or the stand?"

A sheepish smile crossed his face and Spencer scratched the back of his neck. "I, uh, may have spent a few hours this morning putting notes in every book in the first five carts along the river."

How the hell did she get so lucky?

"As I said,"—Spencer raised a hand to cup her cheeks, those blue orbs meeting hers—"for you, there's nothing I wouldn't do."

Their lips met and Lizzie shut her eyes.

Let the future begin.

WANT MORE?

Sign up HERE for a BONUS EPILOGUE. Spoiler alert: It may include cute babies. Just saying.

Pre-order Book Two HOLDING OUT FOR HARPER here.
Read on for a sneak peek of Chapter One!

Holding Out For Harper

Harper Brown is a snarky pain in Sebastian Hasting's ass.

His brother's assistant not only seems to hate his guts, but she's also not afraid to talk back to him and tempting enough to distract him from the billions he should be earning.

Then pictures of their one hot kiss leak to the gossip mags, and Sebastian has a brilliant idea.

What better way to get the gold diggers off his back than to take himself off the market?

It's the perfect solution.

Except as things with Harper heat up, it becomes harder for Sebastian to remind himself that she's only playing his fiancé for the money.

He's a man who always gets what he wants. But is Harper more than he bargained for?

He's a man who always gets what he wants. But is Harper more than he bargained for?

Holding Out *for* HARPER

This is an unedited sneak peek. Don't hate me too much if there's a typo

"You've got to be fucking kidding me."

"It's one week. You'll be fine."

Harper Brown narrowed her eyes at the Head of Human Resources, but Gina's steely gaze told her this wasn't some cruel joke. She was dead serious.

Gina leaned over Harper's desk and dropped her voice. "He's not that bad—"

Harper slammed a fist against the desk hard enough to jolt her green tea. "Have you *met* him?" She felt her nostrils flaring and mentally berated herself. She shouldn't let him get her this worked up. But he was just so damn *frustrating*. At least she'd worked with Gina long enough to be able to speak openly. "I don't work for Sebastian. I work for Josh. It's not my fault Debbie had some mid-life crisis and booked a last-minute trip. He's the one who approved her leave. He can't just expect me to double my workload."

Gina shot a quick glance left and right at Harper's loud rant. They were at Harper's desk, just outside Joshua Hastings' office. Unfortunately, the top floor of Hastings Properties was mostly open-plan and Sebastian's office was just a few doors down. In theory, any of the higher-ups could walk by.

265

"Don't be so dramatic." Gina said, voice still low. "You know very well that Josh is taking some time off too, so you won't be doing double duties."

Harper pursed her lips. She'd been hoping Gina had forgotten about Josh's little trip. He was the best man at a wedding in a few weeks and decided to fly the groomsmen to Vegas for the buck's night. Typical Josh. The Vegas getaway seemed a lot more his style than the no-nonsense groom's.

"I can't work for him, Gina. I just can't."

"Can't work for who?"

She would know that velvet voice anywhere.

Speak of the Devil and the Devil shall appear.

Sebastian Hastings stood a few feet away, navy blue suit perfectly molded to his body. His dark brown eyes glinted as he turned them her way, full lips curved into a smirk. Why did he have to be so attractive? It really wasn't fair. He was a businessman but looked like he could moonlight as a rockstar with his strong jaw, light beard and the silky brown hair that was a bit too long for the boardroom. Harper guessed when you practically ran the company unspoken dress code rules didn't apply.

"Didn't your mother ever tell you it's rude to eavesdrop, Mr. Hastings?" Harper smiled sweetly, pointedly ignoring the horrified expression Gina was throwing her way.

"Didn't yours tell you if you don't have anything nice to say you shouldn't say it at all?"

Harper tensed. She had no idea if her mom had ever said that to her. But her grandma May had *definitely* uttered something along those lines.

Sebastian's gaze clouded with confusion and Harper realized she had gone silent. *Crap.* Couldn't predators pick up on the slightest hint of weakness? Because that's what Sebastian was. A predator. Ruthless. And unrelenting in his quest to find ways to piss her off.

Or maybe that was just his natural personality? Some people had charm. Sebastian had the ability to irk her with a look.

"Mr. Hastings, Harper and I were just discussing how she will move over to Debbie's desk for the first few days to settle into your workload."

Hang on. *What?*

Harper pushed her chair out and the screech echoed loudly against the chrome tiles. "I am *not* moving desks." She gestured around to her perfectly organized workspace. "All my things are here. It would be *stupid.*" Without realizing it she flung a hand towards Sebastian at that last word.

He quirked a brow, "But Miss Brown, how can you be at my beck and call all the way over here?"

Deep breaths. Don't take the bait. Kill 'em with kindness.

Harper smoothed down her skirt to give her clenching hands something to do and tilted her chin up to look at Sebastian. He was wearing a shit-eating grin and had taken a few steps back so Gina couldn't see it.

You know what? Fuck kindness.

"I'm Josh's Executive Assistant, not yours." Harper made sure her voice was sickeningly polite, for Gina's sake. "And I'm not at his 'beck and call'" She made quotation marks with her hands, "I work hard, and I'm busy. I have no time for silly errands."

Harper had worked at Hastings Properties for three years now. When she was first promoted to executive assistant she had been assigned to Sebastian, but he had quickly moved her to Josh. Her stomach clenched at the memory of the conversation she had over-heard between them. Sebastian – the bastard – had no idea she knew the reason why he had reassigned her and she planned to keep it that way. Still, it didn't mean that she hadn't decided to make Sebast-ian's life hell any time she had to fill in for him.

But he gave back as good as he got.

"Gina, would you not agree that the lunch of one of Hastings

Properties' Directors is not some 'stupid errand'?" Sebastian had the audacity to echo Harper's earlier gesture, somehow finding a way to make miming quotation marks look disdainful.

Harper rolled her blue eyes at the memory of the day he forced her to bring him sandwiches from five different shops because he didn't know what he would 'feel like' that day. Then when she had arrived back after an hour of running around the city in the middle of summer to grab them she saw him sitting smug at his desk with an empty bag of takeout. He had just shrugged and said he was so hungry he couldn't wait. Jerk.

"Of course not, sir." Gina said, her glasses bouncing as she nodded. Harper didn't mind Gina. But it's not like they were work besties either. Gina was a stickler for the rules, and she looked as nondescript as her personality: brown bob, brown skirt, beige cardigan. The works. She was the sort of person who would be described as "nice". Harper had too strong a personality to ever buddy up with someone like Gina. Or to suck up to the boss, something Gina did with earnest.

"In my opinion, *sir*." Harper said with a flick of her blonde ponytail, "My degrees in Business and Communications and extensive experience could be better utilized than by fetching your coffee. That's why you have interns."

Gina frowned. "Harper, our intern program is much more than people to organize coffee. It includes work assignments, real opportunities to shadow in the business and—"

Harper held up a hand and Gina shut up. "I'm sure it is." She shot Sebastian a scowl, "Regardless, I'm not moving desks. Not even for a day."

Sebastian's lips quirked. "We'll see about that."

EIGHT HOURS LATER HARPER CARRIED THE LAST OF HER FILES TO

Debbie's desk, fuming. She was so pissed off it felt like steam was coming out her ears.

"Stupid Josh." She banged a folder against the surface, "Stupid Gina." Another. "And stupid, stupid Sebastian." Harper muttered as she slammed the rest of the files down as hard as she could.

The resounding thud felt satisfying at least.

Harper stepped back and grabbed her bag. Josh left for Vegas tomorrow so she would start for Sebastian then. Thank God it would only be a week of dealing with Sebastian alone. Once Josh was back she would at least have a buffer. He didn't let Sebastian give her too much crap: she literally didn't have time for it.

"Who are you rushing off to so fast?" Sebastian's dry voice echoed from somewhere close behind her.

Harper jerked her gaze to him. It was nearing six and he had lost the suit jacket and rolled up the sleeves of his business shirt. It looked good. Too good. She hated the prickle of awareness she felt at the hint of his cologne. It was fruity yet masculine, with traces of spice and darker tones that made her body react in a way it shouldn't.

She tried to convince herself it was just the expensive scent that made her feel that way. *That's the point of cologne, right?*

"Less about who I'm rushing *to*, more about who I'm rushing away *from*."

"So I assume that man who sent you those cheap flowers a few weeks ago isn't waiting at home?"

Harper suppressed a sigh. He was being a dick. *Surprise, surprise.* Sebastian loved to torment her about whatever guy she was dating. Despite its success, at its heart Hastings Properties was still a family business, and all the employees were pretty close. Sometimes on Fridays she would catch up with Josh and some of the other people from work for drinks and bring someone along, but Sebastian never let her hear the end of it. There was always some-thing wrong with them.

But she had never told him about Chad, or the flowers. He must pay closer attention than she realized.

"Chad's my fiancé, actually. And no, I'm not seeing him tonight." She hoisted her bag over her shoulder and turned to leave. "The flowers were perfect. Not everyone needs expensive gifts to win girls over."

He had only proposed that weekend, so Harper hadn't had time to fill in everyone at work. She felt a smug sort of satisfaction at making out to Sebastian that he was out of the loop.

"Fiancé? Are you serious?" Sebastian's face hardened and he shot out an arm to stop her, "Haven't you only just started seeing him?"

Harper shifted away from his touch and sent a stern mental warning to her body to stop fucking tingling when he got close. "It was a whirlwind romance, and it's none of your business."

"They don't exist." Sebastian laughed but it wasn't a nice sound.

"Maybe you don't believe in love at first sight, but I do." Harper's face contorted. How dare he suddenly think he knew her well enough to judge the validity of her engagement? "You don't know anything about our relationship."

Sure, her and Chad had happened quickly. Too quickly in her grandma's eyes but May wanted the absolute best for Harper and had a pretty inflated opinion of what she was worth.

But Chad had swept her off her feet, plain and simple. He was romantic, loving and yeah, a little impulsive but he was a dreamer. He had the golden hair and green eyes of a genuine Prince Charming and when he said he didn't need to wait because he knew she was the one from the moment they met, she believed him.

Ever since she was a little girl Harper wanted marriage, kids, the whole shebang. She loved her work but really, she wanted to be a mom. To have a house full of kids, a husband she loved and a few dogs running around the backyard. The childhood she never had.

"So where's the ring then?"

Harper felt a flare of annoyance at his sharp words. "Of course you focus on the material things."

Chad told her he wanted to marry her the moment he realized it —which happened to be three nights ago. He wasn't the sort of person who could hide his feelings and bide his time waiting to buy a ring or plan a fancy proposal. He needed to share his joy with her from the get-go. It was sweet, not *cheap*.

Sebastian pinned her with those dark eyes, "It's not about the cost of the ring, it's about him not even putting in a tiny bit of thought or effort into one of the most important moments of your life."

Harper didn't respond: she just glared. How *dare* he? Unfortunately, there was a limit to what she could say to someone who was technically her boss, and right now the volley of colorful four-letter words bouncing around her head probably weren't appropriate.

"Even you're worth more than that, Harper."

And with that Sebastian walked away, leaving Harper staring at his back open-mouthed, the ghost of his words echoing around the room…

PRE-ORDER HERE

Coming July 18

STAY IN TOUCH

Connect with Gabrielle here on whatever platform you prefer!

Facebook: http://facebook.com/gabrielleasthonauthor

Instagram: http://instagram.com/gabrielleashtonauthor

Website: http://www.gabrielleashton.com

Or email her at gabrielle@gabrielleasthon.com

She would love to hear from you!

ACKNOWLEDGMENTS

I'd like to say a big thank-you to the real MVP: my boyfriend. He put up with me studying full-time, working full-time and somehow also writing a book. Couldn't have done this without his support. Or his foot rubs.

Thank you of course to my editor Kathy, your help has made this book what it is today. Thank you as well to Angel for your proof-reading skills. I cannot believe how many typos I had. It's a little embarrassing.

I would like to also thank the friends that I've made in the indie community, all my "Chadettes" (you know who you are!). It's been amazing having a group to go on this journey with. You girls all rock, and made this process so fun... And when it wasn't fun you were even more important in helping me get through it all.

Some of those girls are actually talented authors and have books out or coming soon - see the list below!

I don't know her well personally but I would also like to thank Maria Luis. It was through reading her books that I found her reader group (you can find it here) where I got the kick I finally needed to write and publish this book. I've wanted to be a writer my entire life but I always thought it would be too difficult so I gave it up. Well, screw you earlier doubts because I did it! I also stalked Maria hard and listened to a few podcasts where she was interviewed on the publishing process which were super informative so she's helped in a few ways!

And finally thank YOU for making it to the end of this book! I hope you enjoyed reading it as much as I enjoyed writing it.

~

BOOKS BY MY FRIENDS!

OUT NOW: What Doesn't Kill You by Carmen Richter *(a sports romance/romantic suspense)*

OUT NOW: Twisted City by Rebekah Vasick *(a suspenseful Mafia romance)*

JUNE 26: The Devil's Heir by Angel Nyx *(an enemies to lovers slow burn romance)*

JULY 16th: The Awakened by Amanda Carol *(a paranormal/urban fantasy romance)*

JULY 25th: It's Not Home Without You by Claudia Lymari *(a second chance romance)*

AUGUST 1st: One Last Chance by Nicole Cook *(a second chance romance)*

AUGUST 22nd: I Never Planned on You by Stefanie Jenkins *(a brother's best friend romance)*

AUGUST 29th: The Truce by Becca Steele *(an enemies to lovers romance)*

ABOUT THE AUTHOR

Gabrielle Ashton is a contemporary romance author, and self-confessed book addict. She loves to read anything from contemporary, to paranormal, to historical: you publish it, Gabrielle will read it!

When she's not writing about her favourite romance tropes in gorgeously exotic locations, Gabrielle studies law and also works as a television producer. On any given day she wakes up at three in the morning for work, fits in a few classes at university then comes home and writes.

Gabrielle grew up in Australia, lived in Paris, and now resides in Sydney with her boyfriend, two dogs and cat. Although, said boyfriend is making a strong case for a pet bird.

 facebook.com/gabrielleashtonauthor

 instagram.com/gabrielleashtonauthor

Made in the USA
Lexington, KY
07 August 2019